<u>Social Suicide</u>

For my dad, loved and missed forever x

Liz

(Now)

Flash. Flash. Flash.

The stark and sudden difference lit up the room in a heartbeat. It was bright and harsh against the pitch black of the night, and it wasn't alone. Accompanying the light was the sound. The constant noise of the object hitting against the harsh wood underneath. It created a vibration and the longer it went on, the more soothing it became. It was almost soothing enough to allow Liz to ignore the light and let the sound gently put her back to sleep. Almost.

Flash. Buzz. Flash.

As the buzzing continued, it seemed more ferocious. The object began to move across the surface as the sound and light became more consistent.

Flash. Buzz. Move. Flash.

She was tired, beyond tired, her eyes felt heavy, and she could barely force them open, but still…

Flash. Flash. Buzz. Move. Flash.

It was relentless. Before long she knew her phone would move so much it would fall off the bedside table and onto the wooden floor beneath. The noise it would create in the night would be enough to wake the whole household. The fallout from that would be unbearable. In fact, the fallout could already be coming. She was sure she had heard Rob huff at least once already. It must be time to wake. So why did she feel so tired? Liz was a morning person, always had been. It was unlike her to sleep this deep. Rolling over, feeling her head hit the colder side of the pillow, she reached towards her bedside cabinet and looked at the alarm clock next to her bed. Then she squinted her eyes tight, reopened them, and looked again. It was 3am. Why on earth would her alarm be going off at 3am? Unless it wasn't her alarm. Unless someone was calling or texting, but who? Everyone was at home, and she wasn't next of kin for anyone else – she was barely that for her own kids. It had to be emails. It had to be work. The only ones that wouldn't cope without her.

She was about to sit up, unlock her phone and look properly when she heard Rob again. This time there was no doubt. The huff was loud and purposeful. It was over-dramatic. It made her skin crawl. He'd clearly been woken too, and Liz knew exactly what conversation would follow, so to avoid confrontation at this hour, she placed the phone next to her on her bed, to lessen the sound of the buzzing, and started to put on her slippers, which were, of course, neatly tucked by the side of her bed. Then grabbing her grey woollen dressing gown off the hook on the back of the bedroom door and picking her phone back up and placing it in the pocket, Liz was about to head downstairs, when she heard yet another loud huff coming from Rob.

Without turning around to face her, keeping his shoulders hunched and his body firmly on its side looking towards the wall, Rob seemed to growl, 'Liz, it's 3am – sort your bloody phone out, will you?'

'I'm up, aren't I? I think it's the school. I'll take it downstairs, and you can get your precious sleep.'

'Thanks.'

Liz knew that 'thanks' wasn't genuine at all. She knew that he would be in a mood about this all the way until tomorrow evening probably. He would try and start the *your work takes over our whole life* chat in the morning, she wouldn't be interested and then he would stop speaking to her altogether. Liz knew the game well by now. Rob would try so hard to make her feel... something, but in all honesty his feelings never really bothered her as much as he wanted them to. She knew he thought the silent treatment would get to her, wear her down and bring her to tears, but in reality, it just gave her more time to get on with things. Even in a mood, he would take the children to school and sort their dinner when they got in. So why would that be a punishment? Besides, she chose not to linger on why his feelings mattered so little to her. It was a rabbit hole that was always better avoided.

She was itching to check her phone, to open the emails she was sure she had received there and then, but she knew better than that. If she stayed any longer in the room, Rob would claim he wasn't able to go back to sleep... even though he always did. So, she crept out of the bedroom and into the hallway.

As she walked out of her room, she looked towards the two doors to her right, one bedroom for Ellie and one for Thomas. Thomas's door was ajar, as it always was, so he would get some light from the floor lamp perched in the corner of the hallway. He'd always been afraid of the dark, ever since he was small. She was hoping he would grow out of it, yet here he was, at the age of twelve, still running up her electricity bill. Ellie's, of course, was firmly shut. She was sixteen now and typically wanted nothing to do with the rest of her family from the second she came back from school. Apparently, it was bad enough that she had to see her mum when she was there, let alone face her at home too. Liz didn't see the problem. Since she'd become deputy head, she'd only really taught the underprivileged and Pupil Premium kids – the ones with low household incomes – which of course, Ellie was not. But apparently them simply breathing the same air was enough for Ellie to be mad at her mum most days. Liz had told off one of Ellie's friends last week. Ellie told her she had 'ruined her life'… Liz thought that was incredibly ironic.

Stepping down the stairs and into the kitchen, she finally pulled her phone out of her pocket and looked down at it in her hand properly. The brightness on the screen stung her eyes and she shook herself to wake up. It wasn't until she reached the kitchen counter that she noticed the notifications on her phone were not emails at all. They were from Facebook. Liz couldn't help but let her frustration get the better of her. Getting out of bed for work was one thing, but social media was something else. She slammed the phone down a little too harshly on the white granite counter. She couldn't help but flinch as she thought of Rob asking in the morning what the work emergency was and having to tell him it was nothing better than some ridiculous social media notifications. He would feel just as annoyed as she did right now, about being woken at such an hour for something of such little importance.

The frustration of being up, coupled with the curiosity of what lay behind those notifications, left Liz almost frozen to the spot. She wanted to be the bigger person, to ignore this insignificant waste of time, yet she needed to know what was so desperate that it was causing her phone to enter this frenzy. She attempted to leave it where it was and put the kettle on, but the incessant buzzing got the better of her. She rationalised in her head that if it wasn't going to allow her to sleep, she might as well be productive and therefore flicked the switch of the kettle, picked up her phone with one hand and booted her laptop up with the other – seeing as it was still on the kitchen counter from where she had been working on reports late into the night. Swiping the unlock button with her thumb, Liz was brought to her Facebook notification feed.

Ollie Smith and 15 others have tagged you in a post. Go to your timeline review.

Ollie Smith? Liz thought to herself. Now that was a name she hadn't heard in years. He went to her school, the year above her, of course, like so many of her friends at the time. In fact, it was only Rob that wasn't, but the less they spoke about that, the better. She remembered Ollie requesting to be her friend last year. Normally she wouldn't allow people she hadn't seen for so long add her on social media, but she remembered how keen he'd been on her at school, and how it had annoyed Rob when the request came through, so she'd accepted it on a whim, which gave her the exact response from Rob that she was hoping for.

Liz turned away from her laptop to pour the hot water into her coffee cup, all the while still clutching her phone in her left hand. Something in her stomach stopped her from prioritising her laptop for the first time in a long time and she clicked the button to reveal the post that had woken her in the dead of the night.

She wasn't sure what she was expecting, something to do with some God-awful school reunion probably, or worse, a picture of her in secondary school, with her chavvy bangs stuck to the side of her face and the collar on her polo shirt ironed to stand up instead of down – something she would be telling her own pupils off for now. Even that, however, would be better than a picture of her in uniform and pregnant. She'd spent such a long time getting rid of all those photos and she'd be damned if bloody Ollie Smith had managed to get hold of one. That would be worth getting up for at least, just so she could get rid of it quickly.

But nothing could prepare her for the screen she was now looking at. The one that had taken her breath away. Ollie Smith had not produced the original post. No. He'd simply shared it.

Shared it onto her page with a tagline that made her spill the hot water all over the surface and her own hand. She dropped her phone with the pain of the water and threw the kettle back down on the worktop. Running her hand under the cold water of the tap, Liz stared at her phone now laying on the polished tiled kitchen floor, convincing herself that what she had read was wrong. That she must be tired. That it couldn't possibly be... She took her hand away from the tap. The sting in her skin was still there, but her need to re-read the post was stronger than her pain. She crouched down on the floor and lifted the phone back up.

Adjusting her eyes to the screen and ignoring the crack that had now appeared on the bottom corner, Liz read the tagline over and over again, to assure herself she had read it correctly. She tried to convince herself she was wrong, but there was no way she was. There it was. For the whole world to see. In black and white. Her old crush Ollie Smith had shared a screenshot of some pictures that had been uploaded. Photos of her and messages she had sent. And there, on top of the pictures, were his own words:

Ha. To think I used to fancy this woman at school and now she's shagging one of her pupils. It's never who you think it is, is it? @Liz Hall... the paedophile.

Ben

(14 days earlier)

I'm bored. Proper bored. I've got nothing to do, have I? Spent all my wages on these bloody trainers. Good one, Ben. Got nice trainers but nowhere to fucking go. They said they were going to the skate park tonight. Figured that would be OK. I don't have a board, but I could just sit and chat with them. Would have been something. But they changed their minds last minute, didn't they? Decided they'd go to the cinema instead. I ain't got the money for that. Sixteen quid for a bloody ticket now! Are they joking? That's like three hours work down the chippy, just to watch one film. And that's without the popcorn and shit. Can't be the only one not having anything, can I? The one that has to bring a packet of Aldi's own crisps with him like a dickhead. I hate being a dickhead and I hate having nothing to do on a Saturday night.

Saturday is my only night I can go out. I work on a Friday night, you see, to get my spends. And on the weekend, I do the lunchtime shifts, so I need tonight. It's the only time I get to see my mates. They're already getting narky with me 'cause I work so much. I'm sure that's why they don't talk to me as much as they do to each other. Well, unless they're taking the piss, that is. I'm always the butt of the jokes, of course I am – I'm the dickhead, remember? But it's worth it, because for the last couple of weeks, I've been in Mitchell's gang. One of the popular crowd. He's the legend of the school. All the girls fancy him, and all the lads want to hang around with him. And for some reason, the other week, he spoke to *me*. He sat next to me in English and just started chatting. He did most of the talking, of course – I don't have a lot to say – but still… he spoke to me all bloody English lesson and walked out of class *with* me. Well… I sort of followed him, to be fair, to the lunch hall, but he didn't tell me to fuck off or anything. He just put up with me and he's been putting up with me ever since.

Anyway, that's why I don't care about being the one they take the piss out of, because look where it's got me? Feeling like a king, that's where. I'd rather take the shit and stay in Mitchell's gang 'cause not only am I not on my own anymore, but my mates are the coolest kids in school. And that's way more important than standing up for yourself anyway. If I got kicked out of the group, I'd be a loser again, because that's what you are if you ain't in the gang, a loser, and I'd rather be a dickhead than a loser any day.

Tonight though, I'm definitely both, because I'm in, aren't I? In with me mum and her latest boyfriend. Don't even know this one's name. He told me to call him 'Uncle'. As if. I looked him straight in the eyes and told him I'll just call him 'wanker', like I have all the others, and then I clenched my fist. He was dead scared then, honest. He completely bottled it, turned away and pretended to laugh it off. I knew he was scared though. I told Mitchell the next day, said I'd warned him off, made him shit himself. Mitchell wasn't really listening though to be honest. And of course, he made some joke about me mum having someone else. To be fair, I deserve that crap. Mum don't help me look less like a dickhead. But I could definitely see that Mitchell was impressed. I could see that he saw me as a big man in my house, which of course I am. I just need to prove I'm a big man in school now. But I'm working on that.

Fuck. School. Monday's going to be shit. All they'll be talking about is this film they've seen. Maybe I should Wikipedia the plot so I can pretend I went to see it after my shift tomorrow with this week's wages. Yeah, that's a good idea. There's bound to be spoilers online. I'll google it and make sure I know it inside out so if they ask me any questions, I won't get caught short. I could tell them I went with my other friends. Mates from the chippy or something? They don't know anyone who works there, so they wouldn't find out. That will make me look much cooler as well – having other friends and that – much better than a loser dickhead that stays in on a Saturday night.

At least I've got me phone now. Mum had an upgrade and finally gave me her old one. Probably the most decent thing she's ever done to be fair. I did have to bribe her a bit, you know, threaten to tell the school about her parties and getting that whack from that bloke. She went fucking mental when I mentioned it, but she was well nice to me after it happened, so I wouldn't tell the school, but I thought it was worth a try. And it worked. Well, it shit her up enough to give in and let me have her phone. I mean, no, she didn't like it, but it was worth it. Mum won't care again in a few days anyway.

It was the worst at school. Once I had mates, I kept having to pretend that my phone was off for repair. That I'd smashed my screen and it was getting fixed. That's why I didn't have an iPhone 14 like all of them. I was saving my wages to get one, but shit me, they're well expensive, ain't they?! Would have taken me a whole year to save. So, when Mum cracked and offered this one, I nearly snatched it out of her hand. Course, it ain't a 14. It's only an iPhone 5, but I've got one. Even if I did have to spend forty quid getting the screen fixed up at the market to make sure my story added up. They never noticed it wasn't a 14, thank Christ. Well, they didn't really look too hard to notice. But I knew I had one and now I can join in with all the social media and stuff. I signed up to everything straight away. Facebook, Twitter, Insta, Snapchat and TikTok… although I'm proper shit at that one, but sometimes they let me join in with the group dances and I like to watch them when I'm at home. It shows me that I am part of the group. Part of the gang. Yeah, I'm still the dickhead, but I'm the dickhead of Mitchell's gang at Sandi School and that makes me the coolest dickhead around.

I'm about to look up the film when a notification comes up on my phone. Mitchell has put up a new story on Insta. I notice that I go on his page so much that my phone tells me when it's updated now. Something about an algorithm? I don't know, but it's epic. It means I don't miss anything. Obviously, I have to be careful when Mitchell's around because I don't want to look like a stalker or anything, but he's never noticed so far, so that's good. Anyway, I'll have a look first. I hate it when I can't join in with chats, and besides, I reckon that he likes that I'm always the first one to see his stories. Secretly he does, I'm sure.

I assume this one is a nice cosy picture of them in the cinema. I wonder who went? Jack would have, probably Lynsey as well 'cause she's well into Jack at the moment, and Lucy, she don't go anywhere without Lynsey. Then probably the rest of the lads, Josh, Lewis and Ryan. Just me stuck at home. Oh… they didn't go to the cinema. They're at the skate park. What the hell? They wouldn't tell me the wrong thing on purpose, would they? That would be shit. I know we're not besties just yet, but I sit at their table at lunch and that, so I'm definitely part of the crew. Nah, I'm being stupid. They wouldn't do it on purpose. They're me mates. Mitchell said we were mates anyway, I'm certain he did. No, they must have changed their minds, last minute like. Or I bet they couldn't get seats. That's what it was. I bet they went to the cinema, queued up and everything but couldn't get tickets, so they walked over to the skate park. That makes sense. They wouldn't have thought to ring me 'cause it was a last minute thing. I get that. What mate wouldn't?

I reckon if I get a shift on, I could still make it over way before they leave. I'll just message Mitchell and see if they're still there. I'm sure he'll get back to me right away. Course he will. I'll text him now. Or maybe Insta message? Or both? I'll go with both, then he'll get back to me quicker. Fuck it, I might as well send one on Facebook messenger too – you never know what he'll pick up first. I'll stick my trainers and coat on so I'm right ready for when he messages back. I'll just wait. I'm sure it will come soon. Shit, it's hot in my coat.

Liz

(Now)

Liz found herself sitting on the kitchen floor, frantically scrolling through her phone. Refresh after refresh found yet more posts about her: text messages she had sent, photos of her in lingerie, meet-ups she had organised. How could this be? It made no sense. She'd recognised Ben's name as soon as she'd seen the posts. There was no hiding the fact that they'd spent a lot of time together lately. She hadn't exactly tried to keep that a secret, but she'd told the staff it was for her targets, and no one would question how focused she was on those. They all knew she wanted that promotion next year. Besides, no one in their right mind would believe a child like this, with his background. He's a loner, a no one. A statistic. Sure, he'd been hanging around with that Mitchell for a while, but that wasn't enough to give him credibility. In fact, it would probably do the opposite. No teacher liked Mitchell. Every teacher wanted to – well, most of them did – but he made it too hard. He was just that kid that caused grief in the classroom and lowered the percentage of children hitting target. If you got him in your class, you knew you would have to fight tooth and nail to get your pay rise the following year.

Maybe that's what this was. Mitchell had forced Ben to put these things up. She couldn't believe that he would have done this by choice. Although Ben must have said something to him to spark it, but why would he do that? She pulled herself up off the floor and put the phone down on the breakfast bar, avoiding the phone by staring at the ceiling as she did so. She needed to pull herself together. The last thing the school needed was press and police. Innocent or not, they would dismiss her if she brought all that to the door and that was something she couldn't risk. She needed to take back the control on her own. She needed no one but herself, as always.

Turning around to face the sink and leaving her phone exactly where it was, Liz reached for a cloth and started to clean up the mess she had made. As she reached for the tap and stared at the spilt water, however, she couldn't seem to focus on the mess in front of her or just tidy things away in a second like she usually would. This time the mess was in her mind, and her stomach. She felt sick. She stood staring at the running water without blinking for the longest time, yet forced herself to continue, knowing it would clear her mind and settle her stomach.

After everything was clean and put back exactly where it should be, Liz felt herself breathe properly for the first time since looking at her phone. She knew it would help and forcing herself to do it gave her the satisfaction she needed. She allowed herself to turn and look at the phone on the counter, but picking it up seemed impossible. Instead, she decided to ignore it, and leave it lying face down on the white worktop, while she turned to face her laptop once again. She pulled out one of the grey bar stools and sat herself up at the island that dominated the middle of the space. Liz could hear her phone still buzzing next to her, but she left her fingers firmly on the keys of her laptop instead of allowing them to reach towards the noise. It reminded her of a time when Ellie was small. The white noise she used to use to make her fall sleep all those years ago. She would leave it going and Ellie would soothe herself eventually, just like this could. The reminder comforted her now, like it did back then; she was always happier when Ellie was asleep, and she was alone with her thoughts.

Opening her laptop, the screen stung her tired eyes and Liz was instantly reminded of the time. The strip of LED lights under the counters had kept a soft glow in the kitchen, convincing her it was simply early evening, and she would be going to bed soon. The harshness of her laptop, however, assured her that she was awake and not simply imagining some awful nightmare. When her laptop had loaded, she had intended to go straight on to her work emails, to see if anyone had already tried to contact her over these posts… but she needed to get her head together first. To decide what she was going to say and how she was going to react. She knew if she got flustered, things would get worse. A lot worse. And the school wouldn't be the only ones with questions – of course there was Rob and the children to think about too.

Rob and Liz had been together a long time. Circumstances had made sure of that. The teenage pregnancy that had stripped her of everything, other than him. Everyone thought she was so lucky that he'd stuck by her, that she should feel so grateful to him, but Liz was never sure why. Surely Rob should be grateful for her? She's the one that chose to grow the baby and let it ruin her figure and her choices. But no. All praise lovely little Rob that stuck by the teenage slut and her bastard child. Liz didn't feel lucky at all, but she did work hard, and she did change the reputation the teenage pregnancy had given her, and that was not something she was prepared to give up easily.

Work was her control, a way of gaining something just for her and no one else. It was her life, her everything. She'd always wanted to teach, to make a difference. The kids were still a part of it, of course, but really, she was far more switched on than just being the doting maternal type... which, in all honesty, was never really something that came easy to her anyway. Part of her had always wished it had, that she'd gained the same feelings of unconditional love that every other mother seemed to get whilst pregnant, but she never did, and she'd learned to live with that. What she couldn't live with, however, was the thought of her career being taken from beneath her. It had been too planned, too meticulously protected for Ben to ruin everything. Liz knew from the beginning of her career that teaching had the highest female employment rates and the highest percentage of women in leadership and therefore it was the best way she knew of getting the success and salary she really wanted. Sure, she wasn't an accountant or a banker, but women had to struggle to get up the ranks in those jobs, not so much in teaching.

Having the money to buy things she wanted gave Liz more satisfaction than anyone would ever understand. So many times in her teenage years, she was told that she would always struggle with money because of her *situation*. That's what the elderly relatives used to say anyway. Ellie was never Ellie to them, or a baby, or a person for that matter; she was a situation. Something that needed to be addressed and maintained, not loved and adored. Liz had often wondered if this was why she felt the way she did. Even after she had successfully cut her family from her life, she still could not warm to the girl she had been forced to raise and had regularly been left wondering if that was her family's fault, or her own.

She often looked at women in the staff room, announcing their pregnancies and clutching their stomachs with such joy as all the other women cooed around them, and Liz would find herself just standing in the corner, trying to smile but unsure why she couldn't. It wasn't that she wasn't excited for them; it was just that her pregnancy had never been that way. She didn't get to announce it; she got to hide it. People weren't pleased for her; they were disappointed, and this feeling had embedded so much that when Rob was desperate for a second and Liz had reluctantly come off her pill after him promising to do the stay-at-home dad bit, she never really felt excited about that pregnancy either. It was simply an inconvenience by the end. She grew the baby but was excited to hand it over to Rob and get back to work where she belonged. Where she still belonged... despite the next *situation* that was obviously about to upturn her life once again.

A noise from the doorway interrupted Liz's thoughts and she turned to see Thomas standing at the kitchen door, rubbing his bleary eyes. He had thrown his dressing gown over his shoulders, and it always amazed Liz how small it made him look. It was a size 12–13 years – she knew because Rob had made such a fuss of buying it – yet it swamped him. His hair was getting long now too and his fringe flopped forward – almost like his hair was adding to how small his face was. He looked so young still, despite starting secondary school earlier this year.

'Mum? Is it breakfast time?'

Liz couldn't help but roll her eyes as she turned back to her laptop and away from her son.

'Of course it's not breakfast time, Thomas – it's the middle of the night. You have a clock in your room, don't you?'

'Then why are you up?'

As he asked the question, he stepped forward. Liz didn't want him to see anything, of course she didn't, but she also seemed to involuntarily shudder if he got too close. Or if anyone did for that matter. She didn't like people encroaching on her space. It was just something that was a part of her.

'Because I have work to do. And you need to go to bed. Now. Off you go or you'll be too tired for school in the morning.'

'Well, I'm up now. I could make you a cup of tea if you like?'

'I've just had a coffee.'

Well, she had intended to have the coffee and he didn't need to know any more than that. In fact, the sheer mention of it made her realise how much her hand was still stinging. She allowed herself to look down and could see the red spreading across her bony fingers. She hid it from view – from herself and from Thomas – and wished more than anything that he would leave her be, yet he continued to press her further.

'Well, I could get some milk and keep you company?'

'Some milk? Oh, Thomas, when will you grow up? You're in secondary school now. You aren't meant to want to stay up and drink milk with your mum. Go to bed.'

She felt guilty. It was too harsh. She always seemed to know that after she'd opened her mouth. But by then it was too late. It was like someone else took over, especially when she was talking to Thomas, and no matter how much she would think it would change, he always made her irritable and that was something she could never hide. Certainly not at 3am with her phone buzzing, her stomach spinning and her hand stinging.

'Mum?'

'What now, Thomas?'

'Your phone. It's buzzing loads. Do you know? It's right there.'

'Yes.'

'Shall I get it for you?'

With that, he stepped forward, and went to grab her phone from the side. Liz spun around on the bar stool and grabbed his hand instead. It was probably a little too forceful, a bit too dramatic, she had to admit, but she had to stop him from seeing anything else.

'No.'

Their eyes met, but neither of them spoke. Thomas's blue eyes looked like a scared puppy's after being caught doing something they shouldn't. He looked young and innocent. Liz knew she did not. Thomas broke the silence first, wriggling his arm away as he did so.

'OK… Night then, Mum.'

She knew he was waiting for a hug, for some kind of affection, for more physical contact than her just grabbing his arm, but she couldn't. She didn't know why, she never knew why, but she couldn't bring herself to do anything but let go of his arm and turn back around to face her laptop screen.

'Night, Thomas. I'll be at work in the morning when you wake up. I want to get in early, so I'll see you for dinner, OK?'

'Mum… is everything alright?'

'Yes, it's fine. Now go. Goodnight.'

'Night, Mum, I love you.'

The words hung in the air as he left the room and she listened to him climb back up the stairs to bed. Her throat was stuck. She knew what she should have said, but the words never seemed to come out. She wondered if they ever would. But for now, she had more pressing things to worry herself with. There was plenty of time for Thomas later.

Ben

(12 days earlier)

So… I went into school today feeling pretty crappy about the weekend. Two hours I sat on my bed with my coat on. Two bloody hours. Felt like a right twat, I did. What made it worse was that my new 'uncle' reckoned he couldn't remember where the bathroom was and came strolling into my room. Of course, he asked why I was just sat there, on my bed, in my coat. Who wouldn't? When I said I was waiting for my mates to text me back… he creased up… honestly nearly pissed himself there and then. Full blown laughed in my face and shouted down the stairs to me mum, who joined right in. I had to walk round the streets for an hour after that just so I could pretend they'd text me and was waiting for me to meet them. They hadn't though, had they? Obviously. Bloody freezing it was too. And I stepped in a puddle in my new trainers. Fuck it.

Anyway, it's all sorted now. Turns out Mitchell didn't have his phone on him. Said he'd logged on to his Insta account from Ryan's phone to put the story up and then logged straight back out again so he didn't see my message, or my Facebook one, or any of the three texts I sent him. Makes sense though, don't it? If his phone was at home and that. Then he said I should have just come straight down and met them whether I'd heard from them or not. So, I'll definitely make sure I do that next time. Not that it will happen again, mind. I'm going to make sure I have all the money I need from now on, even if I have to go through Mum's purse again.

To be fair though, after my day at school today, they'll probably invite me every time without me even having to ask because today I was a fucking legend. Yes, me, Ben Bridges, once a dickhead, now a rockstar. Because today, we were sitting in English class, me and Mitch, chatting away like mates do, and who should walk in? Only Miss Hall, that's who. Everyone goes quiet as soon as her head pops round the door. Old Mr Bamford at the front looks all smug. He probably thought she'd come to bark at us for being loud and not listening and that, but she didn't. She just looked straight at me and goes 'Ben? Can I have a quick word outside?' The whole class cheer like I'm in trouble and I just sit there… frozen… thinking what the fuck have I done? I don't remember getting in trouble. Sure, I was chatting, but so was everyone else. It weren't just me.

Then… I'm just about to get up and walk over to her when Mitchell grabs my arm and makes me stay put.

'What the hell, Miss? Ben ain't done nothing.'

Shit me. Yup. That happened. He stood up for me in front of everyone. The whole class looked well impressed, not Miss Hall… obviously, but the kids did. She took a deep breath for a second and then just went, in her smug voice, 'This has nothing to do with you, Mitchell. I simply asked to speak to Ben. Let go of his arm. He is not a dog on a lead.'

The class laughed at this. So did I, to be fair, until I saw Mitchell's face. I tried to soften the situation and told him it was OK, that I'd just go see what she wanted, but he was already angry by then. He started swearing at her... actually swearing to the deputy head's face. I mean, not loud enough for her to hear, mind. Mitchell ain't stupid, but he ain't scared either, which is why he said loads back to her, loud enough for me and the people around us to hear... but maybe not her... if I think about it. Still, Mitchell is fearless.

Anyway, she took me outside to the corridor. It's not a wide corridor because of the lockers. Not that anyone uses them anymore. Most of them either have graffiti on them or have been punched in the middle, so they wouldn't lock now even if you could find the key that they gave you in Year 7 and told you to look after. Anyway, she stood really close to me. I assumed it was because the walls always had chewing gum on them and she didn't want to get it on her posh shirt or something like that, but there was something different about her facial expression which made me think it had less to do with the gum and more to do with me. I don't know why, she was just sort of smiling and her eyes are normally dead harsh, but they looked a bit softer today, like sexy soft, and she was using them to make eye contact with me. In a small space. Just us two.

Anyway, there we were, standing well close in the corridor – I mean, good job no one walked past otherwise it would have looked well awkward – and she just started talking straight away about how she knows I don't get much support at home and how my grades were slipping and how she could help me out. I felt pretty embarrassed by this time, I'm not going to lie. I hate talking about shit at home. But when I tried to look down at the floor a bit, I realised, because we were so close, it kind of looked like I was staring down her top. I wasn't. But it was a bit hard not to. I'm quite tall for my age, see, always have been, tall and lanky, not hench like I should be. She's short as well, Miss is. Petite, people would say, I reckon, and she always wears these floaty shirt things with the buttons undone at the top.

Well, when I looked down, I caught sight of her bra. It was lacy and black, and we were standing close... and... well... I had to think of something really gross, really quickly... put it that way.

Basically, the conversation was her offering to do tutoring sessions, one to one like. It sounded lame. Would just mean I was doing schoolwork for even longer – who wants that? I told her I couldn't do Friday after school because of work, and she gave me this, like, sympathetic smile that was weird, but then she said we could do lunchtimes on certain days as well. Me and my big mouth. But what choice did I have? I told her I would do it and I swear to God she squeezed my arm and said she was pleased. It felt well weird. Teachers don't touch you. They don't come within three metres of you if they can help it normally, but there she was, standing close and squeezing my arm, and smiling. I left pretty sharpish after that, otherwise I would have to get that gross image back in my mind again.

When I got back to my seat, I was dreading telling Mitchell. I thought he'd proper take the mick out of me for being a geek, but he did the opposite. He'd chilled out by then. He said he'd wound up Bamford by whistling and making him turn his hearing aid up, then got the whole class to shout, and Bamford shit himself apparently. It sounded epic. Gutted I missed it to be honest, but at least he was smiling again and not angry anymore. Anyway, he said one-on-one time with the fit teach could be quite cool. Apparently, Ryan told Mitchell that you see down her top loads when she leans over in his English lessons and then I told him about the corridor and then he was well interested. Said we could get some pictures for the old bank… I weren't entirely sure what he meant by that, but I went along with it anyway and then Mitchell stood up at the bell and said,

'You coming?'

Yeah… he stood and waited for me. That's right… he *waited*. Don't get me wrong, we've had lunch together loads of times since that first lesson, but normally as soon as the bell goes, he's off and I'm bumping into people and stuffing things in my bag to catch up with him. Not today though. Today Mitchell stood and waited for me to pack up and join him. So, the most

popular kid in school waited for me to have his lunch *and* I saw

a bra. Best. Day. Ever.

Liz

(Now)

Liz's head was pounding like she'd had a night on the town. Not that she really knew what that felt like anymore, but it seemed to be how people spoke about it in the staff room. Storming headache, heavy eyes, and every step she took felt like she was walking through a muddy bog. Yet, she hadn't touched a drop of alcohol. She needed to keep a clear head. She had, however, been up all night, reporting posts on Facebook, thinking of her next move and, much to her own disgust, avoiding her work emails. Whatever was coming today needed to be dealt with head-on and face to face, and therefore, she'd decided that the only logical course of action was to get ready and get to work.

She knew that if she got ready early, she could get there with enough time to sort all this mess out before the school bell rang to start the day. She'd decided overnight that there was no question that Ben would be suspended for making up such wild allegations and this would allow her to continue her life as normal. Therefore, there was no logical reason to disturb Rob or the children or the police for that matter, as it wouldn't even exist by the time school started anyway. With all her reporting, she was sure the post would be taken down and completely removed by 9am, making everything normal again.

The only slight issue, however, was that her phone was still buzzing. By the time she had logged on and reported one post, another one seemed to appear. And they, she had to remind herself, were only the ones she could see. Ben's profile was not private, despite the full e-safety training the school put on last year, and she could see that his post had already been shared over a thousand times. A thousand in a matter of hours. Most of those that had shared it, of course, had not tagged her directly and were people who had the sense to make themselves private, so she knew she could not have reported them all. That unnerved her more than anything. She scratched her neck, the way she always did when she was tense, and tried to put the spiralling feeling out of her mind. She needed to be calm and focused... and she needed to talk to Jo, her boss.

Getting dressed in the bathroom was something Liz had gained great skills in over the years. She had always claimed it was to allow Rob to sleep in later than her, which made her come across dedicated and loving, she was sure, yet in truth, it was mainly so she would not wake the children and she could get ready in peace. When Thomas was younger, he would follow her from one room to the next, wanting to read stories to her at the most inopportune moments. She heard how other mothers adored this, but the only emotion she had was frustration. As Ellie grew a little older, she would beg her mum to let her use her make-up or do her hair in a fancy way like Laura's mum would. Liz would explain she didn't have time for that, and a ponytail would do. She remembered feeling so annoyed when Rob then spent many hours on YouTube learning how to do a

French plait. Ellie was happy, Liz had time on her hands, yet it had always irritated her in a way she never understood. However, at this moment in time, she was grateful for that distance from her family. It was not unusual for Liz to be gone before they awoke. They would not question her slipping out without saying goodbye, knowing that she would be heading to work to get things done, and this gave her plenty of opportunity to set things straight.

As soon as she was ready, Liz grabbed the keys to her Mercedes from the bowl that stood on the dresser in the hallway, brushed down her black high-waisted trousers and made sure her blouse was tucked in neatly. She had purposely chosen a high-necked top today – she didn't need anyone to have any ammunition against her – and put on her Louboutin shoes. She wouldn't usually wear these for a normal day at work – they would be saved for governor meetings and OFSTED – but today she felt like she needed some extra power behind her, and that was exactly what they gave her. The pair of shoes she had bought herself, a promotion present for getting deputy head. When she was head teacher, she would buy herself a Hermes handbag… She already had it picked out and in her online cart.

Driving to work felt different for Liz this morning. Looking out the window, she knew she was passing the same driveways, the same zebra crossings and the same people walking their dogs as every other day, but today she seemed to look a little harder. Usually, she would barely notice things like number 17 having a new door, but today, she did. She looked closely at everything and more importantly, everyone. The people crossing the road – were they staring at her? The people with their dogs – did they turn their head to look in the car? Check it was her? Had they seen those pictures? Read those posts? Liz could feel the anxiety rising in her throat. She swallowed it down and gave herself a shake. At the traffic lights, she pulled down the mirror in the visor of her car and checked her lipstick. She looked perfect… nothing out of place… just the way she should be.

Deciding she was being irrational, Liz pulled into the little shops down the road from the school. She had left without eating and had an instinctive feeling today was going to be a long one, so figured stopping to get some food would not be such a bad idea. She preferred to get her salads from the little bakery in the village, but she wouldn't have enough time today if she wanted to get in early, so she pulled into the parade of run-down shops where the one shiny Tesco in the middle only highlighted the state of the others.

After parking, she crossed the car park with purpose in her walk and headed towards Tesco Express to grab her lunch. Before she could get there, however, she heard the unmistakable sound of a group of Year 10s in the café next door. No wonder they were too tired for schoolwork if they were up at this time to meet for a bacon sandwich, Liz thought to herself. She quickened her steps, but it wasn't enough. As they bundled out of the café door, she was spotted, and they started to jeer across the car park.

'Oi oi, Miss,' one of them shouted towards her.

'Hello, Mr Pickford,' Liz replied, recognising this particular child as Matt Pickford, a boy she was very pleased to get rid of at the end of last year and did not intend on teaching again if she had anything to do with it. Which of course, she did. He had short, ginger hair and freckles. His head was as round as a football and he always looked scruffy. Somehow he had made a name for himself at the school, mainly by just being a loudmouth, but it was enough to get him a gathering that hung on his every word.

'I'm surprised to see you with your clothes on, Miss.' He carried on, spraying crumbs out as he did so and highlighting the smudge of ketchup he still had at the corner of his mouth. 'I much prefer the little black number you showed that Ben kid. Defo would have listened better last year if you had worn that to school.'

The crowd around him cheered. Liz froze. It was only as a car tooted her for standing in the middle of the car park that she was able to move her legs again and reach the pavement opposite Tesco. That made the group cheer again and mumble more mutterings that Liz could barely hear. Much to her own disgust, she put her head down and walked into the shop. The stares that were forming around her were burrowing into her skin, making her face feel hot and her eyes prickle. Every aisle she walked down, she could feel people staring and muttering under their breath. She should have said something. She should have cleared her name, protested her innocence, but instead she did nothing. She was so angry with herself for doing nothing. This was not the person that she was, and she wasn't going to change now. Standing in front of the fridge, she lifted her head back up from the ground, she held the gaze of the people that were staring at her, and she chose her lunch. She confidently strutted towards the tills and purposely chose to go to the cashier rather than the self-serve. She said thank you in a breezy manner and then walked straight out of the shop and towards the group of school children, who of course were still there, hanging around and waiting for her return.

'Mr Pickford,' she called, loud enough for him and the rest of the parade of shops to hear. She saw some kid instantly getting their phone out and starting to record, but she didn't stop. If anything, this would just go in her favour, a way of clearing her name without having to post anything herself, so she continued. 'I don't know what you think you know or think you saw, but I can assure you these allegations are false and will be removed immediately, along with the person that has done the accusing. I am certain Ben Bridges will be suspended by this afternoon and if you do not wish to join him, I suggest you keep quiet about the whole matter. Your shouting is slander, and I will pursue it as such, unless you keep your mouth shut from now on. Understood? Now I will see you later in school, where you will be on time and will have removed that bit of ketchup from the side of your mouth. Otherwise, I can assure you that you will be spending the whole week in detention with me. Have a good day, Matthew.'

His face said everything she needed to know. His pale skin had gone slightly pink and his eyes, despite his white eyebrows, showed more expression than she had ever seen before. He had also pulled his hand into his sleeve and had begun furiously rubbing at the corner of his mouth. She knew nothing else was needed. As she turned and walked away, she heard him mutter something along the lines of 'You'd like that, wouldn't you? Another boy on his own in detention?' It got some reaction from his most loyal of cronies, but not enough to worry Liz. She had stamped him down in public and for a fourteen-year-old boy that was all that was needed to crush his spirit. She also knew that one more suspension for Matt would mean being kicked off the football team, and that was not something he was going to risk easily. Especially with scouts coming to the tournament next week. She got into her car with a new determination for the day. She would no longer fear this stupidity. It could not harm her anymore. She would go to work, speak immediately with her head teacher, who would suspend Ben and put this situation to bed. Of course, that would be a shame for Ben, being stuck at home, but she couldn't think of him right now. She had to focus on her own life.

She put her perfectly polished fingernails around the black leather steering wheel of her car and took a deep breath. Besides, she reminded herself, he had brought this all on himself by creating those posts and opening his mouth. She still couldn't wrap her head around making everything so public. But that could always end up creating another opportunity. If need be, she would lead an assembly about the dangers of social media and then it would be old news by next week. All she had to do was get through this morning and it would all be fine.

It was not fine.

~

From the second Liz entered the school building, there was an atmosphere she couldn't quite put her finger on. There were never many members of staff in at 7am, but more than the general public would think. The Senior Leadership Team would all be arriving within the next five or so minutes and of course the very keen Newly Qualified Teachers would have been here for half an hour already. Her head teacher, Jo Swann, would have barely been home from the night before. She could see her door ajar from across the staff room and knew she had to walk in with her head held high. Liz wasn't foolish. She knew the conversation had stalled since she'd walked into the communal area. She could also see the pink cheeks glowing from the NQTs by the photocopier, but she was not going to address anything without speaking to Jo first. Instead, she put on the most casual voice she could muster and simply stated a generic 'Good morning' to the room before walking into Jo's office and shutting the door. Before she had even turned around, Jo had begun the conversation.

'I'm pleased you came straight to see me, Liz. There's no point avoiding the elephant in the room.'

Jo was older and plumper than Liz. The years of teaching had taken their toll on her and although she still attempted to look professional, her suits often clung in all the wrong places – probably because she refused to buy the bigger size that was so desperately needed – and her hair was always pulled back tight in a clip that got progressively looser throughout the day, despite the layers of hairspray that had been applied.

'I completely agree, as always. I needed to know what we were going to do to squash this little matter?'

With this comment, Jo placed her coffee cup back down on the desk and ushered Liz to take a seat opposite. Usually, Liz would sit on the blue cotton sofa in the corner of the room, they would have paperwork spread out all over the floor, and the coffee machine would be working overdrive. This time, however, she was encouraged to sit at the office chair opposite the desk and it was clear Jo was not about to get up and lounge on the sofa either. Her arms were folded in front of her chest and Liz automatically felt like a child that had been sent here from class. Obligingly, Liz took the seat at the desk and Jo continued.

'The problem is, Liz, this isn't a little matter. In fact, it is the direct opposite. It only came to my attention an hour or so ago. I'm sure it came to yours a lot earlier than that. So I must question why you didn't think to pick up the phone and let me know?'

In truth, Liz had tried many times to ring Jo's number since the early hours of this morning, but she could not once bring herself to press dial. If she was truthful, she had wanted it all to be a dream so bad, or to simply float away before it got too big, but she could see now that was not about to happen. If anything, it was only going to get bigger, and she needed to stay on top of it at all costs.

'Well,' she replied, trying to stay as calm as possible, 'I knew you would not believe a word of it, of course, but I also knew talking to you face to face about it was probably more important. We will need to decide together what happens to Ben. He has a lot going on at home, so I wouldn't want to come down on him too harsh, of course, but he will need to know that situations like this can't be repeated.'

'Situations? I'm sorry, but I need to interrupt you there.' Jo leaned forward on her desk and looked Liz directly into her eyes to ensure there was no mistaking her next piece of information. 'Of *course* nothing too harsh will be happening to Ben. He is a fifteen-year-old boy. A *fifteen*-year-old child who has some very inappropriate photographs of you in his possession and I need to know how he came across them. I am giving you a chance here, Liz.'

'Giving me a chance?' Liz couldn't help but show her feelings now. She didn't want to get cross, no, that wouldn't look good, but she couldn't help but feel annoyed by the fact that he was seemingly being believed so easily. Surely her reputation should be giving her the upper hand in this conversation, especially over a teenager. How did he end up with so much power? Besides, Jo was meant to be her friend, wasn't she? Of course, they hadn't actually socialised out of school, but they had worked together for years, and Liz had spent many an evening working late to ensure that Jo had everything she needed. Liz couldn't help but feel almost stupid for expecting her to just have her back now. The direction this conversation was heading was not in her favour and she needed to steer it back to where she wanted it to be.

'I can assure you those photographs are not of me. I don't even own lingerie like that. Honestly. I don't know how he's done it, but that child has never seen me in any way other than as his teacher.'

'You don't own that underwear?'

'No.'

'So how did he get the picture?'

'How do I know? Photoshop can do wonders nowadays.'

'Pretty good Photoshop then, isn't it? If that's what you're claiming? Even managed to get the tattoo on your leg right.'

The tattoo. Oh God. She'd forgotten about that. Was it really noticeable on the picture? Liz took a deep breath and swallowed the urge to pull her phone out and check the photos once more. She'd had the tattoo for years, one stupid decision when she had just had Ellie. She was good at stupid decisions then, but no one knew about it other than Rob. He'd gone mad when he saw it… and Jo. One night they were working late and discussing times they did things as silly teenagers, trying to relate to the kids they taught. The problem was, Liz hadn't really had the teenage years that everyone else had, so the tattoo had been her one story to put forward in the conversation. She wished, more than anything, that she'd remembered that conversation long before this moment.

'And what about the text messages?' Jo was not giving up. 'He's put screenshots of texts between the two of you up online for the world to see. Telling him that you're waiting for him… yearning for him for God's sake, Liz. I need some hard evidence that these are not from you.'

Liz sat straighter in her chair. She was at the edge of her seat and knew she was starting to look like Jo was getting to her. She stopped herself from scratching her neck again and began to address Jo with as much forcefulness as she could feel being directed at her.

'And what about the hard evidence to say that they are? I can hand over my phone now and you would see no such messages, no pictures, no interaction at all.'

'Easily deleted, I guess.'

'Can't you see? He's fabricated all of this.'

'It's quite a lot for a *child* to fabricate, Liz.'

'But…'

'The point is… Miss Hall… is that I don't know which of you is telling me the truth and that puts me in an impossible position.'

'You don't know who's telling the truth?' Liz allowed her arms to flail into the air in utter disbelief. All aims of remaining calm and professional had gone out of the window and it was all Liz could do to not stand up and pace around the office. 'Come off it, Jo, you know me. You know I would never do anything like that.'

Jo didn't rise to her outburst. In fact, she almost seemed like she was talking slowly for a child that didn't quite understand the assignment they'd been given. She folded her arms on the desk and tilted her head ever so slightly as she spoke.

'I know you as a colleague, Liz. I can validate your work ethic, but I cannot validate you as a person. At the end of the day, I know you as well as I know Ben, and I am a teacher, not a detective. This is not down to me to work out. However, the school is always my priority and therefore I've been in contact with HR and the recommendation is...'

'HR?' Liz couldn't stop herself from blurting out now. What did she mean she didn't know her as a person? She'd worked with Jo for ten years. Ten years they had moved up the chain together, Jo one step ahead, but always keeping Liz as close as possible. They had a career path that had always included each other. When Jo applied for the executive head of the Academy Trust next year, Liz was going to take over Sandringham. Then Jo would move to an advisory role in county, and Liz would take over the academies. They worked together, kept each other in mind, helped one another. Or, come to think of it, Liz certainly helped Jo. Helped run the school so Jo could go off and show her face at Academy Trust meetings.

Helped set up for parents' evenings and open evenings so Jo could make sure she looked presentable for addressing the parents. In fact, Liz had been the one that wrote the speech for the last open evening – Jo had been too busy… Jo was always too busy. But she wasn't too busy now to give Liz a lecture on trust. How could she question what Liz was telling her? Did Jo respect her? Did she value her as a person, as a friend? Or did she just like that she had someone to fall back on? Someone to sort out the details that made her look better. Liz had to admit to herself that, of all the thoughts she'd had during the early hours of this morning, Jo not backing her was not one of them. She'd always been certain that her trust and loyalty was a given.

'Why would HR need to get involved? Surely everyone can see he is just a fifteen-year-old kid with a wild imagination? Surely *you* can see that this is ridiculous.'

Jo took a deep breath and spoke slowly and clearly… much like she did in those many speeches Liz had written for her.

'Like I said, it is an awful lot for a *child* to fabricate. I realise technology has moved on, but seriously... this is Ben Bridges we're talking about, Liz. He can barely string a sentence together, let alone make up all of this. Whatever the truth, having this out in public does not make the school look good, which does not make me look good. If I'm not seen to be taking this seriously, it could have real ramifications on my application for executive headship and I can't have that damaged by anything, or anyone. I must take a purely professional stance and that's something I was sure you, of all people, would understand. I cannot be your colleague in this, Liz. I can only be your boss, and as your boss I am informing you that HR have asked for you to remain at home pending further investigation. It is out of your hands. You will still be on full pay as no decisions have been formally made, but it would be best for the school if you stayed out of the way, while we work all of this out. It is what's best for everybody.'

Liz allowed herself to look into the eyes of the woman sitting opposite her. The woman who had, up until this moment, always been considered as someone to trust. She refused to break eye contact and tried hard to steady her breathing, but the more time she allowed the silence to remain, the more she allowed her emotions to surface.

'Best for everybody, is it? So is Ben being asked to stay at home too?'

'Please don't make me reiterate that Ben is a child again, Miss Hall. And not just any child, but one with a very complicated home life, as you well know. The school and HR think keeping him off would be detrimental to his well-being. Not to mention that keeping him off might prompt his mum to involve the police. Again... because he is a child. I don't think that should be something I have to repeat any more. I hope with all my might that is not something you have ever forgotten previously.'

With that, Jo rose to her feet and indicated the door. Sill sitting, with her hands in her lap, Liz felt the angriest she had in a long time. She grabbed her bag and rose to her feet, but before turning towards the door, she forced herself to look at Jo and cleared her throat.

'I am assuming, as you have contacted HR, that I will receive all of this by letter and that I will have a chance to appeal. Because believe me, *Mrs Swann*, I intend to do so. I will also be writing my own letter about the accusatory tone you have used in our meeting today and will be informing them of the lack of support I feel I have from you.'

Jo took a breath, but no part of her flinched at anything Liz had said. Instead, she met the eye contact and spoke in a calm and almost warming tone.

'Your own feelings and opinions are just that. No one can tell you how you feel, but also no one has witnessed such conversations. I am simply reciting the guidance I have been given and will certainly be in touch later today. I would also advise you to go straight home and await any phone calls that may come your way. Your outburst at the shops earlier today has already been shared on social media and HR will need to be informed of that also. You are not helping yourself here, Miss Hall. We now have a tape recording of you claiming that Ben's suspension would be imminent, as well as your request to have another boy alone in a room with you. Unless you'd like to argue that the video has been somehow Photoshopped too?'

Liz felt herself deflate, like all the air had left her body, and suddenly she was finding it hard to stay on her feet. She felt them wobble in her shoes and she knew her power was slipping through her fingers despite wanting to cling on for dear life.

'For detention. I said the boy would be with me for detention...'

'Something that is no longer your concern, until we have this all straightened out, of course. But for now, as I am sure you are aware, my job is to protect the children in my care and that is exactly what I intend to do. Please do not talk to any other colleagues about this on your way out. I wouldn't want any further damage done to your career.'

Turning on her heels, Liz opened the door and walked back across the communal staff area. She saw the NQTs at the photocopier once again and wondered how much of that conversation they had heard. Then, with a deep breath, she realised that having them as witnesses may not be a help to her after all.

Ben

(11 days earlier)

Shit. I'm going to be late for work at this rate. Got chatting to
Mitchell after school, didn't I? He wanted to know about my
session with 'Hot Hall' at lunchtime… That's what he calls her.
Funny, innit? He said he thought I might get to look down her
top again or something, and he wanted to be the first one to
know about it, so that's why he waited. I couldn't get over it,
walking out of last lesson and having Mitchell actually waiting
for me. In the basketball courts. Just like he was waiting for his
best mate. It was epic.

Even better than that though, I genuinely had more to tell
him. Like, not just getting a glimpse of that lacy bra again,
despite that being fucking awesome, but the fact that I think she
fancies me. Like, honestly, she does. I can feel it. And part of me

is well happy that the fit teacher is into me, obviously, but the other part of me is more chuffed because if I can get her to keep flirting with me, I could finish every day of school with Mitchell waiting for me on the basketball courts, like best mates. I think I'd feel like king of the bloody world then. Even more so than I do right now.

Basically, I had my first one to one with her at lunchtime and she was pretty much all over me. That's what I told Mitchell, and I don't think he really believed me at first, but I told him I weren't lying, said we didn't even do any work really. I went into the classroom, right, and she was there waiting for me. She told me to sit down and then turned her back on me so she could lift her chair over her desk. She could have just walked round or put the chair there before the session, but she didn't, did she? She leant right over the desk to lift it, with her bum pointing right towards me, and she had these proper tight black trousers on that stretched even tighter when she leant forward. And I'm telling you, I couldn't see any knicker line when she bent over, honest, none. The girls at school all wear thongs so they don't get... what's it called? VP something? I heard Lynsey chatting about it the other day at lunchtime. But their thongs still poke up over the top. They defo lift their tops up if they sit in front of you in lessons so you can see it. It's well distracting...

Anyway, she definitely had nothing poking out the top *and* didn't have any 'VP-whatsit', so I reckon she must have been wearing nothing at all. Fuck. Lynsey said her sister does that when she goes out in a tight outfit. And these trousers were tight... not like too small for her... like tight in all the right places. I mean, whether it was a thong or nothing, as soon as she bent over, all these thoughts came into my head, and I had to sit under the desk pretty, bloody quickly. That was definitely her intention though, I reckon, because when she turned back round, she had this smirk on her face and I swear her eyes darted from under the table back up to my face. I felt my cheeks flush, but I didn't tell Mitchell that bit. Obviously.

Then, she sits opposite me and looks at me square in the eyes and she goes, 'OK, before we start, let's just have a chat. I want you to feel comfortable in these sessions, Ben, I want you to feel like you can open up to me.'

I thought, yeah, right, it's you that wants to open up to me... open your legs, that is! Well, that's what I thought in Science this afternoon when I was going over it in my head and I thought I better remember to tell Mitchell. I did as well, and he found it well funny. Proper laughed. It was awesome. Anyway, then she goes on to say that she knows sometimes things are bad at home and I need to know that I could talk to her if I wanted. As she said it, she leant her head on her arm and her hair fell down it like a waterfall. I got a bit distracted then. It's so shiny and dark and I couldn't help but think about touching it, but I didn't, and I snapped myself back into the room. Basically, she was saying that I could come to her whenever I needed to talk about anything. She said it was so that it didn't affect my work and stuff, but I reckon she was talking in riddles. I think she just wanted me to get to know her more, spend more time with her. I

could see the way her mind was working. I told her I didn't want

to talk about home, which I don't ever, but she didn't push it, so

that obviously wasn't her intention in the first place, was it?

Seriously, if she was really worried about me home life and that,

she would have carried on the conversation. But she didn't. She

just kept looking at me, with her hair to the side. So intense like.

Proper eye contact. And I swear she bit the corner of her lip at

one point. Her bright red lipstick looked really stark against her

teeth, and it reminded me of a poster in the front of this old

record shop in town. I knew it was something I'd think about

when I went to bed. And I liked it. But if I'm honest, I definitely

looked away first. Not that I told Mitchell that bit either. I ain't

stupid.

What I did tell him though is that every time she spoke to

me, she leant further across the table and closer to my face.

Those grey plastic tables aren't wide, are they? My books hang

off the end of them most lessons and the edges are always ripped and sharp, so leaning in so close couldn't have been comfortable, but she still did it. In fact, every time she put her head on her hands to look at me, I could feel her breath on my face. Not in a gross way like – she didn't have minging tuna breath or anything. It was minty, proper fresh, like she'd chewed gum just before the session. I mean, the only reason she'd do that was because she was planning to get that close to me, right? She knew I'd be able to smell her breath and she wanted *me* to know it was fresh in case anything happened. Which it didn't… this time, but I can tell it's going to. And I definitely told that bit to Mitchell, but he laughed at that. Not with me, like before, but at me. But I don't think he entirely meant it because he definitely seemed interested. Besides, he wasn't there. He didn't see her staring into my eyes, biting her lip and using moves like the chair trick… that was just for me. She knew I was thinking about her arse, and she liked it. She knew I was staring at her lips, and she liked that too. So yeah, even if he doesn't believe it will happen, it will. It has to. I've been thinking and if this happens,

I'll be the most popular kid in school. That's probably why Mitchell doesn't want to believe me... because then Friday nights would be my choice and not his. That would be immense.

I know I'm probably running away with it a bit now, but if I was the popular one, I wouldn't be running down the street right now trying to get to work on time. Nah, I wouldn't need a crappy job to get money because all the geeky kids would give me theirs. I wouldn't take it or bully them or anything, not like Mitchell does, but they'd want to know all the details of me and Hot Hall, because, you know, they're geeks and that and they don't know what *it* is like, so I'd charge them to find out. Pretty good business strategy if you ask me. I might as well be the next Alan Sugar. As soon as she makes her move, my life is sorted.

But for now, I'm just going to have to leg it to get to work. God, I hate this road. You can never bloody cross it. I can see Mr Chang staring at me through the window, just to the left of the giant blue fish sticker to make sure I can see him looking at his watch. I can tell the sodding time, mate; you don't need to be so dramatic. Thing is, I could walk up the road to the crossing, but it's so far I might as well just run across, if these pissing cars would move. Why is it that everyone needs to pop to the shops after the school run? What do these parents do with their days? I know some work, obviously, not like mine, but they can't have proper jobs if they're around at 3:30 to pick their precious kids up. So surely they could have done it any other time? Then I'd be able to get across this bloody road and stop the daggers I'm getting from the window. The chippy won't get proper busy until five when people come in for their dinner anyway, so I don't know why old Chang is getting antsy now. There's a gap here, I reckon, there's a Range Rover speeding up and an old red banger thing behind. It won't be able to keep up going up the hill, so I'll be able to run across before it. I'd bloody love a Range Rover. Mitchell's dad drives a well nice BMW, or so Mitchell says. We've never actually seen it because his dad works away a lot, but he's shown us which one it is on Google and it's well nice. To be fair, I think I'd be alright if my

dad drove this red old banger. At least he'd be able to see me...
or at least I might know who he is.

I run across the road and the red car honks his horn at
me, there was loads of room, he was being well over the top and
then I lift my bag above my head to weave in between the wing
mirrors of the parked cars. You have to be well careful since
they put CCTV in the car park. It was only put up to watch the
drunks stumble out of the Queenie, the pub on the corner,
because the shopkeepers were getting shitty about vandalism.
Fair enough. Problem is every dickhead now wants access to it
when the tiniest scratch gets on their cars. People are mental
about stuff like that. Mum says it's because all these city
wankers are moving into our town. I overheard her chatting with
some bloke the other night. We live just outside of London, you
see, not *in* London, so you don't pay loads and loads for houses
but close enough to get there by train in about half an hour.
Close enough that the estate agents are now calling it a
'commuter town' and describing it as 'up and coming'. What a

load of shit. There's nothing up and coming about where I live, trust me. Anyway, we now start getting all these pricks in suits living round here and changing the town. You know what I mean, the ones that look down their noses at kids like me. The ones who have no idea what happens to their chips when I go out the back to wrap them up…

Mr Chang ain't impressed when I walk through the door, and I instantly know he's going to put me on fryer duty rather than on the tills. I've been here the longest now out of his weekend workers, so I always get till duty, but old Chang really hates it when you're late and he likes you to know. When I walk in, he already has his arms folded and he meets me right in the doorway. He's dead tall, even taller than me, so he makes sure he stands really close when he's telling you off, so you look as little as possible. He can be a right dickhead sometimes.

'Promptness, Ben. We've spoken about it so many times.'

'I know, Mr Chang, I got caught up at school. Soz.'

'I think the word you're looking for is *sorry*, Benjamin.'

Wanker.

I move forward to try and close the door behind me – it's getting cold in here – but he doesn't move. Honestly, I reckon he gets his kicks by intimidating kids. Not that I'm intimidated, of course. Or a kid for that matter. He don't bother me, but I don't want to lose my job, so I have to make it look like he does. I'm good at that.

'Yeah. Sorry. I'll get my apron.'

I push past him and smell the usual disgusting smell coming from his dirty white apron. It's a mixture of fags and chip fryer and it makes you heave if you stand with him too long, so I need to get away quick. I can see the other lads laughing behind the counters at him calling me Benjamin. Twats. The problem is that ain't even my name. It is just Ben, on my birth certificate and everything. I remember being in primary school and this kid called Jackson said it was 'cause my mum couldn't spell Benjamin. I was angry at the time, but to be fair, it's probably true. My mum really don't help my social status. Anyway, I was right, Chang put me straight at the back on fryer duty. Bloody stinks round here. You know the smell when the oven ain't clean so when you open the door, it hits you in the face? Yeah, that's what I get constantly here, for the full five-hour shift. I swear if people actually came to the back, they'd never eat the food in this place. Well, unless you have to... like me.

~

I'd been at work for about two hours when the bell on the door rang and she walked in. Yup... Hot Hall was here standing in the chippy. She stood by the door in the same tight black trousers from earlier with her car keys swinging in her hand and her sunglasses on the top of her head. I could see her, but luckily from behind the screen there was no way she could see me. Not that I didn't want to talk to her or nothing; I would have bowled right over if we were just in the street, but we're not, are we? I'm stood here in this stupid white hat and pissing apron that makes me look like a right twat. Besides, she wouldn't keep fancying me if she could see and smell the grease dripping off my hair. Don't want to put her off right at the beginning, do I? Not that I think I can now, because it's obvious, isn't it? I told her earlier where I worked. And I told her we had to do a lunchtime session because I was working after school. Which means she *knew* I was here. She knew and she came... to see me. I mean, anyone in their right mind would agree with me now. She's stalking me. And why? Because she wants me. It's the only logical reason she would be in the chippy in the crappy end of town on a Friday night.

I could see her, looking for me, pretending she was looking at the board and checking what to order, but everyone knows what they sell in a chippy, don't they? No one checks that bloody board. It might as well say bloody ostrich bollocks for the amount of people that look at it. So she was definitely looking to see if she could spot me. I mean, she couldn't ask for me, could she? Couldn't make it that obvious. But she was one hundred percent trying to spot me so she could catch my eye. You know, accidentally on purpose like. I was gutted that I couldn't just rock up to her. Stupid uniform. And stupid bloody fryers.

So instead, I grabbed my phone out of my apron pocket. Chang hates you having phones on you when you're working, but he was too busy having a fag out the back to notice and this was too good an opportunity to miss. I hid behind the counter and managed to get a picture of her. I zoomed right in so it looked like we were close obviously, but this should be enough to prove to Mitchell that she wants me. I then made sure I kept my head down while I packed up her large chips and three saveloys. Wouldn't want her changing her mind. While they were cooking, she went next door to Tesco, probably to get herself something healthier. She wouldn't eat the food in this dump; she's too good for that. She must have got the chips for her kids, I reckon. Ellie's in my year, but I don't have anything to do with her. Our year is split into the left and the right side and I'm on the left... We don't mix with the right. Other than Mitchell, because let's face it, he can mix with whoever he wants. Apparently, Ellie hates her mum, but obviously she don't see her like I do. Well, that would be weird, wouldn't it? Still, Ellie don't know how good she's got it. Yeah, her mum might be dreaming about shagging me, but at least she feeds her kids when she gets home from work, which is way more than my mum does. Maybe when we're proper together, she'll get my dinner for me? Can you imagine? Shagging the fit teacher and having dinner on the table. Fuck me, that would be the life.

Liz

(Now)

Still shell-shocked from her meeting, Liz walked through the door of her home, somewhere so familiar, so well known, yet no comfort greeted her. She couldn't remember the last time she'd been here at this time of day. Even in school holidays she would put in a couple of hours at work each morning and the weekends were usually filled with gym classes and hiding at the leisure centre for as long as possible. By the time she got home, the house was full, but thinking about it now, she had no idea where they went while she was out. Did Thomas still do a club? Rob definitely used to take him somewhere, but she didn't know where or when or what it was even for. She couldn't imagine it was anything competitive – he wasn't blessed with thick skin.

As she placed her keys back in the bowl in the hallway, she realised she could barely remember the drive home. It had been a complete blur from the second she left the tall, green metal gates of Sandringham School to the moment she had pulled up on her driveway and put the key into the lock of her front door. The one thing she remembered, however, were the stares. The eyes that had burrowed into her skin as she'd walked out of the school building and through the basketball courts to reach her car. Jo's initiative to have before school booster sessions meant some kids turned up before 8am now. Not enough to cause a huge fuss, but enough to make Liz feel very uncomfortable indeed.

She'd realised herself the irony of how she had strutted across that same car park only half an hour previous. So sure of herself... and of Jo and the commitment and loyalty she would give her. Yet the truth remained. She had chosen to believe the world of social media over her own friend. Well... friend? Really? The word seemed so false now. She had always said Jo was her friend, always believed it too, but clearly to Jo, Liz was nothing but a colleague. Someone to clear up the mess, stay late, be so eager to please that nothing else would matter, nothing other than that next career jump.

Snapping herself back into the room, she pulled off the Louboutins and almost laughed as she threw them off her feet, leading them to fall to the sides and flash the red soles directly into her eyeline. Those soles that had given her so much power this morning were now turned upright on her hallway floor, mirroring the upturned way her life felt at this particular moment. She needed to stop and take stock, decide on a plan of action, and stick to it.

Stepping into the hallway, now barefoot and feeling heavy in herself, Liz managed to tune in to a noise upstairs. The family should have left by now and she should be the only one in, yet she was certain she had just heard a noise on the upstairs landing. She knew Rob had gone in to work early as the smell of the beef stew in the slow cooker was already fragrant in the house. She hated that slow cooker and hated how much it brought odours into her normally pristine home. Regardless, she hated the thought of cooking even more and it wasn't like she even ate the meals he cooked anyway.

Stomp.

There it was again. There was definitely someone in the house. Normally Liz would march up the stairs, determined to find out the cause, but today she didn't feel quite so sure of herself. In fact, she didn't feel herself at all. Tentatively she placed her handbag down on the carpet and stepped towards the bottom of the stairs. Looking up, she could see the floor lamp had been left on and for a second, she felt more annoyed about that than about a stranger in her house. Just as she was about to call up the stairs and demand to know who was there, the person came out of the room and stared directly at her. No awkwardness, just clear defiance in her eyes.

'Ellie! What on earth are you doing home at this time of day?'

'I could ask you the same thing.'

'Don't be smart with me, young lady. Come downstairs now.'

For the first time in what felt like forever, Ellie actually did as she was told. Without another word, she had started to walk, or stomp, down the stairs towards her mother. From this angle, with her arms folded, Ellie seemed almost intimidating. She had turned sixteen in January and that had clearly given her a growth spurt. That teamed with the newly bleached hair and the countless make-up tutorials on YouTube that had helped her to look ten years older than she was made Liz feel like she was facing off with another adult, not her daughter.

The only thing that made Liz realise that Ellie was still her stroppy teenager was the way she kept her head down, allowing her hair to fall into her face and the fact that her hands were still trapped inside the sleeves of her jumper. She had pulled on an over-sized hoody over her uniform, but you could still see the collar and tie poking out of the top of the neckline. Her skirt was barely showing out of the bottom of her hoody, clearly having been rolled up at the waistline, like many of the girls did in her year group. Liz made a mental note that she would have to have an assembly about uniform again soon, before being hit with the stark realisation that the assembly might never happen, let alone that she might not step into that hall as a paid member of staff again.

'Does your dad know you're home?'

'Does my dad know you sleep with kids?'

Wow. There it was. The punch in the gut that Liz had been feeling over and over again this morning. First Matthew at the shops, then Jo and now Ellie.

'Of course not.'

'No, I didn't think you'd tell him.'

'I didn't mean that. I meant there is nothing to tell. I haven't done anything wrong.'

'You sure about that? I can show you pictures that would make that hard to believe.'

By this time Ellie was on the bottom step and it was clear she was trying to intimidate her own mother, just like Matthew and Jo had tried before her. Liz was getting fed up with having the same conversation and this time was determined to come out on top.

'Of course I'm sure. I know what I have and haven't done, thank you very much. Besides, we're not talking about me. We're talking about you. Why are you not in registration?'

'Why are you not at work?'

Silence.

Ellie took this opportunity to push past her mother and walk towards the kitchen. It took a while for Liz to engage her brain enough to follow her, calling as she did so.

'Ellie. How dare you walk away from me. You should be in school.'

Without turning around, Ellie called over her shoulder. Her voice was muffled by her hood, but the words were sharp and clear as day to Liz.

'And so should you, but I bet you worked out pretty quickly that it wasn't going to be much fun for you – or even an option for that matter. Well, guess what, Mum? It wasn't for me either, especially as I didn't know what I was walking into.'

'What do you mean?'

Turning to look her mum square in the eyes, Liz could tell that Ellie was trying to be forceful in her answer, although it was clear that she was as shaken as Liz, perhaps even more so.

'You knew this morning that shit was on there, didn't you? That's why you left even earlier than normal. Didn't think to let anyone else know though, did you? My phone was dead, Mum. Probably all the notifications that killed it off. Thought I'd

91

charge it at school, but I didn't get there, did I? Met the girls at the shops and couldn't even get into Tesco for all the crap I was getting. The girls said they'd tried to ring me but couldn't. *They* tried to warn me, Mum, but you? You just let me walk into it. Shit knows what Thomas is going through now... and Dad. At least I had the sense to come straight home.'

'What do you mean Thomas? And Dad? I reported it all, Ellie. It will all be taken down by now.'

'Will it? Do you reckon, Mum? Wake up! Can't you hear that noise? The dinging from upstairs? That's my phone. I turned it on so the girls could keep in touch. Let them know I'm alright because, you know, they actually care about me. But I had to shove it under the bed. The notifications, the texts, the abuse I'm getting because of you. Because you can't keep your hands to yourself. What is it? Dad not doing it for you anymore? Needed someone younger? We all know that you like them young.'

'What's that supposed to mean?'

'Dad. I'm not stupid, Mum, I can do the maths. I always wondered why we didn't know Dad's age. Why there was never any mention of it. I just figured it was because he hated being old. Didn't like to talk about it, you know? Until last year when someone sent him a thirtieth card through the post. I saw your face when he opened it at the table. You were angry. And why's that, Mum? Could it be because YOU were sixteen when you had me, but Dad? He turned thirty before I turned fifteen, didn't he? He was *fourteen* when you had me, wasn't he, Mum? Fourteen and you were sixteen? You've clearly never got over having it off with kids.'

Before Liz knew what she was doing, her hand was raised, and she had struck Ellie across the face. She'd never hit her before, and she never thought she would, but she needed her to stop. She needed it all to stop. She'd obviously been sat up in her room working all this out and coming up with wild conclusions that she clearly thought mattered. But it didn't matter... did it? Clearly, it mattered to Ellie, so what was to say that it wouldn't matter to Jo? Or HR? Or the police. If they found out, would it make everything look worse? She couldn't let this get out of hand… or get out at all. Raising her hand was the only way she could make it stop. And it did. Completely. Ellie didn't move and neither did Liz and suddenly the clock on the wall in the kitchen felt louder than it ever had before.

Silence engulfed the room completely as the two females, who looked more alike than either of them liked to admit, stared anywhere but towards each other. It was Liz that broke first as she looked up to see Ellie's face; a mixture of shock and surprise remained, the anger briefly gone. Liz was trying to calm her brain enough to think about what she would say next. How she would get out of the situation and move on from the pain she had caused her daughter. But all she could think of was what Ellie had said about Rob and how that could damage her reputation further. As much as she knew she should put her arm around her daughter and apologise, getting through to her about not discussing Rob's age was more pressing. Her and Rob knew there was nothing to it, but would everyone else?

'Now you listen here, Ellie.'

'Listen? Listen to you?' Ellie shook her head and turned her back on Liz. Leaning her hands on the kitchen worktop behind her, she took a deep breath. After a second breath she turned back to face her mum, only this time the shock had been replaced, and the only emotion that remained was anger.

'You've just hit me.'

'Don't exaggerate, Ellie. I snapped you back into the room.'

'Oh, you snapped me back… of course… you didn't hit me round the face. I must have got that wrong. Just like everyone in the whole town has got it wrong about you and Ben.'

'They have got it wrong. Well, they've been lied to…'

'Just like I have. About this… about Dad.'

'Look, I need you to understand. The age of your father when you were born has absolutely nothing to do with this. Yes, I was sixteen but only just. My birthday is only a week before yours, isn't it? We were *both* young and *both* stupid. I am neither of those things now.'

'Oh really? Stupid? Nice, Mum. Seems to be your track record, doesn't it? Stupid to have me, stupid to get caught with Ben…'

'Watch it, Ellie.'

'Or what? You'll hit me again?'

Liz kept eye contact with her daughter despite the overwhelming urge to look away. In fact, the urge was to run away, not just turn her head. She wanted the ground to swallow her whole or to wake up and let this all be a dream, just like the bad endings she had read so many times in her students' stories. No matter how hard she wished though, the look of disgust on her daughter's face was burning her eyes and etching onto her mind forever. Before she could say another word, Ellie gained the momentum to walk away and storm back up the stairs to the bedroom she had left moments ago. Liz, alone in the kitchen, allowed her daughter to go. What else could she do? For the second time in twenty-four hours, she had a stinging in her hand. This time, however, it was the only feeling left in her body. The rest of her felt completely numb.

Ben

(10 days earlier)

Fucking hell. Sometimes I just hate being me. Being shitty Ben Bridges with the shit clothes and the shit hairstyle and do you know what? The shittiest life on the planet. Yup, that's me.

So, I got up to go to school this morning and as always there was no uniform clean. I went through the wash basket and grabbed a white shirt; I thought it was the one I had on yesterday and chucked it on. It fit alright, which is worrying when I think about it now. Anyway, Mum was still in bed when I left, same old same old, lazy cow, which meant I didn't see anyone before I got to school. Maybe if she'd actually been awake for once, she would have seen it first and warned me, but she wasn't, was she? She won't get up until *This Morning* starts. That's pretty standard in our house. So, there I was, merrily walking through the big green gates – who the hell thought to paint them dark green? – and I'm strutting over to Mitchell, who was sitting under the basketball hoop, when all of a sudden, he starts pissing himself. Then he nudges Lynsey and Jack, and they start laughing too. I turned round to see who they were laughing at and that just made it worse. By the time I got over to them, they were howling on the floor, with their phones in their hands taking pictures of me.

'What you laughing at?' I said to them. In a way that I thought sounded casual and cool, not wound up or anything, obviously. I didn't want them to think they were bothering me. But they didn't stop. I don't think it would have mattered how I had said it now to be fair. They probably didn't even hear me.

'Oh, nothing, Ben... or should I say... Betty?' Mitchell said and then laughed even harder. Then they all joined in.

'How about Becky?'

'Or Belinda?'

Mitchell loved that one.

'Fucking Belinda! That's a great one, Jack! Fucking Belinda Bridges has come to join us for the day! Go on, Belinda, pose for the camera. Give us a twirl!'

I still didn't have a clue what they were on about, just stood there looking like a right mug. I took my bag off my shoulder and as I looked down, I caught sight of the shirt I'd put on this morning. I never wore a blazer to school. For two reasons really: one, it hasn't been washed since I was in Year 7, and two, it hasn't been *replaced* since I was in Year 7. Mum always said she'd bought it big so it would last the whole time I was at school. But all that meant was that I looked like a sack of shit in it from the beginning and it's only got worse as I've moved up, which is why I just gave up altogether. I wouldn't mind, but it wasn't even new. Some other kid's name was written on the label from the day I got it. Most kids get in trouble for wrong uniform, but the teachers kind of leave me alone about it. Probably 'cause Hot Hall fancies me, I guess. All makes sense now. Never understood why they didn't say anything before.

Anyway, there I am looking down at the shirt I've got on, and that's when I realise that the only time I've looked in a mirror all morning was to gel my hair in the tiny bathroom mirror we have. I haven't seen the rest of my body and I haven't seen the shirt. The shirt that now looks distinctly like a woman's shirt. It's got pleats for the bloody boobs and everything. And to make matters worse, there's little stitched flowers all down the side. How the hell did I miss that? So there I was, stood in the middle of the playground, in me mum's fucking shirt while my so-called mates rolled on the floor pissing themselves and taking about a hundred pictures. Where the fuck are they going to end up? All over bloody Facebook and Insta probably. Well done, Ben, you dickhead.

Mitchell didn't stop with Belinda either, no way. That was only the beginning.

'I didn't realise you were getting hand-me-downs from your mum now too? Shitting hell! Benefits dried up that much, have they? You'll be turning up in those shit pink tracksuits she wears soon! Or are they just for special occasions?'

Everyone laughed. Fucking hell, even I laughed. What else could I do? It was awkward though. Standing there laughing at yourself. Even I could feel it, but I couldn't do anything else. I couldn't turn round and tell Mitchell he was being a twat, could I? Tell him to put his phone away? He'd fucking eat me alive. When he takes the piss out of you, he's got this face on him. Hard to explain, but his eyes go dark and even though his mouth is laughing, his eyes tell you he's ready to knock you square out. That was the look he was giving me, so I had to play along. It weren't the time to stand my ground. It never is with Mitchell to be fair.

Jack said later that Mitchell had been in a right mood that morning. Something about his dad not showing up at the weekend. He said it was a good job I'd made him laugh otherwise he would have been in a mood all day. What a good mate I am, huh? Stand there like an idiot and take a shitload of abuse just to make life easier for the rest of the group – top

bloke, me. Besides, bit rich, ain't it? His dad don't show up for

one weekend and he lays into everyone around him. Try never

meeting the prick in the first place. My dad did a runner before I

was even born, but you don't see me laying into people for it, do

you? I know I should be well chuffed that Mitchell has let me

hang out with them all, and I am, but days like today it don't feel

completely worth it. Not that I'd ever say that. I mean, he's still

the best mate I've ever had, but that ain't saying much, is it?

The thing is, without Mitchell, I'm back to being a

nobody. And now I know what it's like to be in the right crowd

and I can't let that go for anything – even if it does mean taking

a load of abuse while I'm stood in the basketball courts, wearing

me mum's shirt, and watching them fill my Facebook page with

so much evidence I'll never be allowed to forget it. My face was

bright red, and I was standing all awkward. And just as I was

thinking *What the hell am I going to do now?* It got even worse.

Because who walked past? Right then, as I was stood looking

like a twat? Only bloody Hot Hall. I thought I was going to die. I wanted the ground to swallow me up there and then. I mean, how the fuck was she going to fancy me when I was stood in full view looking like something off Ru bloody Paul?

She stopped when she saw me and came right towards us all. Mitchell was howling even harder now, and the others where all trying to calm down so they wouldn't get in trouble, but Mitchell couldn't care less. I'd love to be like that, but all I could think of was that she was going to have a go at me for wrong uniform in front of everybody, or worse, laugh along with them. And I didn't move. I hadn't the whole time. I was rooted to the spot and all I could do was just try to swallow over and over again where my mouth was so dry. I took a deep breath as she got closer and prepared myself for the roasting I was going to get when something bloody amazing happened. Because she didn't shout, or laugh for that matter. In fact, she showed no emotion on her face other than concern and care. And then, she reached out and put her arm on me, gently moving me to one side, all the while keeping the most intense eye contact I've ever witnessed in my life.

'Are you OK, Ben?'

'No.'

I said that a bit too quickly. I weren't keeping cool like I wanted to, but I think I said it quietly enough, so the others didn't hear.

Then she moved in even closer and kind of walked with me, right to the side of the basketball courts. I thought my legs wouldn't work, but they did. With her arm on mine, I was able to put one foot in front of the other. I reckon I even looked like I was strutting off. Bet I did.

'What's happened?'

'I put me mum's shirt on by accident. I didn't realise until I got to school.'

I smirked then, you know, tried to show her that I wasn't fussed and found it all really funny. Tried to show her that I was just taking it all on the chin, but she looked at me like I was upset about it.

'It's OK, these things happen,' she said, all the while with her arm on mine. 'It's nothing we can't sort out.' And then she sort of squeezed my arm in this playful way and smiled. I was so shocked by what was happening that I couldn't respond. Literally just stood there saying nothing. I mean, I knew she fancied me, of course I did, but I didn't expect her to make it so obvious in plain view of everyone else. She obviously mistook my silence for worry because she looked straight in my eyes and went, 'Don't worry, Ben.'

And I weren't. Well, I was a bit when it was all happening, but I weren't crying or nothing. Shit no. I was laughing in front of the others. She must have seen that. But... I did feel like a twat, and Mitchell did say some stuff about me mum that was a bit below the belt. I mean, I take the piss out of her, of course I do, but when other people do it... I don't know. It's just harder to swallow, ain't it? Anyway, I thought it was best to let Hall think I was upset because she was so bloody close to me, and I could feel Mitchell staring. This was definitely going to back up what I was saying the other day, so what was the harm in looking like I was worried?

'I didn't know I looked like this before I got here,' I said. 'Honest. I wouldn't have done this for a laugh.'

'Oh, I know, Ben. It's just a mistake. Look, there's some spare clothes in reception. If you come with me, you can get changed in my office and no one else needs to know.'

Shit. That's right. She said... *come with me and get changed in my office*, with her arm around me, and then she said... *no one needs to know*. In fact, thinking about it now, I think she smirked when she said that bit. You know, like a playful, sexy smirk. I'm sure she did. I mean, I was looking at the floor quite a bit, but I'm sure that's what I saw when I looked up. She wanted me to take my top off and not just anywhere but in front of her *and* not tell anyone. Then, to make it even better, she shot Mitchell a look to shut him up and told me to follow her.

I was thinking of maybe telling the gang she'd had a go at me. Maybe mouth to them that she was walking me off to get a detention slip for wearing something like this as a joke. You know, try and brush it off that way, but then… then I saw Mitchell's face and I knew he'd seen what I'd seen because he had shut up, not because of the look she gave him, but because her hand was still on my arm. He kept looking from her arm up to my face and back again and then doing this thing with his eyebrows where they went up and down. Not only that, but she was standing close to me, proper close, like that day in the corridor, and I knew exactly what he was thinking. It was obvious there and then, to me and to Mitchell, that she does want me, and she doesn't care who sees it. I mean, how many other kids would she have done this for? None. None except for Ben

Bridges. Because from then on, I could tell I wouldn't be Belinda Bridges again. No matter what pictures they had, it didn't matter, because I could see it in Mitchell's eyes, that I could laugh this off and still go down as a legend because he was impressed.

He even winked as we walked away. And I winked back. Fuck. I've never be the lad that winks at his mates. I've never been the lad that has a mate to wink at for that matter. But there I was, with a secret code. A secret conversation between my best mate and me. Because he is my best mate really, even though he's a twat sometimes. And on top of that, it's not just any conversation, is it? It's not one about football or weekend plans. It's the one where a fit teacher wants to take my top off in her office while she watches… I mean… that bit didn't actually happen in the end. She got me the shirt and when I went into her office to get changed, she got caught by Mr Smith and ended up chatting to him outside the door for a bit while I was inside. I did it as slow as possible, but Mr Smith had a lot to say. When I finally came out, she looked gutted that I was leaving. Even made some joke about how long I took to cover up her disappointment. Honestly, cock-blocked by Mr Smith. Who would have thought it?

Liz

(Now)

Looking around the downstairs of her home, Liz knew there was nothing left to clean. There was nothing out of place and not a speck of dust left on the surfaces. The home was pristine, everything in its rightful place, yet she couldn't gain any satisfaction from that. Her home may be in order, but her life was not. Ellie had stormed up to her room hours ago and her music could be heard blaring through the ceiling. Usually this would irritate Liz, but today it gave a little sense of relief. A moment of shutting out the world or drowning out her thoughts. Either way, as she scrubbed the skirting boards earlier with Radio 1 bellowing through the floorboards above, she had managed to zone out from the hell of the past twelve hours. Now though, now it was done, her mind had moved straight back to that conversation with Jo. Liz couldn't help but relive every second of it, kicking herself for all the things she should have said, and what she could have done.

She should have refused to leave. After all, what real evidence did they have? Yes, they had some pictures, some supposed messages, and a stupid post, but is that really enough to ask her to leave the premises? She should have stood her ground more. Maybe threaten *them* with police involvement? Not just HR. After all, this was slander – she'd said so herself to Matthew that morning. But she'd been so intent on protecting the school she hadn't even stopped to think about who was protecting her. She also couldn't shake the feeling that by leaving so willingly, perhaps she had made herself look guilty. Or whether shouting and standing her ground would have looked worse. One thing that she knew wouldn't go in her favour, however, was the fact that she'd lied.

When Jo had spoken of those pictures, the ones of her in the black lingerie, she had sworn she didn't own them. Had never seen them before in her life. Yet she knew that if she went upstairs, they'd be there, in her drawer, for anyone to find if they were looking. She'd always enjoyed wearing nice underwear; it made her feel empowered, and it made her feel wanted. She knew when she got undressed, Rob's eyes would dart towards her. Remind him of what he had, despite the fact that she rarely let him have it at all. But she knew he wanted it and that was enough. That was the part that made her feel powerful. The reason for the purchases in the first place. So why did she say they didn't exist? Walking out might have been a slip up, but saying something wasn't real when it was, that was a huge mistake. What if the police did get involved and searched the house? Would it come to that? Or would they even need to search for that matter? Would Rob just tell them all they needed to know? Would he clarify that they were hers? He may have been looking less recently, she had to admit that, but surely he still noticed enough to know the truth. And he would be angry enough to tell them.

Pushing Rob to the back of her mind once again, she found herself racing up the stairs towards her bedroom. She knew the set was in the wash basket, so all she had to do was dig it out and throw it away. The bins would be collected tomorrow, so if she could get them in the outside bin tonight, without anyone seeing, she wouldn't have to worry about that mistake again. It would just be one more thing out of the way.

Tipping the wash basket out on the bed, she immediately saw the black lacy bra, in between the mass of hers and Rob's clothes. The knickers, however, were harder to find. In a mad rush to look through, Liz hadn't even noticed the door swing open behind her, let alone her daughter standing in the doorway.

'What are you doing?'

Startled, Liz turned to meet her daughter's face. There was a red mark on her cheek where her hand had hit it earlier. Surely she didn't hit her so hard that it had bruised. Perhaps Ellie had been rubbing it on purpose, or used some blusher to make it look worse than it was. If Liz was honest, she wouldn't put either option past her daughter. They were too alike for that.

'I'm just sorting out the washing. Figured I'd make myself useful while I'm at home.'

Liz took the opportunity to shift her whole body towards Ellie and stuff the bra back under Rob's jumper behind her as she did so. The last thing she needed was for Ellie to put two and two together and come up with five. She knew she needed to start a conversation, to keep Ellie's eyes firmly on hers and stop them wandering. It was the only way to get her to leave without anything looking suspicious.

'Look, about earlier, I'm sorry I hit you. It's been such a whirlwind and I... I... just don't know what to do.'

Ellie lifted her head slightly and looked towards her mum. Her hard eyes seemed to soften, and Liz couldn't help but wonder if that was the first time she'd ever apologised to her own daughter. It didn't feel comfortable, but it needed to happen. She needed to soften Ellie and keep her on side, stop her digging any further.

'Well. I get that. I guess. Still a shitty thing to do though. And I still think you should've told us all this morning. But whatever. I only came in to tell you your phone has been ringing. I went downstairs to get a drink and it was buzzing in your handbag. Thought it was nothing, but it's the school number that's coming up, so I brought it upstairs for you.'

Without thinking any further about what she was concealing, Liz jumped up to grab the phone from her daughter's hand. She had pulled it out of her hoody pocket as she was talking, and Liz had reached for it immediately. Ellie was clearly shocked at the quick reaction, but Liz couldn't stop to think about that.

'Ellie. Why is my phone disabled?'

'Because I tried to unlock it to pass the message on to you. They've left a voicemail. But I didn't know your passcode.'

'No. Exactly. Because the passcode is there for a reason. I can't even call them back now.'

'You'll be able to look in a minute. Calm down, Mum, it unlocks itself.'

'Don't tell me to calm down, Ellie. My life is upside-bloody-down right now and I can't even listen to a pissing voicemail.'

Ellie pulled her hood up over her face, all softness immediately gone, and the harsh stare returned in its place. All hopes of reconciliation had abruptly vanished. Yet rather than stomp off, as would be the usual, she slouched against the doorway; she was obviously just as eager to hear this voicemail as Liz was and that unnerved her. Pacing up and down the bedroom staring at the countdown on her screen, waiting for it to unlock, Liz wished she could make her daughter leave.

'For Christ sake, Ellie. This could be important.'

Shrugging and returning to her normal stroppy teenage voice, Ellie mumbled, 'Well, excuse me for trying to help.'

'Trying to help? Trying to help? Don't talk rubbish. You were trying to snoop, trying to look in my phone, find something, weren't you? Well, there's nothing to see.'

Ellie stopped mumbling now and looked towards Liz. She lowered her hood and pushed her hair back from her face, either to show she was serious, or to show the mark more clearly. Whatever the intention, it made the room feel stifling and her words seemed to ring as if they were in an empty building.

'Show me then.'

'I can't, can I? You've bloody blocked it!'

'Convenient.'

Without another word, Ellie pulled her hood back up over her head, turned and stormed back out of the room and across the hallway to her own. She slammed her door with such force that the painting framed on Liz's bedroom wall shuddered, as if it was trying to escape the volatile home this had so quickly become. Staring at the painting, Liz realised she hadn't truly looked at it for so long. It was hung just above her grey headboard and was a wash of bright colours. Poppies, daisies and other wildflowers blew in the wind. A snapshot of a field, a dream, an escape. It was the only bit of colour in the whole room, perhaps even in the whole house unless you count the kids' rooms, which Liz often didn't. She had come home one day to find it hung on the wall by Rob. A grand gesture of love, a way of bringing back their childhood, the childhood sweethearts he always thought they were. Because the painting wasn't one you'd just find in a shop. It was Liz's GCSE art piece. Her last moment of pure creativity. When Rob looked at it, he saw the happy and colourful life they had as teenagers. When Liz looked, she simply mourned the freedom she once had. She'd painted this just as she had found out she was pregnant. Everyone assumed it was the blossoming of the baby inside her, but for her it was a dream of escape. The life she longed for.

In her hand, the phone rang, and Liz dropped her eyes from the painting to the phone screen brightly displaying the school's phone number. She had stopped watching the clock, distracted by the painting, yet they were obviously trying her again because she hadn't even had a chance to pick up the voicemail yet. She felt her hands trembling, and in that instant, she didn't know if it was fear or anger. Either way, she would use the emotions inside of her to her advantage this time.

'Liz Hall speaking…'

'Hello, Jo…'

'I left my bag downstairs.'

'No, I wasn't ignoring you on purpose…'

'I'm sure you can understand that I needed a bit of time to clear my head.'

'Oh, trust me, I am aware of the importance of this communication. I'll make sure it doesn't happen again.

Although, of course, if I was in school, I wouldn't have to wait by the phone...'

'Well, that's the problem. I don't really understand why I am at home.'

'Not if I'm innocent.'

'I didn't say *you* didn't think I was innocent. Though, you haven't actually said that you do. Come to think of it, I've never once heard you say that you believe me.'

'Then what is the point of this conversation, Jo?'

'Yes, I gave Ben tutoring sessions.'

'Because he is in my targeted children that were working below age-related expectations. Is that not my job?'

'He's a Pupil Premium child, which is why he is on my radar. Those children's targets reflect directly back onto mine, as you are well aware.'

'I understand his background...'

'Well, that's why I gave him one to one. I didn't think he would respond well in a group.'

'Because he's shy. I wouldn't get the best out of him with other pupils looking on.'

'Oh, you know what I mean…'

'No…'

'I'm not doing any other one to ones at the moment because I just don't have the time. As you may have noticed, my workload is pretty high as it is. I just thought… Ben needed it the most.'

'Because of *who* he is.'

'Yes, exactly… because he's vulnerable.'

'Wait…'

'Look, I know what you are trying to do.'

'No, I am not disputing that he is…'

'Yes, he is a vulnerable kid. Like so many in that school as you well know.'

'What do you mean "then why Ben"? Surely I have explained that already.'

'No...'

'Because why would I need another staff member there to watch me teach the kid how to write a bloody sentence?'

'I don't need to calm down. I need you to listen.'

'Oh really? Well, unfortunately, you've also shown *me* a different side to *you* today. I always thought I had worked with someone that showed respect and trust to their staff members, but obviously...'

Pause.

'Yes...'

'Yes, I'll be there.'

'At the meeting? Why would I...'

'Look, I've said I'll be there, but no, I will not be bringing a union rep. Is that all?'

Liz didn't even need to hang up the phone as she could already hear the beep before it had left her ear. Whatever was going to happen at this meeting, she needed to be as prepared as she could be, and therefore she found herself cursing inside for never paying to join a union. At the time it seemed ridiculous; all they did was strike and that was something she was never going to do. It wouldn't be worth the risk to her career. But she also had never pictured something like this happening. Maybe now it wouldn't be so bad after all. Although there was no point wasting time thinking about things like that. She put her phone in her pocket to ensure Ellie didn't get hold of it again and turned back to the matter in hand. Rifling through the washing with more determination than ever, she sourced the black bra and matching knickers and stuffed them under her top. Then without another thought in her mind, she walked purposefully out of her bedroom and down the stairs. As she reached the front door, she passed Thomas. Her son had also come home from school apparently, but she didn't stop to question. Moving past him in one swift movement, she walked out of the front door and round the side of the house to the bins. Lifting the lid, she found a plastic wrapping laying on top. After a quick look to check no one could possibly see her, she stuffed the undergarments from beneath her top in the plastic bag and buried it below the rubbish as far down as she could reach. Carefully placing the lid back down, attracting as little attention as possible. Then Liz allowed herself to take a deep breath. Now no one would need to know she'd lied. It was a daft, impulsive reaction, but it wouldn't come back to harm her now. As soon as that bin was collected in the morning, the only scrap of evidence they had on her would be on its way to a landfill, never to be seen again.

Ben

(9 days earlier)

I was just looking through Instagram and saw the gang were all down the skate park again. I weren't going to sit around this time, so I was just putting me trainers on and was about to head out the door when I heard me mum crying in the bathroom. I ain't a fucking monster, so obviously I knocked and asked if she was OK. She didn't answer, so I turned the door handle and went to walk in, and she slammed it shut before I could walk through the pissing door.

'For fuck's sake, Ben. I'm in the loo. Give me some bloody peace, will ya?'

'Yeah, alright. I was only seeing if you were OK. I heard you crying, that's all.'

Bloody ungrateful cow. Honestly. I was only trying to do the right thing. When she didn't say anything else, I went to walk down the stairs. It's not like I don't care or nothing. It's just that she obviously don't want my help and my mates were waiting for me. Well, they weren't actually waiting because they didn't know I was coming. But then if they don't know I'm coming, they wouldn't wait for me either, so I definitely needed to get a shift on. Then, just as I'm about to bomb down the stairs and out the door, I hear her again.

'Ben. Where you going?'

Now don't get me wrong, my mum ain't completely shitty. She has her moments, but she's never asked me where I was off to before. Sometimes she might ask if I'm going past the shops to get her something, but normally I just wander in and out without a care in the world. When I got my job at the chippy, it took her four full weeks to notice. Which was amazing because I didn't have to give her any of my wages then. Should have kept quiet for longer, thinking about it.

Anyway, I shouted back that I was off to see my mates at the skate park and she didn't even scoff at the word 'mates'. She just said 'OK' and sniffed a bit more. I knew something was wrong then. I backtracked up the stairs, avoided the one that creaks so much you think you're going to go through it, and stood back outside the bathroom door.

'Mum,' I said through the wooden door. Honestly the number of times I've looked at the white paint cracking off that door with Mum on the other side of it is ridiculous. It's especially bad at the bottom, around the dent that some prick kicked in a few years back. 'Are you alright?'

'He's gone, Ben. Dylan. He's gone off with Laura from down the street. Fucking slut. She knew we were together.'

And here it was. Dylan, the latest 'just call me uncle' had been knocking about for a few weeks now. Even in Year 11, a few weeks is nothing, but to me mum, it's always the world. It's always the time that she falls desperately in love and starts picturing a wedding dress and a tiara as big as the one Katie Price had when she married Peter Andre. Mum still has the *OK!*

mag from their wedding in her drawer. I see it sometimes when she asks me to get her fags for her. I know it's what she's always wanted but she never gets. I did remind her that they are divorced once when I caught her looking at the mag and she rolled it up and belted me round the head with it. She's a bit of a fucking psycho sometimes.

For me though, as sick as it sounds, I always like this break-up bit. She leans on me then. I make her tea and we watch telly together. She ugly cries and I call the bloke a twat and then we actually have a laugh, just us. The problem is, I help too much. I make her feel better and that's when she fucks off again, to the next idiot that tells her he loves her and she's dumb enough to believe it.

'You want a cuppa, Mum? I nicked some biscuits from the tea room at the back of the chippy as well. They're in my bedroom if you want one?'

'You sneaky fucker. Hiding biccies in your room. Yeah, go on then, mate.'

With that, the bathroom door unlocks and there she is, standing in her pink fluffy dressing gown that ain't so fluffy anymore. Her hair is standing on end and the black roots are more on show than ever. I don't know why she bleaches it blonde. I've seen pictures of her when she was younger, and she looked well good with dark hair. More than that though, she'd look more like me with her hair dark and I think I'd like that. Not in a weird way. Just a way where people knew she was my mum, you know? And they knew it because we looked alike, not because she was the one making a show of herself, screaming my name down the street to bring the washing in.

Anyway, we went downstairs and sat on the sofa. I put the kettle on and watched as she fiddled with something in her pocket. I wanted to ask what it was, but you have to be careful with Mum. One minute she's happy and smiling and the next she's shouting her head off over something shitty. So, I kept quiet and just made the tea instead. Brought her in the biccies, proper posh ones with chocolate on them... thanks, Mr Chang... and sat down next to her.

'Fucking hell, Ben, you ain' 'arf getting lanky. Put your legs down, will ya? you're digging into my bloody side.'

It's true. The sofa is well small for us now. I didn't tell Mum it was probably because of the weight she'd put on lately. Shitting hell, I ain't that brave. But it was also because we'd had this sofa for as long as I can remember and the slats in the middle had definitely broken so when you sit on either side, you immediately roll towards each other in the middle. I pushed myself back to the side and put me legs down and asked me mum if she wanted to stick a film on or something. One of her mates had broken the firestick and we could watch any film we wanted now... as long as you were alright with seeing people stand up from their cinema seat to go to the loo midway through. That's when she went, 'Ain't you supposed to be meeting those mates of yours?' and I realised I was.

I hadn't thought about Mitchell or any of them for a bit then. It felt weird. Honestly, since we've started hanging around together, I swear all I do is watch their Insta, look at their Facebook and their TikToks. Anything really, in case I miss out on something. Like today. Mitchell had said that I didn't have to ask to join them, that I could go straight down and hang and that was what I was going to do. I was going to head straight to the skate park and hunt them down. It weren't until now that I was thinking, what would I say? I could have been all brazen and be like 'Where was my invite?' and laughed and that, but then if they'd said, 'Oh, we didn't want you to come,' I would have been fucked. I was thinking I could just pretend I'd gone for a walk and had bumped into them, but I've done that before, and they said they knew I'd watched their Insta story, so I must have known they were there. That was well awkward. I hate that you can see who's watched yours. Mitchell never seems to watch mine.

So, I told Mum that it weren't important and picked up the remote to choose a film. That's when I noticed she was fiddling with that thing in her pocket again, so I said to her, 'What's that you got, Mum?'

She looked like someone that had been caught behind the library at school. You know, where they all go for a fag during free periods. I knew I shouldn't have asked. What a twat.

'None of your business, nosy bollocks,' she goes, and I knew I should've left it, but something was nagging at me more than ever.

'It's alright, Mum. You can tell me if something's bothering you.'

'The only thing bothering me right now is you. Are we watching a film or not? I don't want to watch no love shit though. I've had more than enough of that crap.'

Again, this is where I should have kept my mouth shut. Should have put the film on, drank me tea and enjoyed my time with her. Not thought about Mitchell, or the thing in Mum's pocket, or anything else. Just me and Mum. But I couldn't, could I?

'Is the thing in your pocket to do with Dylan, Mum? Has he done something?'

'For fuck sake, Ben. I told you to leave it, didn't I? You wanna know what it is so badly, do ya? Got to be nosy. Well, here. Have a good fucking look.'

With that, she threw her hand in her pocket and shoved something out towards me. I knew what it was straight away and there was no way I was touching it. That's fucking gross. She must have only just bloody peed on it.

'Fucking hell, Mum, not again.'

I couldn't help myself! This weren't the first time I'd seen a positive bloody pregnancy test in this house. I swear she thinks it will make them stay. Then they don't, so neither does the baby. She'll be phoning the doctors tomorrow morning, I'm sure. Then who has to look after her? Me, that's who. Me running the warm baths and putting the stinky lavender bag in the microwave. Sod that.

She weren't happy with me swearing at her. She was shouting back at me, saying that she should have got rid of me too. That her life would be better without me screwing it up. It's nothing I ain't heard before, but it still hurts if I'm honest. I mean, I ask myself too. Why did she keep me? She clearly don't have a problem getting rid of the others. This will be the fourth, I reckon. And in PSHE the other day, Miss Barker said they only let you have five. It wrecks your body or something. So Mum is definitely going to have to keep one soon or just be more careful. They taught us how to put a jonny on a banana. Surely she had the same bloody lesson?

Anyway, I didn't want to sit there and listen to any more of her shit. For once I had places to go, so I got up and walked out the door. She'll be fucking livid when I get home, so I'll have to be out for ages and sneak back in late. By the time I'm back from school tomorrow, she'll be over it, so I just need to wait until then. I checked Insta to see if they were still at the skate park, but nothing had been uploaded. Besides, is that actually where I wanted to go? My life has been so much better with mates, I ain't saying otherwise, but after the shit I'd just had from Mum, did I really want to go and get more? Be the butt of someone else's jokes? Not like I could tell them, is it? 'Oh, sorry, guys, I was coming earlier, but my mum's got herself knocked up again and needed me to make her a cuppa before she phones her mates down the abortion clinic.' Fuck sake, Mum.

So I found myself walking around the streets, not really looking where I was going, and that's when I realised I had walked into the posh side of town. The one where there are cul-de-sacs and cars on driveways that haven't been burnt out or keyed. I was certain this was where Hot Hall lived. I'd seen her daughter Ellie walk back from school this way once. To be fair, she's well fit too, if you like girls our age, only no one will go near her because of her mum. Mitchell would, obviously, but he said he would only hang out with a teacher's kid if he got to bang her, and he said Ellie is well frigid. Not like her mum... well... I reckon. I heard some boys in the changing rooms say that they had tried to be mates with her, so they got invited over to the house and could have a rummage through Hall's underwear drawer, but Ellie never let anyone in the house, so they'd ditched her. I get it. I've pictured myself in her bedroom loads of times. Laying there waiting for her... I mean, I'm defo going to see it one day for real anyway, just a matter of time, but it's good to imagine while I'm waiting.

This is what I don't get, see. Ellie must be fifteen or sixteen and her mum looks well young, so she must have had her when she was a teenager too, just like my mum. But they don't live in shit like we do, do they? They live in this big fancy estate and drive fancy cars and have a dad at home. Mum always blames me for everything. Says it's my fault Dad ain't around, and my fault she couldn't work, and we have to stay in the estate. Every time something breaks, and she can't afford to fix it, that's my fault too. But Hot Hall has all those things. I bet she can afford to fix things. And she has proper designer stuff. Not knock-offs from the market. So, it can't just be my fault, can it? Otherwise, Ellie would be on the estate with me and not in her fancy house with everything she could ever bloody want.

I decided to try and look for the house – I needed to see it and take it in – so I slowed down my walking and started looking in all the windows. Not in a weird way, just looked like I was casually out for a walk, that's all. And that's when I saw her. Standing in an upstairs window with the curtains wide open. I stood in the street and stared and then realised it would look well weird if I just stood in the middle of the pavement, so I tucked back into the bush across the street. Crouched down like, so no one could see me. You know, didn't want to look like a weirdo. And that's when it happened. There she was, curtains open, standing in front of the long window, and she started to get undressed. I couldn't believe my fucking eyes. Had she seen me? Was she doing it on purpose? I mean, who gets undressed with the curtains open unless they want people to see? Old Dirty Dom, round the back of ours, is always doing it and Mum reckons it's so he gets her attention. So that must be what Hot Hall was doing for me. She saw me standing in the road and she wanted to show me what was to come. I mean, how rude would I be if I didn't stay and watch the show?

It was getting dark out and the lights were on in the room, so it made everything proper clear. First, she took off her top. Her hair, fuck me, it swayed down her body like it does in films. Still fell perfectly as she took off her silky top and showed the lacy black bra underneath. Then... shit... then she bent down to take off her skirt and that's when I saw the mirror. The fucking full length mirror behind her. So when she bent down, I saw her whole, perfect arse. She was wearing a black lacy thong to match the bra, but it was bloody tiny, barely there, so everything, and I mean everything, was on show. I could feel myself getting a stiffy and I knew I needed to remember this forever, so I took out my phone and took as many photos as I could. She was doing it for me anyway, so what was the harm of taking the pictures? Not that I think I could get the image out of my brain if I tried, but just in case. My boner was making it so hard to carry on crouching in the bush, but I couldn't move, not in the middle of everything. I mean, I ain't stupid. I know what it would look like if someone walked past. How would they know that she was doing this for me? They wouldn't understand.

So, I stayed there, taking pics and watching until she turned around and walked out of view. She was still in her underwear when she walked away, and I thought about staying huddled there in case she took off even more, but I didn't want to risk being caught by anybody. She obviously only wants private moments between me and her and I respect that.

Before I went to leave though, she came back into view. One more perfect time. She'd put a black silky robe around her... God, I wish I was that robe... and she walked right over to the window. She stared for a minute, right at me, right in my direction, and I swear I ain't making this up, I swear she fucking winked. She winked right at me, in my direction, and she closed the curtains. Shit. She fucking wants me. I've said it all along and now I know. Now I know everything I need to know. Fuck. I thought of Dirty Dom and got rid of the boner quick. Then I ran home to look at the pictures. Fuck Mum, fuck Mitchell, fuck the lot of them. Ben Bridges is about to actually fuck Hot Hall. Tonight, that might be in my mind… but tomorrow… Who knows? Shit me. This is happening.

Liz

(Now)

'Liz? You home?'

He knew she was home. He knew they were all home. The car on the drive, the shoes in the hallway; it wouldn't take a rocket scientist to work out where they were. The doors to the kids' bedrooms were firmly shut. Liz hadn't even questioned Thomas. He had walked in as she was walking out to the bins and by the time she'd got back in, he was upstairs. She knew she should have gone and checked on him. He hadn't hidden the fact that he was crying, but right now it was the last thing that she wanted to do. As she sat on the sofa, her car keys firmly in her hand, she had wanted nothing more than to run. Run from the kids, from Rob, from the many questions that were bound to follow. She wanted to run so much, but she knew that wasn't the answer. How could she prove anything to anyone if she wasn't around to face them? So instead, she waited. Waited in silence, watching her chest rise and fall as if she was breathing underwater, gasping for air. She finally understood what it was like to be drowning, but she knew in an instant Rob would pull her up to the surface and make her face the horrors that followed.

'For fuck sake, did you not hear me calling?'

She didn't turn around. She stared forward, focused solely on the black TV screen in front of her. There was no life in the box. It was comforting.

'So? What have you got to say for yourself then?'

Still, she didn't turn her head. She didn't say a word. The car keys still firmly in her right palm. The vision of escape still firmly in her mind.

'Liz? I'm talking to you. For Christ sake, have the decency to answer me. That's the least I deserve, isn't it?'

With that, he walked around the sofa and stood directly in front of her. Towering over her as she stayed seated. He had dirt on his hands from work, yet he was continuing to rub them all over his face. His clothes were as scruffy as always, a light pink T-shirt with holes under the armpits and a pair of jeans that were so baggy and washed out he could look like a teenager. If it wasn't for the lines around his eyes, of course. Yet, they were almost hidden by his light brown hair covered in oil and grease and desperate for a haircut. He didn't sit, his arms were folded, and his eyes were burrowing straight into her forehead, almost egging her on, daring her to look back at him.

'So, it's true then. You've been carrying on with a kid the same age as Ellie? What the fuck is wrong with you? It's fucking sick. *You're* fucking sick. And to not even warn us? That's why your phone was going off this morning, wasn't it? What was it? Was he texting you? Telling you to leave me or he'd tell everyone? Is that why you scurried downstairs like a little girl? Only you're not the little one in this, are you? He is.

He's a bloody *child*. Do you know how much stick I've been getting at work? Walked into Dave asking if it was the first time. Can you imagine what that's like? The whole fucking town knowing your wife's been shagging a kid behind your back. Oh, I've had it all today, Liz. The blokes couldn't wait to tell me how shit a man I must be if you'd rather have it off with a kid. A fucking kid. You're sick, do you know that? Fucking sick.'

The spit was flying from his mouth as he was pacing up and down in front of her, rubbing yet more grease through his hair from his hands as he did so. She wondered how long he'd been practising that little speech, probably the whole car journey. From looking down, Liz could only see his feet. His grey socks were padding on the carpet and a part of her was pleased that, even in this temper, he had remembered to take his shoes off in the porch. He was so scruffy when they first moved in together and moments like this made her realise how much she had helped him. How much he had developed over the years. If he did choose to leave her, his next wife should be so grateful.

After all, she made him like this. Not that he ever gave her any thanks for that.

'So, you're just going to sit there, are you? Not try and defend yourself? Tell me I'm wrong? Why aren't you telling me this is all bullshit? Why aren't you fighting?'

Liz knew she should be. That she should be fighting for the man she'd spent over half her life with to believe what she was saying. But she couldn't… or wouldn't… she didn't know. She just felt numb. Completely and utterly numb.

'Would you believe me if I did?'

For the first time, Liz lifted her head and looked Rob in the eyes. Between Jo and Ellie and the underwear now sat in the outside bin, she was exhausted. In reality, what could she say? She'd not managed to convince anyone of her innocence thus far, so maybe she was protesting too much? Maybe if she kept her mouth shut, they might want to believe her more.

'I've been sat in that car, parked up on the road for half an hour. I've looked at every picture and text and post in detail. He knows everything. He's seen everything. The way you write your messages, no abbreviations, all punctuated, one single kiss at the end. It's exactly how you write, Liz. The picture. That's the same underwear you were wearing last week. Don't think I didn't notice.'

'Shut up.'

The mention of the underwear had somehow lit a fire inside of her. The last thing she needed was him spouting off about that, especially after what she had told Jo.

'What?'

'Shut up. That picture is not me. That underwear is not mine.'

She didn't have enough energy still to rise to her feet, but she had shifted forward. She was on the edge of the sofa, and she didn't take her eyes off him. He needed to know how serious she was about this discussion. This one could ruin her, and she hoped her eyes showed forcefulness and truth, rather than the overwhelming sickness she felt inside instead.

'Are you kidding me? What, you think I'm going to believe that bullshit? I've seen it with my own eyes.'

'No, you haven't.'

With this, Rob knelt down so his eyes were directly in line with hers. If she wasn't going to stand, then he would ensure she saw him closely. His eyes were dark and bloodshot and there was spit in the corner of his mouth. Liz could see his whole body was trembling, yet he spoke with nothing but venom in his voice.

'Yes, I have, and you know I fucking have. Look at the background of the picture, Liz. I zoomed in. Most people are so distracted by your slutty picture that they can't look past it. But I can. I don't need to see you anymore. Look behind it and what do you see? Our fucking bedroom, Liz. Our paint on the walls and the door to our en-suite. Anyone that steps foot in this house will know that the picture is you. Taken in our room. Was he in our bed? Did you have that slimy teenage kid in our bed? You fucking whore.'

Standing up and pushing him away, Liz ran to the door of the living room. In her hand was the keys to the car still. She looked down at them and then at the door. She knew what she wanted to do, but she knew what she needed to do as well and the pull of that was stronger. She raced up the stairs and into her bedroom. She pulled out her phone and found the picture Rob was talking about in an instant. She diverted her eyes from the amount of likes and shares it had received and looked at the detail. Rob was right. You could see the paint and you could see the door, but the door was to her left. If the door was to her left, she wouldn't have been facing the bed. He couldn't have been lying there. He would have been...

'Oh God. It was that night.'

'What night?'

Rob had followed her into the room and was blocking the doorway. Liz knew he'd been working out a bit lately but only just realised how much of a difference it had made. He was broader than she had noticed, and she couldn't help but wonder when that change had happened. When did she stop noticing him?

'What night, Liz?'

'I didn't say that. I was talking to myself.'

'You did. I heard you. What night? You just said it was *that* night. What does that mean? Was he here? Where was I? I mean, let's face it, we don't spend much time together, so it could have been anytime. Any of the kids' sports events that you miss because you have to "work". Any of my networking events that you can never possibly attend. There I was thinking you were hardworking and dedicated and the only thing you were dedicated to was getting your leg over a teenage boy.'

'STOP IT! Stop it NOW!'

Liz stood up from the bed and made sure it was her that met his gaze this time. She was not down and out yet and the fight in her was rising. She had been through enough today and this was not something else she was prepared to just sit and take. Especially from Rob.

'How dare you! Do you not think I've been through enough already?'

'*You?* What *you've* been through? Are you kidding me? What about us, Liz? What about the kids? What must they have been through today? Did you even check on them while you were there?'

'I... I wasn't there.'

Liz looked at the floor. Her blood was boiling, and she could feel the pink rising to her cheeks. She was so angry at Rob. He always said he would protect her. He said he loved her. Yet here he was, believing the word of a child over her. She always thought she had the control in this relationship. Never worried because, in the cold light of day, Rob would always need her. He wanted the family unit, and he wanted the trophy wife and that was exactly what she gave him. She never feared he would actually walk away, no matter what she did. Yet here he was, broader, stronger and more confrontational than she had ever known him. Maybe it was him that had found someone else, maybe he was the one with the bit on the side that had given him all this confidence that, in reality, Liz had been trying to knock for years.

'What do you mean you weren't there? Have they sacked you?'

'No, they haven't bloody sacked me. Don't be ridiculous.'

'So...?'

'So… they just needed me to be at home while HR sorted all of this out. It's fine. I'm going in tomorrow and it will all be forgotten.'

'Oh, it will, will it? What about when I tell them the picture he posted was taken in our bedroom? Will it all be forgotten then?'

'Rob. You can't say that.'

Liz had meant for this to sound forceful, like she had control, but in truth she was pleading, begging the man she thought she knew to believe what she was saying. She couldn't believe what had happened to her, but she needed him to keep quiet. She couldn't have him telling the school anything of the sort.

'I can say what I want.'

'No, you can't. I'm telling you, you can't. I told Jo it wasn't mine.'

'And why the fuck did you do that?'

'Because I knew how it looked.'

'How it looked? How does it look, Liz? Like you're guilty. Because that's what you are, isn't it? You make me sick.'

'No, Rob. No, I'm not. I didn't…'

Liz fell onto the bed and flung her arms up in the air. How could she explain this without it looking even worse? She looked up at Rob, hoping to appeal to his softer side. Wishing with all her might that he would see her looking vulnerable for the first time in a long time and it would do something to change his heart. To make him remember that he could trust her. Because he could… couldn't he?

'Didn't what? Didn't parade around in your fucking underwear to seduce a teenage boy? Didn't bring him up to our room in our family home and show him what a real woman looks like? A real woman that's old enough to be his fucking mother?'

Spit flew from Rob's mouth and landed on Liz's cheeks. Any hope of a softer side of Rob appearing had vanished and Liz couldn't tear her eyes away from the redness of his cheeks. He spoke to her and looked at her with so much hatred all she could do was stare deeper into his eyes and hope that the old Rob was in there somewhere. But from the words that followed, she knew that Rob was buried too deep to reach today.

'What was it, huh? Didn't get enough kicks when you were his age, did you? Felt like you'd missed out? Is that what it was? Tied down to one man for so long you felt like you needed to explore? Jesus, Liz, we may have been teenagers, but we all know you'd done plenty of exploring way before me. All the shit you give Ellie for having boyfriends. I always assumed it was so she wasn't a slut like you. Little did I know it was so you could keep all those boys for yourself. I forgot… you don't share.'

'Enough.'

Liz stood up and pulled herself together. Letting Rob get this irate would do nothing but hinder the situation. If he was too angry to see her vulnerability, then she would have to talk some sense into him. She'd been doing it most of her life, so she was sure she could do it this time.

'Rob, this is ridiculous now. What do you want from me? You want me to tell you that I shagged him right here on the bed? Well, I didn't. He wasn't here. He's never set foot in our home.'

'What then? You sent it to him? Little teaser to remind him what was waiting for him?'

'Don't be ridiculous! Look where it's taken from. Go on! You reckon you've studied it so much, then tell me what angle it was. I'll tell you where. From the window. The kid took it from the fucking window, Rob, can't you see? He must have been out there. I thought... I thought I saw someone... I didn't realise... I would never have known.'

'What are you going on about, Liz? You thought you saw someone and... so you what? Got undressed by the window? If that's your cover story, then that's ridiculous. So desperate for attention that you flaunt yourself out the window for any Tom, Dick or Harry to see? How long did it take you to come up with that one? If it's been taken from there, then you've either had him sitting there, or you've propped your phone up on the windowsill to send him one of those stupid selfies Ellie is always harping on about. Either way I don't need to be here or be anywhere near you.'

Rob turned to walk out the door and Liz found herself grabbing on to his arm. Was it to gain control, or an unconscious act to cling onto the life she had worked too hard to achieve?

'You can't. Where would you go?'

Without hesitation, he pushed her arm away and started to root around the bottom of the wardrobe for a bag.

'To my mum's.'

Looking down at him on the floor, Liz caught herself in the bedroom mirror. Her hair was tangled like a mop on her head. Her make-up was smudged and barely there and her face was as red as her lipstick. How had she allowed things to get like this? How could she be living in some kind of scene from *EastEnders*? It was ridiculous and it needed to stop.

'Honestly this is daft. Put the bag down. We both know you're not going anywhere.'

'Oh really?'

'Yes, really. You won't leave and you won't tell the school anything about the picture because what would that do? Really, think about it. Our whole lives would be shattered. Everything we have worked towards. Seriously, Rob, you know me, and you know I would never ever do anything like this. I would never jeopardise anything.'

Rob stood up with the bag in hand. He looked crumpled and this time he didn't make any eye contact.

'Do I? Do I even know you anymore?'

For the first time, there was silence in the room. Liz knew the answer. The truth was, neither of them knew each other at all anymore. In fact, had they ever? Or had they just gone through the motions they were supposed to? Rob too loyal to leave his pregnant girlfriend and Liz avoiding the shame of being a single mother. Could they have really spent their lives like that for the last sixteen years? Sixteen long years of going through the paces of life. Spending more time in the office than at home, resenting spending time together. Even having sex on every fourth weekend because she knew she should. Had Rob noticed the pattern she had committed herself too? Is that why he didn't try it on with her anymore, no matter what she wore. Is that why... why she got excited at the thought of someone watching her through the window... No matter who that person was.

'Look. You know me enough to know that I wouldn't do something like that. I wouldn't risk my job.'

'And there it is! There's the reason we all knew was coming! You wouldn't dare shack up with a teenager… not because of your partner or your kids, or because it's against the pissing law, but because of the one thing that really matters to you – your job!'

Rob's whole stance had changed. The anger was back in his eyes as he rushed around the room pulling things out of drawers and putting them in the bag.

'That's not fair.'

'No, Liz… *this* isn't fair. Being second, third, fourth best isn't fair. We will leave you trying to sort out your precious job. We wouldn't want to get in the way of that. Besides, how else are you going to find your next fuck?'

Taking the bag and opening the door to leave, Rob was stopped in his tracks by their two children on the other side. They had obviously listened to the same conversation, yet their expressions were so different. Ellie's matched her father's. An inexplicable anger that showed through every inch of her rigid body. Thomas's, however, was sullen and soft. His eyes were red as if he had been crying some more and he looked straight at Rob, avoiding all eye contact with his mother. Ellie's eyes were burrowing into Liz's skin, yet it didn't feel uncomfortable. Anger she could cope with. Ellie's reaction was just as hers would be. It left her feeling nothing at all. But Thomas... Thomas was different. The hurt and the fearfulness in his face were new sensations to Liz and it left her almost urging him to look at her. If anyone was going to believe her version of events, it was going to be him. She could feel it. She wanted him to look at her, so she could almost explain everything without words. So she could tell him that it would all be OK. She surprised herself at how much she wanted her son to believe her, or just to look at her, but he didn't and neither did Rob.

He sent the kids to pack an overnight bag, which they dutifully turned around to do. Leaving the hallway bare, with just Rob's back left in her eyeline. The whole time, Liz was rooted to the spot. Standing by her bed, she moved her toes up and down to feel the thread of the carpet between them. It was something. Something that reminded her that this whole nightmare was playing out in front of her. She really was losing everything. They were all about to leave the home… and worse, publicly. It wasn't late. The neighbours would see, they would gossip. The gossip would spread… to the streets, to the town, to the school. How would the school react if they knew Rob had left?

'Rob? Rob? Please. Don't do this. What would the school think? If you leave, if you all leave, they'll think I'm guilty.'

'Aren't you?'

The voice wasn't Rob's. It was Thomas's. He was stood back in the doorway with his rucksack over one shoulder. This time he did look her square in the eyes. The tears were already brimming. Liz found herself so shocked by this question, by the accusatory tone she had heard, especially from the mummy's boy that she always thought would have her back. She held his gaze, but no words came out and he didn't wait any longer to listen. He walked down the stairs followed by his sister and his dad, a unit, a group all walking out together. She listened as Rob embraced Thomas and how he allowed himself to sob into his dad's arms. Then she heard them put on their shoes and walk out the door. She heard it click close and still she did nothing. She didn't move, she barely breathed, she was alone.

Ben

(7 days earlier)

I'm not going to lie, the walk to school this morning felt epic. I couldn't get the picture out of my head... and I couldn't stop staring at the one on my phone. I was going to make it my wallpaper, but then I thought anyone would be able to see it and I didn't want that, did I? That show was for me and only me. Well... maybe Mitchell too. The thought of Mitchell being jealous of me could be even more awesome. Well, maybe not... Shit me, she really is fit. Like, I knew she was fit, but I didn't realise she was *that* fucking fit, do you know what I mean? I didn't realise someone's mum, someone older, could be that hot underneath. Honestly. She's better than the girls on the sites Mitchell showed me. *And* those girls haven't got a clue who I am. Whereas Miss... She knows me and she wants me... It's so good it makes me shudder.

Anyway, there I was, walking down the street on my way to school, buzzing and that, when I see Chris walk out his house and cross the street. Fucking hell, I thought, how have I managed to avoid me mum all night, yet I can't avoid this wimp? He lives a few doors down from me. Used to hang about a lot when we was younger, but then my mum fell out with his mum – because my mum was flirting with his dad… standard – and then 'the thing' happened and I haven't seen him since. Thank God. Never would have made it into Mitchell's gang with him still sniffing about. I got my phone out and tried to walk past him, kept my head down, you know? I don't want to be mean to him – he gets enough of that from his dad – but I can't be seen to walk in with him either. Honestly, walk into the quad with Chris and try and meet up with Mitchell? He'd laugh in my face… even more than usual. Anyway, I look up from my Facebook feed and he's there, next to me. He's not said nothing, just walking, like we're mates who usually meet up and that. Shit.

'Alright, Chris,' I say. Well, what else am I meant to say? The twat was right bloody there.

'Alright, Ben.'

That's it. That's all he says. Then he just carries on walking next to me, with his fingers in his rucksack loops and his floppy blonde hair in his pissing eyes, like we speak every day. I mean, who uses both straps of their backpack? Everyone knows you only put it on one shoulder. Obviously, unless your Mitchell because he doesn't even have a backpack at all. He's such a rebel. Anyway, all I'm thinking is, how the hell am I going to get him to bugger off before we get to the school gates, so I says to him, 'Did you want anything?' and he just shrugs and keeps on walking.

'Seriously, Chris. I get that you ain't got any mates and that, but I do. I don't know if you've seen, but I'm in Mitchell's gang now. So, you know, I can't really walk in with you, can I?'

Yeah, I know, bit harsh and that, but it had to be said. I've waited so long for friends like this, to have places to go at the weekend, I'm not about to ruin it now. Besides, Chris... well, there was that thing... Basically, me and him used to hang out still after our mums fell out. Mum wouldn't have liked it, but she didn't know, did she? And it was nice having a mate. Until... until he pissed himself on the stairs. Honest to God right in the middle of main block. And it was in between lessons, so everyone saw him piss his shorts. It dripped on the stairs and everything. I mean, there were kids blocking him from getting down. They cornered him where the stairs turn, but still, we were in Year 9 – surely he could have held it? So, from then on, he became Pissy Chris around school, and I knew I couldn't hang out with him again. Being on your own is better than being mates with Pissy Chris. Staying loyal to him would be stupid. Obviously, I felt a bit guilty about it at the time, ditching him like that, but it was clearly the right decision. I wouldn't be mates with Mitchell if I still hung around with the boy that pissed himself on the stairs during school.

'Don't worry, Ben, I won't walk through the gates with you. I just need to be with you until we get out of the estate.'

I knew what that meant. I looked back and saw his dad sitting in his car on the street. His face seemed angry, and it did shit me up a bit. The eyes on him. He's a right psycho bastard. Me and Chris had been through this enough for me to know the drill. His dad wouldn't touch him in the street with witnesses – he's on bail. If he walked with me, he'd be safe. And obviously he ain't cool or nothing, but I don't want him to take a beating either. So I was stuck with Pissy Chris until we got out of the estate. Just enough time for him to go ahead before we got to the gates of the school.

'Alright, Chris. I'll walk with ya. What's the crazy bastard doing now?'

I saw him flinch at that and he flipped his head round so fast his hair nearly whacked him in the eyes. He's obviously shit scared today. Things must be bad.

'Don't. Keep your voice down.'

So I did and we carried on walking in silence. I'll be honest, I wanted to tell him all about last night. I wanted to tell him that Hot Hall had stripped for me and winked through her bedroom window. That she wanted *me*. But how do you bring shit like that up? And why did I need to impress Chris? Of all kids. Jesus, he'd seen me walk into lessons with Mitchell. He was already impressed.

'I take it you've seen me with Mitchell,' I said to him.

'Not really. Is that who you're hanging out with now?'

Was he shitting me? As if he hadn't noticed. What a prick.

'As if. Don't talk crap.'

He's well full of himself. How do you get that much sass when you're the kid that pissed themselves in front of everybody?

'I'm his best mate. We hang out together all the time.'

'OK.'

'Do you have Insta? You should follow me. Mitchell is always on my Insta stories because we're always together. And Jack and Lynsey and that. We do loads together.'

'OK.'

Honestly, that's all I was getting. He barely even lifted his head or looked at me. I know he was trying not to draw attention to himself and that, but he had a chance to chat to someone in the popular crowd and he was totally blowing it. He's such a dickhead. He must be well jealous.

'So do you have Insta?'

'No. I don't have a phone.'

'Nah, guess you don't need one. No one to text.'

Cheap shot, I know, but there I was helping him out by letting him walk with me, which, let's face it, could totally ruin my rep, and he was giving me nothing. I was getting bored. Then, all of a sudden, he stops walking and looks up at me, straight on like, and that's when I see why he's grown his fringe so long. His forehead is covered in little circles. I think they're burns from a ciggie or something. That's defo what it looked like anyway. Shit. His dad must really be on one at the moment. I was just about to feel sorry for him, you know, lay off him and that, when he opens his bloody mouth.

'Look, I get it, Ben. You reckon you've got mates. Congrats. Can we talk about something else now? Or not talk at all?'

What a prick.

'Alright. Calm down. Besides… it's not just mates. I've got a girlfriend too…'

'Have you?'

'Yeah, only no one knows yet.'

That's when he gives me this sideways look and starts smirking.

'Oh right. Course you have. Imaginary, is she?'

Fucking hell, Chris was getting lairy. Apparently pissing your pants and having no mates gave you a load of fucking confidence – who'd have known?

'She ain't imaginary. Idiot. She's just loads older, so we have to keep it quiet.'

'How much older?'

Fuck. How old is she? I don't know.

'Like, thirty. She's a proper woman. Not like the girls at the school.'

'Erm. You know that's illegal, right? You're not sixteen until August.'

Smarmy prick. How the hell does he remember when my birthday is? He better not shoot his mouth off, because I told Mitchell the other day that I was already sixteen. It kind of slipped out. He was talking about what he wanted to do for his birthday and was saying about a house party and that. I knew I'd never want any of them to come for a bloody party at mine with my mum, so I told him I had my birthday at the beginning of the year. Thought it might buy me some time, you know... to think of something else. Mitch would definitely remember that conversation, so he'll a hundred percent think I'm sixteen. I needed to shut Chris up quickly.

'Oh yeah, and you'd know all about illegal stuff, wouldn't you?'

Yeah, another cheap shot. He hates the fact that his dad deals drugs. When he started, we thought it might be alright, you know, could flog some weed or something on at school, make some mates and some cash. But when it carried on, it just meant he had a load of crackheads knocking on his door at all hours of the night. It must be shit to be fair. He stuffed his hands in his pockets and his eyes went red. I couldn't tell if it was anger or if he was going to cry. I mean, walking into school with Pissy Chris would be one thing, but walking in with him crying would chuck me out of Mitchell's group for good. Luckily he started talking before he could get too emosh.

'What, like everyone on our estate? Look, do what you want. If you want to shag some woman old enough to be your mum, go for it. You better keep it secret though or the pigs will get involved and no one wants that in our street, do they? Anyway, me dad's gone now; I'll walk ahead. Don't want to ruin that fantastic fucking life of yours, do I?'

And with that he does one. Starts running up the street with his backpack swinging. Dickhead. What does he know? I was going to shout after him, tell him to stop running in case he pisses himself again, because let's face it, that would have been fucking hilarious, but I didn't 'cause I didn't want anyone to draw attention to the fact that we'd been together. That would have been worse than talking to him in the first place.

So, I got to school just in time to see Mitchell and the rest of the gang by the basketball hoops. I kicked myself because I thought, if I'd walked a bit faster, I could have shouted at Chris running in front of them. You know, the bit about pissing himself again? Bet that would have got some laughs. But I was so scared to be seen with him I slowed down instead. I shouted at them when I got close, and went and joined them, but they were all just sat on their phones. No one looked up or nothing. I could see Mitchell was smiling, so I asked him what he was looking at. He ignored me, so I went and sat next to him to look over his shoulder. That's when he turned.

'Fucking hell, Ben. Move back. You stink.'

Everyone started laughing then and Mitchell pushed me away and put his hoody up over his nose. I stuck my nose under my shirt, and I swear I didn't smell that bad. It must have been walking with Pissy Chris. His smell must have rubbed off on my clothes. Not that I could tell them that, could I? That would have been well worse than whatever this shit was. He kept the insults coming though, and then they all joined in. After ten minutes of them wafting their arms and pretend retching, I'd had enough. I'd tried to laugh it off, honest I had, but fuck me, how much could I take? So I grabbed my bag and started to walk towards main block.

'Where you going? Don't be a pussy,' Mitchell shouted after me.

I turned back to face him and said, 'I'm not. I just need to be somewhere.'

I should have said I needed the loo or something. That would have made much more sense, but I didn't. Can't think that fast... dickhead.

'Oh yeah,' Mitchell said, the grin on his face widening. I knew I should have shut him up, spoken over him with some other excuse, but for some reason I was totally distracted by the amount of spots he had around his mouth. I'd never noticed them before, probably because of the beard he was trying to grow. Everyone was well impressed when it started, but mixed in with the spots, it didn't look that impressive anymore. Then my mind wandered, and I remembered the other week. I got a right massive spot on the end of my nose, right, and I stressed all morning in the mirror because I knew he'd take the piss out of it. Only he didn't... and now I know why. I mean, he ain't got a leg to stand on, has he? Why had I not noticed that before? In fact, as I was looking at him closely, I couldn't help but think, what did Mitchell have that I didn't? Other than a loud gob, of course. I'd started gelling my hair, had the right trainers on, had a phone; why did I put up with his shit? No wonder Hot Hall wanted me and not him and his spotty gob. So, I told him... well, not that he's got a spotty gob... I ain't that brave... but I told him the rest.

'Yeah. Got to run. I've got to go and meet my missus. She'll be waiting for me.'

I thought that would wipe the smile right off his face, but if I'm being honest, it did the direct opposite. He fucking fell about laughing and so did the others. It was so dramatic, like he was on a bloody cheesy comedy show. Honestly, he rolled back on the playground and held his stomach. It really pissed me off.

'As if,' he said through his fucking shitty laugh. 'As if anyone wants to go out with you, smelly bollocks!'

'Well, shows what you know then, don't it? Because they do. They want to go out with *me*, and they want to shag *me* and they're fucking hot too.'

I thought I'd said this well loud, but I can't've done because Jack said later that he couldn't hear me – said I was mumbling or something. But in my head, it was loud and confident and bloody epic... until Mitchell stood up. His hood fell off his head and I could see he hadn't gelled his hair or anything. He'd obviously had a shit morning and now he was going to take it out on me. So he walks right up to me, all slowly and menacing like, and goes, 'Prove it.'

Fuck.

There I was, in the middle of the courts, me bag swinging on my back, and I thought… well… either I prove this and although I might ruin my chances of anything *actually* happening with Hot Hall, my mates will think I'm a legend and my life will get instantly better. Or I keep it all a secret, genuinely get a shag, but Mitchell's going to think I'm lying to him, and he'll deck me for it. I know he would.

The problem was, the way I'd said it, it sounded like we'd already shagged, didn't it? It sounded like we were an item and I'm not stupid; I know she's not technically my missus yet, but she's going to be, isn't she? Especially after last night. But I couldn't tell them that. Tell them that she wanted me, but we hadn't done anything. That just sounds pathetic. Besides, they'd never have believed me if I didn't have something to show them. He said it. He said, 'Prove it,' so what else could I do?

Luckily, he'd walked so close to me by now that I could almost whisper the conversation. I didn't need it getting any further than Mitchell. He was the only one I needed to prove things to anyway. He was the one with all the power. The others just followed him about.

'Alright then. I will. But you ain't to tell anyone, alright?'

'Oh yeah, why not? She ashamed to be with you?'

Mitchell didn't clock on to the whispering bit and looked round to the others for back-up, but they'd stopped laughing. They knew Mitchell had switched. I knew he'd switched.

'No. It's just... she's got someone else, ain't she? She needs to end it first.'

'So, you're the other bloke? Second best?'

He had his arms folded now and he was smirking. He was enjoying making me squirm. I could feel it. I couldn't let him take this away. It was epic – *I* was epic – and I needed to show him that.

'I'm the one she'd rather have, mate.'

I sounded right cocky, I knew I did, but he was getting under my skin, and I thought maybe that sort of confidence would make him respect me a bit. It was obvious that he didn't believe me, and I couldn't have that. Besides, what I said was true… probably. But the only way to make him believe it would be to show him the photo.

The problem was, I didn't want him taking my phone. I didn't want him to show it around to everyone. It was mine. She was mine. I weren't about to just give her away, not when she'd done that just for me. But she'd understand. She knows how this school works and she'd know that I'd need to tell Mitchell.

Otherwise, I'd be back to being a loser dickhead and then she wouldn't fancy me anymore. So really, I was doing it for us.

'Look, I'll show ya, but you don't touch my phone, alright? You look. Just you, mind. The others can mind their own, then I'm putting it away. We ain't ready to go public yet and I ain't about to spoil it.'

'Fuck me. Listen to old Cocky Bollocks over here. Reckons he can tell me what to do?'

He still hadn't grasped the whispering and he turned round to the others and goes, 'Soz, guys, you can't play. Ben says you're not allowed.'

Then the others start groaning and booing like they're in a bloody pantomime and I can feel my cheeks heating up. I was trying too hard to stay calm and in control, but I'll be honest, I just wanted to run. Turn around and get away from all of them, but how could I? Besides, Mitchell leaned right in then, and finally did whisper. Only not in a 'we've got a secret' way, but in a 'I'm going to kill you' way. And he goes, 'They better be good pictures, 'cause I ain't about to hang out with someone who wastes my fucking time.'

And there it was. The moment I knew I had to do it. If I didn't show Mitchell these pictures now, if I didn't get the respect from him that I needed, then I'd lose everything. All my fucking mates in one fell swoop. I couldn't risk it. I was kicking myself for opening my mouth in the first place. Stupid twat. Should have kept it quiet for longer, got some real stories to tell them, rather than this one, but what could I do? So, I moved further back and looked at Mitchell to follow me... and he did. I knew he was pissed, obviously, but having him follow me felt so good I almost started to enjoy myself. I mean, Mitchell had never given me this much attention before. Not one on one. Yeah, we sat together now, but he was always so busy performing to the class and getting on teachers' nerves that we never really spoke. But here I was, in the courts, just me and Mitchell, and I thought fuck, don't screw this up, Ben, make sure he gets a good look. Make sure he believes that she did it for you. Make sure there is no doubt in his mind that you are having an affair with Hot Hall.

So I reached inside my pocket and pulled out my phone. Without another word, I unlocked the screen and went to my pictures. Obviously, I didn't need to do that. It was still open where I'd kept looking at it, but I didn't want him to think I weren't playing it cool. I held it close to me while it was loading. I could feel Mitchell's breath on my forehead as he tried to lean in for a quick look. Shit me, he'd had a lot to smoke this morning. His fag breath was worse than me mum's and that's saying something. But I didn't get distracted, and I held on to it tight. I finally felt like I was in control, and I needed to make sure it stayed that way.

'Fuck. Off!'

Mitchell had caught a glance at the screen, and it was obvious he'd seen who it was. I was looking at the picture too and to be honest I was a bit nervous to look up at his face. I couldn't read what he'd said. Did he believe me?

'Mate. Is that Hot Hall?'

This time he did whisper... but not because he was threatening me. Definitely not. It was because he was impressed, because he couldn't believe his bloody eyes. Just like I couldn't last night. Only his excitement was at the picture, and at me. I could feel it. All ideas of having the hump at me had gone right out the window. Now we were just two mates standing together. Because that's what he'd said, hadn't he? 'Mate'. It hadn't come from my mouth; it had come from his. And it made it all official, didn't it?

I looked up and saw how excited his eyes were and realised it matched the excitement in me. My heart was thumping. All aims of playing it cool had been lost, but I didn't even care.

'Yeah, it is. I fucking told ya she fancied me, didn't I?'

'Shit. No way. Is that in her room? Have you been in her house then?'

'Yeah. She invited me over last night. Put on a show for me, didn't she?'

Alright, it weren't quite like that, but it's bound to be next time. She knew I was there, didn't she? The problem was, then he started asking loads of questions.

'And then what happened? Did you fuck her?'

'Er... no... not yet... She likes to tease.'

By this time, he's almost gripping my coat. He pushed my shoulder as he talked. Not in an angry way, but in banter, like mates would do.

'No fucking way. So, when did it start? In the tutoring sessions?'

'Yeah... course... we ain't been doing maths, put it that way...'

Well? We hadn't... we'd been doing English. See? I didn't lie. He came up with the answers he wanted. Besides, we'd *nearly* done lots of things. If I'd kept my mouth shut for a little longer, I would have loads of stories to tell. It's not like anything would be a lie for long.

'Fuck. You've got to tell the others. This is epic.'

That's when I panicked a bit. He grabbed me by the coat and almost shoved me towards them. I shook him off and stood my ground. Adrenaline was pumping around my body, but I had to stay strong. I told him, 'No,' and he looked at me like I'd just pissed on his cat. Not that I know if he has a cat, but you get my drift. I don't think anyone has told him no in his whole life, not properly, and he weren't happy about it. But I couldn't risk it getting out. Not before I'd made my move. It would blow my chances.

'And why not?' Mitchell continued, crossing his arms over his body, and giving me this look that nearly made me piss myself there and then, just like Pissy Chris for fuck's sake.

'Because... mate... because she'd be pissed, and then what would happen? She'd fucking go before I got you any more decent pictures. See? This could be our secret. Just between me and you. You keep my secret, mine and Hall's, and I'll get you all the pics you want.'

Mitchell liked this. He liked that he was the one back in control. Thing was I knew it, but he was wrong, weren't he? I was the one playing him. I mean, sure I needed to get more pictures and fucking pronto, but this way, he was keeping his mouth shut just like I wanted. You could see he was about to answer, about to throw another idea on the table, when the best thing that could have happened, happened. Her. Hot Hall. She walked right up to us both. She defo looked better without the trousers on, but fuck me, these ones were nice. They were so tight against her skin I couldn't help but picture what I now knew was underneath. And it was definitely less than yesterday. There was no way she was wearing those lacy things today. No space. That was obviously the teaser for me. Today there was nothing underneath and she wanted me to know that.

I quickly put away my phone and looked between her and Mitchell. I was begging Mitch not to say anything, but I didn't need to worry because he didn't get a chance.

'Ben. We've got an early one to one this morning. Did you forget?'

I'd thought about this moment overnight. I wanted to show her that I'd seen her last night, and that I had understood her message and now I had Mitchell watching as well, so I couldn't fuck it up. I took a deep breath and went, 'Course not. You know I'll always *come* for you.'

I could feel Mitchell smirking, but I couldn't break eye contact with her. I needed to know that I wasn't imagining anything. And I definitely wasn't because then she replied with,

'Good. So you should' (with a smile, I should add, the same kinky fucking smile as last night). '*Come* on then, Mr Bridges.'

Then she walks me back into the block to do the lesson. Mitchell couldn't help himself and he wolf-whistled as we walked away, but Hot Hall pretended not to hear it. Or heard it and liked it? Fuck knows. But it felt good. So fucking good. The look on Mitchell's face as we walked away was bloody brilliant and now Hot Hall wanting me to come. Shit. I couldn't believe me luck. I mean, who'd have thought it, hey? Me, Ben Bridges, the loser, the dickhead, now besties with the most popular boy in school and fucking the hottest woman on the planet. I mean… yeah, we ain't fucked yet… but that's still to *come* remember?! Besides, she definitely wanted to, but the only classroom that was free was the one with no blinds, so we couldn't exactly do anything. She looked well disappointed when she realised. She said it was because I'd get distracted, but I knew what she meant really. Plus, she touched my leg loads in the session, and kept bending over in that way she does just for me. She obviously likes a little tease and I'm happy to sit there and take it. She knows what she's doing and so do I... well, Google is helping me learn... but I reckon she'll like telling me what to do anyway. She's got that side to her for sure. Fuck me, life is bloody awesome right now.

Liz

(Now)

Once again, Liz was alone. Alone in the house she was so proud to have bought only a few years ago. The house that had given her the sense of pride she had always wanted. Not only was her name on the mortgage, but it was the one with the higher income. The one that had been the main contributor. Signing those papers had given her the boost she'd needed after all those years of disapproving looks as she boarded the bus with the pushchair and her college lanyard round her neck. Those faces that had stared at her then seemed to disappear as she signed her name on the contract and up until very recently, she swore she would never picture them again. The faces she thought she could banish with her three-bedroom detached home in the nice side of town. Sure, it wasn't the best place to live in the country, but it was where they'd made a base and where she'd proved everyone wrong.

For the first time, however, she felt daunted by it and by the silence that engulfed it. She kept expecting to be interrupted by the buzzing of Ellie's music or annoyed by Rob's inability to turn off the television set, despite leaving the room. More than anything though, she kept turning around expecting to see Thomas behind her. He did that a lot. Always trying to spend time with her. Liz knew it was his cry for attention. She had mentored many parents on it throughout her career and she knew all the strategies to aid him, but, in all honesty, she just didn't have the time, or she just didn't want to. It was something she knew deep down, but burying it was easier than dealing with it. She told herself it was because she was busy. But even now, even at her lowest and her loneliest, she wasn't sure whether she would be pleased to see his face appear at the doorway.

Thomas had been Rob's idea. He wanted to 'finish the family' as he always said. The perfect life, perfect home…

Mum, Dad, a boy and a girl. Obviously, the genders weren't planned, but she remembered his face when they announced it was a boy. The sheer elation at having the stereotypical family. The man getting his little boy. It made her sick then and it still made her sick to this day. Why did it matter what they had? Would it have been less idyllic if they had another girl? Or if they had stayed put with just one child without ruining her body any more? Apparently, it did, although Liz had never understood why. This was why she was so hell bent on not getting married, despite the amount of times Rob had asked over the years.

'It doesn't have to be a fancy do, Liz. We can just go away, just the four of us, elope somewhere exotic. You could leave as Miss Hall and return as Mrs Kirby. Wouldn't that be romantic?'

'What makes you think I'd take your name?'

'Well… it's not just mine, is it? It's the kids' as well.'

And he was right. Liz had allowed the children to have his surname. At the time, she saw it almost as an escape route. They had their name and she had hers. It put a distance between them that made her feel more at ease. She remembered Rob ringing her from the registrar's office with Ellie, explaining that they wouldn't let him register the birth even though he was the father as they weren't married. At the time, they were kids; it wouldn't have even come into anyone's thoughts, but by the time they had Thomas, Rob had discussed getting married while she was pregnant and had used the registrar's office as an example of why they should.

'Are you being serious, Rob? You want to get married so I can stay in bed while you go and do the paperwork? Wow, I'm so lucky!'

'No, not just because of that and you know it. I want to marry you because I love you and I want us to be a proper family.'

'We are a proper family.'

Because they always were really, to him. Even remembering the words she'd said then made her feel uneasy. He'd been so happy, pure elation. It had amazed her how much those words had meant to him. The problem was that to him, a proper family meant they were a unit. To her, it meant that she was trapped. Maybe that's why she hadn't rung the police herself. Yes, the school was the main factor, but perhaps, deep down, she thought that allowing this to surface and unravel gave her a get-out clause to the life she had been living for all these years.

Liz allowed herself to sink further into the sofa. She took in her surroundings as if she was watching a film. She saw the vase of fake flowers in the corner of the room. Of course, the vase was grey, and the flowers were white. She didn't need bursts of colour, but she did need practicality. The vase was placed on the floor and underneath it was the stain Thomas had put there on the day he spilt his blackcurrant juice. The cream carpet had been ruined… on the exact day it had been laid. Staring at it was never going to be an option, so a floor vase became the solution. That was how she lived her life. She saw a problem, she fixed it. So why couldn't she fix this?

She allowed her eyes to move from the vase to the grey mantelpiece. It was clear and mess free, other than one photograph in a frame. It wasn't in the middle, so it didn't block the view of the mirror above it, but it was on the left-hand side at a slight angle so you had to turn your head to look at it properly, meaning you could avoid it altogether if you so wished. The frame was spotless, of course, and looking now, Liz was faced with a picture of her and Rob. His arm was around her waist, yet hers were firmly at her side. Only now did Liz realise how stiff she looked standing next to Rob, who was always so relaxed. She knew she'd only framed it because she looked skinny in the jumpsuit she was wearing. Anything more than that hadn't really mattered.

Leaving the sofa, Liz climbed the stairs to remove her make-up. The irritation of the day had taken its toll on her eyes, and they were now stinging with the mascara she had plastered on this morning. As she got to the top of the stairs, however, she heard a pinging noise coming from Ellie's room. It was a ping she heard a thousand times a day coming from her daughter's laptop, and she knew someone must be messaging her on one of the social media sites; Liz lost track over which one was most popular at the time. However, it was very unlike Ellie to leave her laptop unattended. Rob must have really hurried her out of the door when they left.

Ellie, much to Liz's distaste, loved a drama. Despite their family situation, she was probably loving all the attention this was giving her and relishing in her newfound fame at the school. It made Liz roll her eyes, despite no one being around to see it. She had intended to walk past the room, to ignore the sounds and focus on herself, but with every step she took, another ping happened. Ellie had to be messaging someone back through her phone, not realising it was coming up on her laptop. Without a second thought, Liz found herself pushing open the door of her teenage daughter's bedroom and clearing the clothes on the chair in order to sit at her desk and look at the laptop screen in front of her. It was black, but the pings continued. All she had to do was wiggle the mousepad and she would see everything that was being discussed. Was that what she really wanted?

As she took a breath, a mixture of cosmetics, overpriced perfume and wax melts filled her nose. The sickly-sweet smell masked the smell of the empty plates and cups that were accumulating under her bed and for once Liz was pleased about Ellie's new addiction to reed diffusers as well as everything else. The room was its usual state. Clothes draped over every surface, as well as spilling out of every drawer. Her bed was unmade, and the clean laundry Rob had put there at the weekend was still folded on the end of the bed, not looking like it had been touched at all. How on earth had Ellie managed to sleep in such a way that the pile was undisturbed? Surely it would be easier for her to just put it away.

Liz had always been frustrated by Ellie's lack of organisation, especially with her GCSEs coming up. She had wanted to see revision notes stuck to her walls, but instead there were posters of bands she'd never heard of and magazine clippings for her 'vision board' to help with the YouTube channel she wanted to create. Liz knew she was a young mum, but even to her the world had changed dramatically since she was a kid. She knew Ellie would not be seen dead with her mum's pencil thin eyebrows and slicked back hair from her teenage years. Although Liz could admit, that was probably a good thing.

On the back of her desk, her copy of *Catcher in the Rye* had been pushed to the side and her make-up tidy was in its place. Liz loved teaching that book and there was a time when she thought she and Ellie would bond over discussing the themes for her coursework. Obviously, that wasn't to be. She doubted her daughter had even read the book, let alone be prepared to discuss the topic of her essay with her mum. In some ways Liz resented how naturally bright Ellie was; it almost made her try even less. But Liz didn't have time to dwell on it. That was for Ellie's teachers to work out. She had other children that needed her help.

With the laptop noise continuing, Liz knew what she was about to do was an invasion of privacy, but seeing as that was not something she had been awarded today, why should she feel the need to give it to anyone else? Besides, this could give her an insight into what she was facing by going back into work tomorrow, and it would give her the upper hand she so desperately needed right now. So, she placed her hand on the mousepad and watched the screen flicker to life and immediately load Ellie's Facebook page. No wonder there was so much noise coming from it; there seemed to be dozens of chats open in little windows at the bottom of the screen. Liz quickly scanned them, looking for names she knew, and instantly spotted some usual suspects. Chloe had written, *u ok hun?* at least four times, but

Ellie had yet to respond to any. Laura or 'Lauz' as she was

clearly known had also tried to contact her friend, *WTF! Wt is ur*

mum doing? U must be devo'd! Liz shuddered at the fact that

these children were in her English class. One because of the

embarrassment, of course, but also because of the poor spelling

and grammar. How on earth were these children meant to do

well in life if this is how they typed?

The most striking thing to Liz, however, was that Ellie

didn't seem to be replying to any of these girls. The ones she

would class as Ellie's closest friends had been completely

ignored by her daughter. In fact, the only conversation that was

flashing consistently was with a boy that Liz had never heard of

before. Harry. He was under Harry George, but Liz suspected

that to be his first and middle name. Apparently, a lot of the

children were doing that now and the only reason she knew that

was because Ellie had been very angry not to have had a middle

name. Thinking of one name was hard enough; Liz had no need

to think of a second. She clicked on the conversation and tried to scroll up to the beginning, but the pair were typing so fast it kept bringing it back down to the bottom. Liz knew she was playing with fire even opening it – one wrong move and her daughter would surely know that she was spying – but curiosity had taken over her senses and she needed to see what this conversation was about. She decided to sit back and witness the second half until they stopped typing and then read up when she could.

It must be so hard for you babe.

Babe? That was a bit over friendly for someone she had never been introduced to. Liz racked her brains. There wasn't a kid in that school that she didn't know, and the only Harry in Ellie's year was a little wimpy kid. There was no way Ellie would let him call her babe, was there?

It's just so hard H. Y wood she do stupid shit like this? I didn't even no she had any spare time on her hands, it's not like she ever spends it wiv us. She had it for him tho didn't she?

Don't sweat it. I've got all the time in the world for u.

Aw I know. I just can't get over who it was tho. Like, if Mum is a slut then fine, fuck it, it's her life. But y wood she choose someone like that loser? He's a no one.

Well course he is to u. Ur used to a real man.

Liz stopped reading the conversation and immediately clicked on his profile. She no longer cared about how noticeable this would be to Ellie. She needed to find out more about this so-called 'real man'. The first thing that rang alarm bells was that his profile picture was of a cartoon. Some Simpson-looking character with a backward cap and chains around his neck. Did Ellie even know this person? Know what he looked like in real life? Had she met up with him? How many times had Liz spoken to her about meeting people off the internet? Well… she may not have had it directly with Ellie, but she had done the assembly that her daughter was in, and Ellie clearly should have listened harder.

With further investigation, Liz could see that the profile was sketchy to say the least. His only friends were girls, young girls, around Ellie's age, yet his profile said he was twenty. Why wouldn't he have any friends his own age? And why are none of them male? Had Ellie even looked at this? He seemed to only post pictures of his torso as well, none of his face. These abs Liz was staring at could belong to anyone. Surely Ellie wasn't stupid enough to think she was talking to the person this body belonged to? As she scrolled down further and further, all she could see was the likes and comments Ellie had given him.

Looking good babe… Yum… Yes please.

Yes please? Yes please to what? What exactly was her daughter asking for from this supposed twenty-year-old? She tried to go back to the message, but it had gone. Had it been deleted? Or hidden? Apparently, there were ways of doing that now. Liz knew she was losing track a little bit with how fast technology was moving, but she never expected to feel this out of touch. They must have stopped speaking, but was that because

Ellie knew she had been snooping? If she knew already, there was no need to hide it. Liz picked up her phone and called Rob. She hadn't expected him to answer first time, of course not, but she knew that if she continued to spam call, he would answer eventually.

'Liz, now is not the right time.'

'Oh, get over yourself, Rob. I'm not ringing to talk about you. I'm ringing about Ellie.'

Probably a little too harsh, but she needed to get the point across. Rob was always one to hang up the phone and run away from confrontation, but she knew the idea of his precious daughter being involved in the discussion would stop him from doing just that.

'What about Ellie? She's at Mum's.'

'Why have you left her there? Where are you?'

'I thought this wasn't about me?'

'It's not.'

When did Rob get so cocky? Apparently, he'd grown a pair of bollocks recently and Liz was not a fan.

'Look. Her laptop was making this pinging noise for ages, so I went in to see if I could turn the volume down and I saw her chatting away to this man.'

Nearly the truth. She didn't need to explain herself anyway.

'So, you were snooping on our daughter? Trying to see if your lover boy was talking to her as well, were you?'

'Rob, enough. I wasn't snooping. Not for any reason. I told you the noise was giving me a headache and I was going to put the laptop on silent until I saw these messages.'

'Oh yeah, and what was so horrifying about these messages then?'

She knew he was goading her. Using his smug, sarcastic voice, but she needed to get her point across.

'They weren't normal messages. She was… flirting…'

'She's sixteen for Christ sake. She's going to be flirting with boys from school. She's your kid, remember.'

Cheap shot. One Liz knew was coming but didn't hit any less hard. Couples did that. They knew which buttons to press, and this was always the one Rob chose when he was particularly angry at her. She knew, however, that this time she needed to swallow it.

'That's what I'm getting at though. You're not even listening. It's not a boy, not someone from school. It's a man. He claims to be twenty on his profile, but I don't even know if he's that. There's not pictures of his face, just his body, if it even is his.'

'What the hell are you talking about? Ellie isn't stupid. She wouldn't talk to someone she didn't know in person.'

'Well, that's what I thought, but here we are. Either she doesn't know this bloke, or she's met up with him, and whichever option it is, it doesn't feel right. You need to talk to her. Take her phone away until she tells you the truth.'

'Down to me, is it? As always.'

'Oh, grow up. You took them and left, remember?'

'Grow up? That's rich considering your preferences.'

'Now you're just being childish.'

'Guess you'd fancy me more that way, wouldn't you?'

Liz, who knew she had been pacing around Ellie's room the entire conversation, stopped and walked into the hallway. She needed a bigger space, a cleaner space, and she needed to take a deep breath. She couldn't allow his goading to distract her from what was important.

'Rob... will you focus? Ellie is talking... flirting... with a man she doesn't know. He could be twenty, he could be forty for all we know. And as you said, she's sixteen for Christ sake. You need to talk to your daughter.'

'She's your daughter too.'

'You think I don't know that? She was the one that started this hell, remember? Being her mum set my life up for failure, didn't it? I had to work so hard to get all of this, to get rid of the sordid reputation. I don't want her to go through all that I did. That's why you need to talk to her. She can't make the same mistakes as me.'

'See, that's where we're different, Liz. You have called that kid a mistake for her whole life. But to me, she never was that. She was a surprise, yes, but she was a fucking brilliant one. She made us a family. But you could never see what she'd built. Only what you saw her as destroying. I'll talk to her, of course. I want her to be safe and I want to protect her, but I will do it in a way that *I* feel is right. Seeing as they are just *my* children anyway.'

Liz could feel the phone making her face hot. Or was that just her face? She knew her hands were trembling, and she could feel the anger boiling over. Was this through frustration? Or just the harsh reality of Rob explaining exactly how she felt so clearly and precisely in a way she never could. Yes, she had seen Ellie as a mistake, but it didn't mean she had no care for her at all, did it? That was a completely different discussion.

'Don't give me that. Don't act like a martyr. You knew I didn't want her. I said it from the offset. I would have just gone and got the abortion. No one would have known, and our lives would have carried on the way we planned. But *you* convinced me. *You* said it would be like a fairy tale. Well, some fucking fairy tale this turned out to be.'

'And whose fault is that?'

'Yours. *You* wanted to keep Ellie. *You* made me have Thomas. *You* wanted this pretend perfect family, not me. The only reason I agreed to Thomas was because *you* said you would take responsibility for all the shit. So take it. Deal with the daughter that is so full of herself she reckons she can flirt with men on the internet and take the boy that's too wimpy to sleep without a light on in secondary school. I'm done with all of it.'

'Liz...'

She couldn't stop. Her eyes were brimming with tears and her mouth was out of control. Everything she had felt over all these years needed to come out. They needed to be said, to be shouted from the rooftops. They needed to be out of her brain and in the open where they could breathe, where she could breathe, finally.

'No, Rob. I'm over it. Maybe all this is a blessing. Maybe it's the escape I needed. You told me I would change. You told me that I would love them, and I don't...'

'Liz...'

'I don't love them, and I don't love you. But remember that just because I don't want to fuck you doesn't mean I want to fuck a kid.'

'Liz…'

'What?'

'I'm on the car phone.'

'And?'

'And Thomas is in the car.'

'Shit.'

She slammed down the phone and threw it onto the hallway floor. Looking through her open bedroom door, Liz saw herself in the full-length mirror that was opposite her. She no longer recognised the person staring back. Her hair was all over the place, her face was red, and her make-up was smudged. She looked a mess. She felt a mess. And there was nothing she could do to stop it. Nothing that would make it better. And no one that cared enough to help her. She dropped to her knees and closed

her eyes. With only her own breath for company, she allowed

the tears to fall.

Ben

(6 days earlier)

I told Mitchell to keep it a secret, so he told everyone…
obviously. Well, not *everyone* everyone, but everyone in our
gang, everyone that mattered. I'll be honest though… it felt
awesome. I walked into school like a baller. The whole gang
came running up to me as soon as I walked through the gates. I
didn't have to walk round trying to find them, like usual. They
were just there – waiting.

The only problem was, they wanted to see more pictures,
more evidence. And I ain't got any. Nothing more than I had
when I told Mitchell. I went in for my one to one yesterday, but
other teachers kept walking in and out, so we didn't get a chance
to talk about the *incident*. I wanted to tell her that I saw it and
that I liked it. That I more than bloody liked it… but she got out
a copy of *Romeo and Juliet*, like nothing had happened. I mean,

Mitchell has said loads of times that girls are weird, but I didn't know they were this weird. Stripping for me one minute and trying to teach Shakespeare the next. That's well screwed up. I tried to show her I was annoyed, show her that I wanted to talk about the other night instead, so I went, 'We ain't doing that book – we're doing *King Lear*,' but she just acted like nothing had happened. Said she wanted me to just get used to the language and read all sorts of his plays. So, that's what happened.

It weren't until afterwards that I'd realised what a dickhead I'd been. I was so focused on people coming in and out, and her ignoring what happened, that I didn't even pick up on what she'd done. How could I be so stupid? *Romeo and Juliet*? Two people that fancy the fuck out of each other but they ain't meant to. Two people that have to hide their love from the rest of the world. Shit. It's us, innit? Me and Hot Hall. We want to be together. She wants me bad, but we can't, just like the characters in the play. I wish I'd cottoned on sooner because she kept saying things like, 'Do you get it, Ben? Do you understand what I mean?' And I'm sat there with a face like a slapped arse, not actually getting anything she was saying.

So, when it hit me in the afternoon, I stayed late after school and went into the library. I knew I weren't going to bump into any of the gang in there, so I could get on with my plan quickly. I printed off a picture on the school computers of Romeo and Juliet from the internet. If anyone checks, they'll just think it's to do with my lessons – clever, right? Then I wrote on the back of it, *I get it now. My Juliet. B x.* I think it's subtle enough that if someone else found it, they'd think nothing of it, but obvious enough for her to understand. Honestly, maybe this tutoring is making me well smart because I thought that was an awesome idea. Then I snuck into her classroom and left it on her desk. Wish I'd waited to see her face when she picked it up, but I had to get to the bloody chippy. Chang was pissed that I was late again, but it was worth it.

So, there I was, thinking of my Juliet, away with the fairies, when I stepped onto the basketball courts and the whole gang swarmed around me. I should have been annoyed, should have been pissed at Mitchell for telling everyone, but I couldn't be. And I couldn't because of the way they were looking at me. Honestly, it was incredible. Jack pushed to the front first. Mitchell had hung back on purpose; he wanted to make sure everyone knew he already knew everything. But the rest of them were right in my face.

'Fuck me, Bridges, is it true? You banging Hot Hall?'

Jack was so excited that his cheeks were a bit pink under his freckles. The rain was dripping off his gelled spikes at the top of his head, but he didn't care. Plus, I couldn't get over the fact that he'd called me by my surname. It was like a nickname, right? Like I'd been proper accepted. That's why I stuttered a bit, but it didn't matter because the next questions came thick and fast.

'Let's see the pictures. Mitch says you've got some.'

Then Lewis joined in. He looked just as excited... though no one wants him to smile too much – his skin is so dry if he moves quickly, it cracks. That's what Mitchell says anyway and so obviously we all think it's well funny.

'Yeah, come on, mate, don't hog it all to yourself. We all need that material in our brains for later. In fact, send it on, will ya?'

The girls tried to act cool, but you could tell they were interested. They were lingering at the side, but it was Lynsey who spoke first. She flipped her hair back over her shoulder and made sure she stuck her tits out as she talked. She all thinks we don't know she does it, but we definitely do. I mean, we don't mind obviously, but no one stands with their backs arched like that for no reason.

'Fuck sake, guys, you're acting like you've never seen a woman before. You're so gross. She probably looks all wrinkly. She's had children, remember.'

'She don't actually,' I piped up. I felt like the biggest bollocks in the school, and I weren't going to let Lyns ruin it. She's always looked down her nose at me and it was obvious she was jealous. I weren't going to let her fuck it up. 'She's well hot, beyond hot, and I'll show you. But I ain't sending it. She won't want you all having it on your phones.'

'How will she know?'

I mean. Jack was right. How would she know? But I couldn't be giving out my picture, could I? She did it for *me*. She only wants *me*. She doesn't want all the others fucking gawping at her any time of the day. So I ignored the question and got my phone out, keeping it close to my chest so they couldn't grab it. I knew once they saw it, they'd shut up anyway. Not that I really wanted them to. When they all got proper close, I felt my heart pump and my cheeks go red. I didn't know if it was because I felt awesome or because I was nervous, but I thought, what am I worried about? I'm not lying… well, not really. Yeah, sure, they think I was inside rather than outside, but that's the only difference, ain't it? So I showed them. And they fucking lapped it up.

They were cheering and shouting so loud that everyone on the courts turned round. Thank Christ the rest of the year are too shit scared of Mitchell to actually come up and bustle in. But they turned and they saw. They saw me. Just me. In the middle of my crew. While they told me what a fucking legend I was. Honestly. Rockstar material.

The only problem was… pissing Lynsey. You could see the photo had made her jealousy boil over. She didn't like Jack looking at my missus in her sexy underwear. She'd probably never looked that good in her life. She ain't experienced like my Juliet, is she? I mean… Hall's tits are something else. Nothing that a Year 11 girl could contend with. No matter what push-up bra she wore. The thing was, she weren't the only one that was jealous. It was obvious that Jack was too. He'd stuck with teenage Lyns while I was out there banging a proper woman with proper experience... well, nearly banging, not that they knew that... and it was written all over his face. Lynsey clocked it and barged right through the middle of everyone so she was right in front of me, which takes some doing seeing as she's the size of a fucking Oompa Loompa, and flicked her stripy hair in my face.

'So, if she's your girlfriend... or your missus as you say... why is this the only picture you've got?'

'It ain't.'

'Well, where are the others?'

'On my laptop.'

'Why the fuck would you put them on your laptop? Who does that?'

She looked round then to get some backing. Lucy smirked, of course she did, but the lads were too busy taking in the image. I could see it in their eyes, so they gave her nothing… not even Jack. I knew the boys were ignoring her, so I made sure I sounded proper cocky… even though, to be fair, I had no fucking clue why someone would put it on their laptop… I don't even bloody have one.

'So not everyone sees. You might have forgotten, Lyns, but she has a fucking husband, *and* she works at the school. We have to keep it quiet.'

'Yeah, she has a husband… and you're a fucking child.'

There it was again. The same thing Pissy Chris said. Why are people so obsessed with age? I thought they'd make a point about her being my teacher, I get that, but it ain't like I'm seven, is it? You can shag at sixteen and that's what they all think I am anyway, so what's the problem? I tried to show her that I weren't a pushover no more, not now I was the hero of the group, so I stepped forward. I probably spoke a bit too loudly, especially to a girl, but she was getting under my skin.

'Well, she obviously don't see me as a child, does she? She sees me as a fucking man.'

'Or she sees you as the same spotty kid that we all see and that's what turns her on. Fucking weirdo.'

'She ain't a fucking weirdo. She's fucking class and hot as shit and you're just jealous. End of.'

Yeah, I know. Proper bold from me, but she was pissing me off. This weren't just about Hot Hall. It was about me and my moment. I've waited my whole life to be the centre of attention. Not for something shit either, for something good, really good, and she was ruining it. She's always taking all the attention. She knows the boys fancy her and she plays on it big time. Walks round in the tightest trousers, not a skirt like the other girls, because she knows she can stick her bum out further in her trousers and make it look more noticeable. She always refuses to wear her blazer too, so her black bra shows through the back of her shirt. She never wears a tie and leaves the buttons open so you can see down her top. We all look, of course we do, but now... now she'll realise that she ain't the fittest girlfriend in the group no more. When Hall ditches her feller and comes to me, she'll come and hang out with us all and Lynsey knows that will be the end of her. Why would the boys drool over her anymore when I walk up to the skate park with Hot Hall? I mean. It's never going to happen, is it? And you know the best thing? I won't even be worried about Hall fucking off with one of the other blokes, like Jack does, because she knows us all. She knows all my mates, yet she chose me to start this with and I'll always know that.

Lynsey still wouldn't leave it though. After my outburst the blokes had all made an 'oooo' noise and she'd got the hump and stropped off, giving Jack a right glare as she did, but he didn't chase after her like she wanted. He just rolled his eyes and then winked at me. Honest to God. I reckon he liked that I stood up to her. Someone needed to. It was epic… until she was back –

obviously pissed that only Lucy had followed her off, so she

started shouting her mouth off again.

'I think this is all bullshit,' she announced to the group.

'There is no proof really. One slutty picture. That could have

been taken anywhere. For all we know you could have been a

creep, hiding in the bushes, taking the picture through the

window.'

Fuck. I mean, when you say it like that, it don't sound

good, but it weren't like that, was it? Before I could answer it

though, Jack had piped up as well. Clearly the bro code had gone

out the window and now he was scared he wouldn't get a shag

later. Epic mate.

'Yeah, to be fair, Ben. What else have you got? Surely,

you've been texting and that if this has been going on a while?'

What a fucking turncoat. What happened to the wink he

gave me seconds before?

'Yeah, course we have.'

Shit.

'Show us then. Show us the messages.'

Double shit. I fumbled with my phone and stuffed it back into my pocket. I didn't want them getting hold of it. This was turning. I could feel it.

'I can't.'

'Why not?'

'Because I have to delete them, don't I? It's like that when you are the shag on the side.'

'So that's what you are then? Her bit of rough? Can't really say you're her boyfriend if she pretends you don't exist.'

Jack smirked and turned round to look at Mitchell, who was standing right at the back of the crowd. I'd almost forgotten he was there for a moment, but when I caught him, I saw that he was smiling. Not in a way where he was encouraging me or anything like that but in a twisted way, like he was enjoying watching me squirm. Sick bastard. I needed to get him back on my side.

'It's complicated, innit? You lot won't understand. We're going to go public and that, 'course we are. It's just…'

'Just what?'

'Just that we have to do it in the right way.'

'Oh, this is bullshit!'

Yep… Lynsey was back on her mission. She'd let Jack do the talking for long enough and now she was going to spout her mouth off again. I knew I never liked her. Not really. Well, definitely not now.

'We need some more evidence before we're going to believe your crap. If I don't see messages or more pictures, I'm calling bullshit and I won't be spending any more time with you. And neither will you, will you, Jack?'

Jack didn't look at Lyns. He looked at Mitchell and Mitchell looked at me. I could see everything fucking crumbling and I hated it. Mitchell was clearly thinking, which ain't something I see him do that often. He scratched his spotty chin and then spoke for the first time in ages. He made sure he looked straight at me while he was talking. It was well awkward.

'Yeah. Show us some more, Ben. I ain't saying I don't believe you… but I hate being taken for a mug, so I need to know you're not doing that. You understand, don't you, mate?'

Something about that 'mate' didn't feel friendly. If anything, he sounded like he was threatening me, like something off *Peaky Blinders*.

'I ain't taking you for a mug, Mitchell. I wouldn't do that. I've got loads more proof at home and I can show you all of it. In fact, I'll show everyone. I'll put it on Facebook. By the end of the week. I will. I'll put it online.'

Why the fuck did I say that? They hadn't asked me to put it out there for everyone to see, only them, but I'd made it bigger. Me and my bloody gob. I knew I needed to backtrack, so I added, 'I just need to chat to her first.'

But that gave Lynsey all the ammunition she needed.

'Need to get permission from your imaginary missus, do you?'

She looked at Lucy as she said it and obviously Lucy laughed, then she glared at Jack, so he laughed too. Mitchell weren't laughing though. He was just staring. Hadn't taken his eyes off me for ages. I didn't know if that was because he believed me, or because he was pissed off, but I knew then I had no choice but to follow up on what I'd said.

'No, Lyns. I don't need permission from no one. But I don't want to fuck it up either, do I?'

'Why not?' Jack muscled in. 'Look, Ben. You're fucking the hot teacher... or so you say... That gives you, like, legendary status. No doubt about it, you'll go down in school history, but let's face it, you ain't going to settle down with her and start a fucking family, are you? She'll stay with her feller, and you'll just get to be a legend forever more. So, you might as well show us the pictures, show the whole bloody world and enjoy every second while you can. That is… if it's true, of course.'

Now look, I ain't stupid. I know he was goading me. I know he was seeing how far he could push. But what could I do? He said the word legendary. I've never been a legend in my life… not unless you count being the legend of sad, loser dickheads. This was my chance to finally be the popular kid. Not because of Mitchell, but because of me. I *had* to show them what they wanted. As soon as Hall saw the note about the Shakespeare book in her drawer, she'd know I was up for it, and she'd act on it. I knew it. So now, if I just make it happen before the end of the week, I can still put everything up there for them to see without having to lie at all. It would be simple.

So, I told them I would. I told them that I'd do it in a few days. I stuck to the story about deleting text messages, so I said I needed time to get some more. I also said I'd put it online, so that they would see the same time as everyone else. Fuck. Mitchell told me he'd be well pissed off if I didn't live up to what I'd said, and I know that would be the end of me, so I have no choice. It's out of my hands. I just need her to find that note and quickly. Then I can keep hold of everything.

Thomas

(Now)

Mum didn't know I was in the car. She didn't know I was listening. She probably wouldn't have said that if she thought I was there, but I keep thinking… does that matter? Did she just say it because she was angry? Or does she not say it to me because she knows the truth hurts? Because it does, you know. It really, really hurts. I always knew I wasn't her favourite. If she had a favourite. I knew I annoyed her, that she found me too wimpy, but I didn't know she didn't love me. Because that's what she said. Her words. She said she didn't love me, she didn't love Ellie and she doesn't love Dad. So why has she stuck around all this time?

My mate Pete, his dad did a runner when he was four. He said his mum told him it was harder for dads to bond, because they didn't have you kicking around in their stomach for nine months. She said that's why they have this mother's instinct thing. So what happened with me? Why does my mum not have that? Because in our house, it's always Dad. He drops us off and picks us up, even though Mum is going the same way. He watches my hockey matches and Ellie's netball matches even when she says she doesn't want him to because it's embarrassing. But Mum just works and goes to the gym and… well, obviously the other thing too… with the older boy. The one from the school.

As soon as I walked in this morning, it started. I don't have Facebook. It says you have to be thirteen to have it and I'm only twelve. I'm one of the youngest in my year. My mates said they all made up their dates of birth so they could download it when they were like ten, but I hate lying. Besides, Dad said I could have a phone only for calls and texts, so that's what I have. He trusts me to stick to the rules and I like that. So, no, I hadn't seen anything. Ellie said Mum must have seen it all because it was linked to her account or something, but she didn't tell us. I wonder why? Why didn't she warn us? To protect us? Ellie said it was because she only likes to protect herself, but I think she's wrong. After what Mum said today, if she was only interested in protecting herself, she would have left ages ago. Walked out on all the people she didn't love, like Pete's dad, but she hasn't, has she? She's stuck around for something, so maybe she just thought we wouldn't see it? Or maybe she hadn't checked her phone? I don't know what happened. I mean... it would have been nice to know. To have warning. Because today was horrible, from start to finish.

I walked into the playground and immediately felt like everyone was staring at me. I keep myself to myself at school, always have done. I spend most of my time with Pete and that's how I prefer it. Ellie's always calling us gay, but I don't think we are. I just like being around him. We like the same stuff. No other boys in our year would spend lunchtimes creating a full A3 chart about who would win in a fight between Iron Man and the Flash, would they? But we did. Even though it's probably a waste of time as they would never cross paths because Marvel and DC are different universes anyway… obviously. (Besides, we both know Iron Man would win, but it was fun coming up with the pie chart.) So… yeah… normally it's just Pete who knows I even exist at school. But today, well, it felt really different. I felt like people were pointing at me when I walked past and stuff. I thought I was imagining it until I met Pete at the entrance of the Science block where I meet him every morning. He looked awkward and asked if I was OK. He cottoned on pretty quickly that I had no idea what he was chatting about, so he pulled me into the loos to show me his phone. I swear I nearly died on the spot. I didn't want to look at the pictures, but I had to check it was her. And it definitely was. It was definitely my mum looking like something out of Pete's brother's posters on his bedroom wall. It made me feel sick. I couldn't look at it any longer, let alone read the posts, so Pete had to fill me in. Tell me how this kid reckons he'd been shagging my mum. Can you imagine it? Said he had text messages between them and everything. I didn't want to hear what they said, but Pete said

they were graphic. I almost got annoyed at him for reading them,

but then I thought… well… thank God he did, because if he

hadn't told me, who would've done?

Pete said I just had to keep my head down. He said he'd

stay with me, and we'd just ignore it. I thought that was a good

plan until I walked into registration and everyone, and I mean

everyone, looked up. Me and Pete are normally the first ones in,

sitting at our table in the back corner, but we'd spent so long in

the loos coming up with a plan to deal with it all that we were

pretty much the last ones through the door. Miss barely even

looked at us and just told us to sit down. Even she looked

embarrassed. And then everyone else started whispering. The

noise was unbearable, like a bee buzzing too close to your ear.

We rushed to our table, wanting Miss to just start the register,

when Mickey shouted across the room,

'Thomas. Your mum been shagging that Ben kid or what

then?'

My heart dropped. I felt so sick, like when you go on a rollercoaster, and you go down the dip part. I've only been on one and this feeling was the reason I've never been on another one. I tried to ignore him and sit in my seat. Pete sat down with me, and I've never been more grateful to have the chair closest to the window. It was like a barrier he created between me and them. I knew my cheeks had gone red, I could feel it, but I refused to answer. I just kept willing Miss to start the register and quiet Mickey down, but it was like she wanted to know the answer too.

'Don't ignore me, Tom. I asked you a question. Did you know she was shagging about?'

'No,' I mumbled, wondering why the hell I'd answered him in the first place. Pete shot me a look. He'd told me in the bathroom not to speak to anyone and he was right because answering Mickey just spurred him on even more.

'Shit, so she was proper sneaking about? Bet you had a right shock this morning then, didn't you? Jesus… Didn't realise she liked kids. Maybe I should have tried it on with her myself.'

'Enough, Mickey… and watch your language. This is still a classroom and that's still your deputy head you're talking about.'

'Oh yeah? For how long do you reckon then, Miss?'

With that, Miss Preston just started the register. She looked as awkward as I did. It was obvious that she didn't think Mum was going to keep her job and if she thought that, then she must think she's guilty. Just like everyone else in the world, even Dad. I couldn't make sense of it.

When it got to my name in the register, she didn't even wait for me to answer before she moved on. It was like she didn't want to acknowledge that I was in the classroom. Miss Preston was young. Mum called her an NQT, which I think meant she'd just started teaching. I remember Mum saying it was a shame she had Mickey in her form one night because she knew from his primary school what a pain he was. I remember telling her that I would stay away from him, and she just laughed. Even she thought I was too much of a loser to hang around with a popular kid like him. I mean, to be fair, she was right. Not only am I a bit geeky, I admit it, but I'm also super scared of kids like that. The ones that don't care what anybody thinks. Me and Pete both are. We can tell that to each other, so that's why we just stick to the two of us. Today though, for the first time ever, I really could have done with more friends. More people to crowd round me as I walked down the corridor.

As soon as I left my form room, it started. The bell had gone, and everyone was walking to their next lesson. The corridor was crowded, and I thought I'd be able to sneak past everyone. Get to the next lesson and the safety of the classroom without bumping into someone as vocal as Mickey. But of course, that wasn't the case. There's too many kids like that in my school to avoid them all.

'That's Hall's kid.'

That's all I remember hearing. One voice from the other end of the corridor and then it was like I was a piece of discarded fruit and a whole swarm of ants were all over me. They were shouting things. Asking questions, but I couldn't hear them, let alone answer them. Then all of a sudden, I heard one of the older lads saying that Mum wasn't there, that someone had seen her leaving earlier and then that was it; it was game on, like they could get away with anything.

They started shoving me down the corridor, from one side to the next, cheering each time someone had a push. I could hear people shouting, calling Mum all sorts of names... slag, slut, even paedo. It was horrible. I couldn't stop myself crying. The tears were rolling down my cheeks before I could do anything about it. Part of me hoped that they would see, and they would stop, but they didn't. It was like seeing me hurt just spurred them on even more. I'd lost Pete in the crowd. I tried to call for him and that just made them laugh even harder. They kept repeating it, 'Pete? Pete? Where are you, Pete?' Poor Pete, honestly, that must have been so bad for him. He didn't need to be involved, did he? They were getting rougher and rougher with their pushes, and it took everything I had just to stay on my feet. I just clung to my backpack straps and hoped they would push me towards the stairs soon so I could run down them and escape.

That's when I heard a different voice. A teacher. It was Mr Smith. He must have heard the cheering and come out to see what was going on. He grabbed me by my bag and pulled me out. There was no kindness in him. He didn't ask if I was OK. He just told me to get to class and told everyone else to do the same. So, we did.

By the time I got to Science, Pete was waiting for me outside. He said he was sorry for losing me and that there wasn't anything he could do, but I wasn't really listening. I couldn't get over what they'd said about Mum. The words they'd used. Was she really those things? Was she a slut? Was she a paedophile? They told us in PSHE that sixteen was the age of consent and I thought you were sixteen in Year 11. I spoke to Pete about it later though and he said he might not be sixteen yet, but it would be bad anyway because she was his teacher. He said she could get in a lot of trouble, with the police and things. And I thought, if that happens, where does that leave us?

For the first time since the start of the day, in that Science lesson, I thought about Dad. I'd been so wrapped up in my own stuff that I hadn't even thought about him. If it was true, if she'd been with that boy, then she's had an affair, right? She's cheated on Dad. I knew then that when I got home Dad wouldn't want to hang about. But I couldn't help but wonder if he'd take us with him? Mum works so much that Dad does most of the stuff with us anyway, but it doesn't mean I don't want to see my mum again. Or do I? I wanted to know how Ellie felt. I looked for her all break time, but I couldn't find her anywhere. I saw her mates in the quad, but I didn't want to walk up to them. They were scary at the best of times, let alone today. Besides, wherever I walked people said something. Some said quiet things that only me and Pete could hear. Others shouted it for the whole world to hear, but they all said the same sort of thing. They all told me what a slag she was. I mean… if the whole world is saying it, it must be true, right?

By the end of break, I couldn't cope anymore. I told Pete I was going to say I felt sick and go home. He didn't blame me and almost looked relieved that he would have more of a peaceful day without me there. Who could blame him? So I went up to the school nurse, ready to fake an illness, and as soon as she saw me, she just said she'd ring my dad. Nothing else, no lying needed. Of course, I was secretly relieved about that bit… but still. She called Dad and he told her I could walk back, and he'd meet me at home. Normally they wouldn't allow that, normally they'd speak to Mum, but she didn't. She just told me to go. It was like she was almost wanting me to run away from there. So, I did.

The thing is, I've only just realised now that I didn't defend Mum. Not once, not all day. I let them say what they wanted, and I kept my head down. I just kept thinking that if I got home, she would tell me things that made sense. Dad would explain how they'd got it wrong, and Ellie might even let me hang out in her room to make me feel better… you never know. Only, it didn't happen like that, obviously, because Dad thinks she did it, doesn't he? And he knows her better than anyone. Mum says she didn't, but she didn't say that to me. She said it to Dad… and her boss… She said it to Ellie apparently as well, but not me. She didn't care what I thought. The only thing I heard was when they were on the car phone. I hadn't been listening to the whole conversation because my phone had been going off. The same messages over and over again from numbers I didn't know. I'd stopped looking at them and tried to ignore them, but by doing that I listened to the argument she was having with Dad instead. I listened to her say she didn't love me, that she never even wanted me. And that's when that sick feeling came back – the one that's like the rollercoaster – only this time it was worse. The worst feeling I've ever felt in my whole life. My dad hasn't spoken to me since, my sister never speaks to me anyway, my gran is with Dad saying horrible things about my mum, and my mum… she says her own horrible things about me. Now I'm on my own, the sick feeling in my stomach and the sick text messages are all I have for company. Yet I keep going back to the fact that I didn't defend her. Maybe… maybe if I'd stood up for her… maybe then she'd love me. Who knows?

Ben

(5 days earlier)

I thought it would be easy. I thought she'd see my note, we'd

have a one to one… you know… of the physical kind… and

everything would be hunky bloody dory. Only that hasn't

happened. Of course it bloody hasn't. She hasn't even seen my

note for starters, and I haven't had any one to ones this week

because she's always in stupid meetings. Typical. Why did it

have to be the week I'd opened my mouth that she went AWOL?

If I'd have just waited a bit longer or made my move straight

after the strip tease at the window, then maybe I wouldn't be sat

at home thinking about what the fuck I'm going to do. What's

making it worse is that the gang are constantly messaging as

well. They keep telling me how many days I've got left and how

I need to make my move, show them the evidence, but they

don't get it, do they? They think it's all happened already, that I have everything I need and I'm just sitting on it for some dickhead reason. God if only that was the case. Not the fact that I thought it would happen this week, that I could just expand it a bit and have everything I promised. But now... now I need to show them something I don't fucking have.

What the hell am I going to do? I need more time. I could have everything they want if I just had more time, but they ain't going to give me that, are they? No excuse in the world would give me even one day more without losing all my bloody friends. Shit. If it had happened, this would be piss easy and nothing would be hard... Well, the right thing would be hard... obvs... but that's not the point right now. Now I just need to get out of this because it's all my fault, me and my fucking mouth. I thought... I thought if I could just get back to our one to ones, I'd have a chance to tell her, tell her that I'd seen everything, tell her that I understand everything, then she would have fucking jumped on me, we'd exchange numbers and I'd have everything I need. But I can't. And I can't speak to her at school when the other teachers are around, and I can't exactly rock up to her house, can I? What would I say if someone else opened the door? *'Oh, hello, I'm just here to see if your missus still wants to shag me?'* or *'Hey, Ellie, can I fuck your mum quick?'* Yeah, that would really work. Dickhead.

Mitchell just sent another text. He keeps telling me that I better not be lying to him. He keeps saying that if I am, if I'm talking shit and I've lied to him, then he'll knock me out. I think it's just banter, I hope it is, but what if it ain't? What if, come Friday, I have nothing. Nothing to show, nothing to say. Then what? Then I'm royally fucked. No hot teacher to shag and no mates to hang around with. I'd be back there again, Ben the dickhead, the loser, like nothing's changed. The problem is, it's all fucking changed. Everything in my whole life has changed and it's epic. Every day I wake up knowing I'm going to walk into school and into a group of people that actually want me to be there. Not rock up on my own, or hang about on the outskirts of the group trying to join in. Not with Pissy Chris desperately trying to make me look even more like a twat. I get to walk in and hang out with the coolest kids in school, sit with them at lunch, say bye to them at the end of the day. And I have people to follow on Insta, pictures to put on Facebook. People like my posts… They actually like them. I mean… yeah, sometimes I ask them to, but everyone does that nowadays. Lynsey is always sending messages round to say she's updated her profile pic and everyone needs to like it. Obviously… I've normally already liked it by then, but that's not the point, is it? She *wants* me to like her pictures and sometimes she likes mine.

And it's not just about her and the others… it's Mitchell. Mitch, the most popular kid in school, likes *my* pictures. Everyone sees that. Everyone knows. They know on Facebook, *and* they know when I walk around the quad with him, or into classes with him, and it makes me feel like a fucking king. Proper awesome. And for the first time in my life, I feel like I'm noticed and I ain't losing that. Not for nobody. So, I know it's shit and I know it ain't fair, and I might lose my chance of ever shagging Hot Hall, but I need to make some stuff up, because let's face it, it's better than losing everything I've got.

All I need to do is convince the gang that I ain't talking rubbish and then everything can go back to how it's meant to be. So, I've been googling. There's a programme where you can easily Photoshop pictures. There's a YouTube video showing you how to do it and everything. The only problem is, you need to use a laptop or a computer to do it. It don't work on phones, and I can hardly use the school ones, can I? So I'm going to have to nick my mum's for a bit and hope to fuck I don't get caught. Then the pictures should be easy enough to do. Obviously, all I have at the moment is the one in the window from the other night and clearly it looks like I was closer than I was because they all thought I was in the room with her. But one picture ain't going to be enough, is it? I have the one I took in the chippy too, but she's just standing there in her clothes, so that won't be enough to convince them either. I mean, by watching this vid, it looks like I can get a picture from the internet and put her head on it. So maybe I could get a picture of someone in their underwear and use that? Obviously I'd have to find someone with the same type of body, but she's banging fit, so that shouldn't be hard.

Actually, fuck it, I've already got one in her underwear. Maybe I should keep her clothed but put me next to her, so it looks like we're having a selfie together? I could make it look like we're in my room. Mum wouldn't have a clue who's been and gone, not that she'll find out about all of this anyway, so I could make it look like we're on my bed. That will look insane. Proper good. Actually, the more I think about that, the more I reckon that's a better idea than the underwear. Fuck, I reckon I could pull this off. Make it proper convincing. If I take a selfie of me, on my bed, and put her picture next to me, no one's going to know any different.

All I need to do now is get into Mum's laptop when she ain't around. I know her password – I've had that memorised since I was about ten. She really should change it once in a while. Before I had a phone, I didn't know how to wipe the search history, so she always knew when I'd been using it. Now I've googled that, I'm ready to go. Actually, it's been quiet downstairs for a while now. The new feller was round earlier. I knew it wouldn't be long, but I haven't heard them for ages. Maybe they've gone down the pub. Fuck it, I'm going to risk going downstairs. Her lappy will be in the living room, so I'll spot it straight away.

God, I hate how much these stairs creak. Mum keeps saying how she's going to ring the council to get them fixed, but she never does. She never does anything she says she will. Definitely still seems quiet though, and her fake UGGs from the market are gone from by the door, so I reckon she's out. I could be quids in here. I just need to grow some balls and push the living room door open. It's either closed because they're out or it's closed because they're doing something else... I'm praying that they're out. Oh, thank Christ, they are. To be fair, it was way too quiet in here to be the other thing anyway.

And there it is. The laptop. The golden way of keeping my life just the way it is. I knew she would've left it in here – right on the tray she has her dinner on – in front of the telly. Oh yeah… she always manages to make herself dinner. Cheers, Mum. Hold on… What the hell? It's not just her laptop on the tray… It's her bloody phone. She's left her phone at home. Shit.

'Mum?'

No answer.

'Mum?'

I had to check. She never leaves her phone at home. She must be proper loved up with this latest knobhead to forget that. I thought for sure she'd still be knocking around here somewhere. Wait a minute… oh my God. I've just had the most banging idea ever. Photos are good, the one in her underwear is insane and us being in bed together will be mint, but they ain't going to be enough, are they? Yeah, they'll show us together, but YouTube just showed me how easy it is to fake shit like that, so no one will fully trust it, will they? But they will trust a text. Think about it; if it's in black and white too, then there is even more evidence. Who would shag someone and never text them? That just wouldn't happen. And now I've got Mum's phone right here in my hand, for me to use, well… that's exactly what I can do.

If I save Mum's number as Hot Hall instead, I can send any texts I want, that can say anything I want. I can text myself and make it look like I'm texting her. I could write some proper raunchy shit, like proper *Fifty Shades* stuff and then there would be no denying it. There would be flirty fucking texts between me and Hot Hall for everyone to see. If I screenshot them so I can put a picture up and then make sure I delete them off Mum's phone, I'll have them saved and Mum will never know. Then I'll have everything I need, and I'll be able to show Mitchell and the rest of them and my life can carry on being epic. The photo can wait. Mum leaves her lappy around a lot more than she does her phone. Even when she's passed out pissed, she's bloody hugging it. I'm never going to get this opportunity again, so I need to do it right now. Fuck, I hope she don't walk through the door. What do I write? I think Mum's got *Fifty Shades* upstairs, the only book she's ever read in her whole life. I could look at that for ideas of things to text myself… Fuck, this could actually end up being quite fun… I might need to take some tissue upstairs with me too.

Liz

(Now)

Still sitting on the hallway floor, Liz turned her back to her room and the mirror, wiped her eyes and looked towards her daughter's bedroom. The door was open, and she could see the circle she had made through the mess on the floor as she was pacing around it. She seemed to be surrounded by mess and carnage and it was moving into her brain, creating questions she would never have asked herself before. Her daughter's messy room, the lack of care she showed, was that because of her? Because she didn't care about Ellie, so why should Ellie care about the home that meant so much to her? The plates under her bed, another sign to Liz of her inadequacies as a mother. Liz didn't make her any meals, so why would she know that there were plates missing? She ran a tight ship; the rooms she went in were spotless… but only because she barked orders. She paid for cleaners, for gardeners, for dry cleaners and the rest. Well, Rob did. She couldn't, could she? She was the breadwinner, the one with the career. What did he have? Sure, he was a mechanic, but that's a job, isn't it? Not a career. He would stay the same every day and she was going places, so of course he needed to step up and get the rest of the stuff done. That's why the pile of ironing had been left there by him, the meals had been cooked by him, yet it was never good enough to her. She was too busy to change it though. Besides, she pretty much paid for it all anyway. Rob's half barely covered the bills. He definitely didn't have anything left over from his share to buy nice crockery and clothes.

She turned away from Ellie's room and saw the floor lamp. The one that had illuminated the hallway in the early hours of this morning. Had it really only been one day? It felt like the longest in history. The bulb was still fighting to shine its light despite the strip of late afternoon sunshine coming in through the blinds. All day it had shone, so unlike Liz not to have switched it off by now. She remembered telling Rob that if it got left on again, she would get rid of it altogether – the black cable looked unsightly running across the floor anyway. But Rob had put a stop to that because it was the one Thomas needed, the one he couldn't cope without. Oh Thomas. He had heard all of that. Heard her say she had wanted an abortion, that she never wanted him in the first place and that she didn't love him. Not just that, but how had she reacted? Had she stayed on the phone and fought for him to understand? Had she tried to make him feel better? No. She'd hung up. She didn't even tell him that it was just said in anger and that she didn't mean it because... well... she did...

No matter how hard she'd tried, she'd never been able to warm to Thomas. She thought she would because the pregnancy was so different. People around her celebrated this one. They kept telling her that her and Rob had beat the odds, proved the world wrong, and she'd liked that, but deep down she knew it wasn't true. She'd felt so forced and so trapped by Rob. The world thought he was so kind and loving, but when she looked back now, she felt nothing but resentment. He had pestered her for so long to have another baby and make a 'proper family'. He'd told her how people would look at them better if they stayed together and raised another child well. And he was right, they did, but every time someone said it, he would give her this sickening smile. One others thought was love, but one she knew to be full of smugness, his way of showing her he was right all along.

Thomas inherited that smile. Every time he got full marks on a test, she would see it. Every time he won an award at school, she'd see it. In fact, every time she should be bursting with pride, he showed that smile, and rather than gushing over her wonderful son, her stomach would flip, and she would have to walk away. She knew, deep down, it wasn't fair, but she could never handle how much he looked like Rob, barely any of her genes in him at all. And the way people talk about him, just like they do about Rob, how kind he is, how loving. Even when he was a toddler, people would stop her in the street to say, *'Oh, your Thomas, he's such a sweetie, isn't he? So kind and caring, not like the other boys.'* They'd meant it in such a kind way, of course they had, but Liz couldn't bear it. She didn't want a kind man, she didn't want another Rob; she was surrounded by these men that she should spend her life being grateful for according to everyone else, yet she wanted nothing more than to escape from. Not only that, but those people that had stopped her were right. He was so different from the other boys in his class, and she hated that. Why did he have to be so wimpy? The other boys always laughed at him, and he never stuck up for himself. He'd just come home and ask for a cuddle. Rob would scoop him up and he'd sit him on his lap for hours. Liz… if she was honest with herself, would do anything but. The thought of it made her skin crawl; him clinging on to her for dear life like a spider monkey gave her nothing but a feeling of sickness that she couldn't get rid of. But as she sat on the floor, looking at the hallway lamp, Liz couldn't help but wonder that if she had given him that attention – if she had held him tight in her arms like a mother should – would he have grown up quicker? Would he still need that light on to sleep at night, or would he feel secure enough without it because he had a mother that loved him?

She shook herself. This was ridiculous. She knew this wasn't the case. She'd been on enough safeguarding courses to know about neglect and her children were definitely not neglected. Just looking at Ellie's room told her that. Designer clothes strewn on the floor, china plates thrown under the bed and a top of the range laptop that was still insistently sending messages from people that were clearly meant to be having dinner or doing homework by now. Besides, they had plenty of love from 'Dad of the Year' and they had mates. Ellie was surrounded by a gaggle of girls wherever she went and Thomas… well, he had Peter… and they were obviously very close, so he always had someone to talk to. Liz had provided them with independence, which was a gift that had been stolen from her. They should be thanking her if anything.

Brushing herself down and standing up, Liz picked up her phone from her pocket. There was no point hiding from this anymore. She knew people from work would have messaged to see if she was alright. Perhaps even old acquaintances would be trying to get to her on Facebook to check if she was OK, and she shouldn't be ignoring them. She should be thanking them for their kindness and their support. As soon as Jo saw how many people were on her side and knew her well enough to believe her over a child, this would all be over, and she could get back to work where she belonged.

The phone had more notifications on it than she thought was possible. Streams of the obvious, stupid children in the school who she would reprimand for sharing the post when she returned to the building, and old school friends who had nothing better to do with their lives, clearly. But then... there was a lot of people she didn't know at all, yet they were all speaking about her as if they knew her personally. Mothers, grandmothers, all detailing their disgust in her. How had it reached so many people? Of course, she knew it could. She had seen the teachers that had put a post up to show their pupils how far it could travel, but that was because they had asked them to. They requested that people shared the post all over the world. Liz had not requested anything of the sort, and by the looks of it, neither had Ben. Yet there it was. People up and down the country sharing their opinion on the teacher that had seduced a pupil.

Liz ran downstairs to get her own laptop. She found herself sat on the same kitchen stool as earlier, the same stinging in her eyes and the same feeling in the pit of her stomach. No matter how unrealistic she knew it was, she hoped with all her might that if she opened it up on a different device, it would all be gone. Of course, it was not. There it was again, only bigger this time. The shares upon shares of that post. That stupid post that started all of this. She couldn't get over how trying to help someone had led to all of this. Of course, helping Ben had not been completely selfless, but only in terms of her own career, not in terms of anything else. If only she had known it was him at the window that night. She knew there was someone. but why didn't she care who? And then…

Liz stopped looking at the screen and allowed her head to fall into her hands. The note. The picture. She'd found it in her desk a few days before all of this had started. She thought it was nothing. Perhaps a note confiscated by one of the supply teachers who had been covering her lessons. But now… it couldn't have been. It must have been from Ben. She'd been showing him *Romeo and Juliet* in their sessions. She'd wanted him to get used to Shakespearean language… nothing more. But what had he taken from it? She racked her brain to remember exactly what had been written on it – she'd looked at it so fleetingly – something like, *I get it now, my Juliet.* Was it from him? Is that what he thought this was? That she was some star-crossed lover who couldn't be with the one she wanted? He thought it was a hint, between the play and the window display…

Liz frantically switched the screen from the horror display of Facebook to her own work emails. Someone must have messaged her, someone that understood. She would use that person to get into her desk and remove that picture. She would explain and they would understand, but if she left it in there, if Jo searched her desk and found it, it would definitely not be understood. She couldn't ask one of the Senior Leadership Team – she knew they were all in Jo's back pocket – but her English department was full of people that she chatted to every day. They were her colleagues and her friends. They knew her better than anyone in the school, despite what she used to think. They would help her if she asked. In fact, they'd all probably been sending emails for hours now. Liz never gave out her phone number – it was personal – but they knew she would always reply on email at the drop of a hat, so that's where they would have sent their messages.

Logging on seemed to take forever. As Liz watched the spinning wheel load in the middle of her laptop screen, all she could hear was the thumping of her own heart. Not just in her chest, but through her whole body. It felt like her head was going to explode, like her body was attacking her from the inside. How could she have been so stupid? Lost so much control? How can she be the one fighting while he gets to continue his life like a... what? Like a hero? She knew this would give him major popularity points. She heard them call her MILF and things behind her back. Even those fake messages he'd put on the post, the number was saved under 'Hot Hall'. Liz couldn't believe how much she used to relish in that. How, deep down, she loved the attention. That part of her had never left, not really, no matter how old she got. Yet, here she was, wishing she was some ugly cow that could just keep going with her life... Things really had got bad. Once her emails had loaded, she looked through all the new ones for the names of the people in her English department. Tina was always sucking up to Liz, inviting her out to the pub on a Friday night – not that she ever went. Surely Tina would have sent a message. Liz looked again at the unread messages but could see none from Tina, or Martin, or Amy. In fact, nobody from the English department had emailed her at all. She looked further. Liz had never not looked at her emails for this long. She had all the generic ones to sift through, the staff meeting agendas and the like, but nothing personal. No messages of support or to ask if she was OK. Nothing. She looked again and again and again and still no word from anyone.

She flicked back to her Facebook page and took a deep breath before she opened the messages tab. Again, lots of unread words to sift through, but none of support and none from anyone she would see on a daily basis. Her account was private, but she could still get message requests from people she didn't know and there they were. What felt like hundreds of messages, not of sympathy or understanding, but of abuse, just loads and loads of abuse. The words in these messages, even in just the first lines that she could see, hit her like a punch in the stomach… *Slut… Whore… Paedophile…*

That was the one she'd never had before. Sure, she'd been called a slut, a whore, a hussy, many times in her life. That happens when you're pregnant in school uniform, but a paedophile? As if anyone could think she would do such a thing. Yet here she was, staring at message after message of people that obviously believed all the lies they had been fed. Without thinking, she opened a third tab on her laptop and typed her own name into Google. Sure enough, there it was, a write-up in the local online newspaper. Her work picture from the school website had been used, with the tagline, *Liz Hall allegedly used her position of power to lure a young student into her bed.* Sickness rang through her body, and she ran to the downstairs bathroom and put her head over the toilet. With her last bit of control finally lost, Liz watched the vomit splatter onto the white porcelain bowl before pushing her hair back over her shoulders and slumping herself on the floor in a heap. She was a mess. Because that's what her life had become. One giant, unsolvable mess. This time, Liz allowed herself to sob uncontrollably, for the first time in many years. Streams of tears ran down her face as she sat on the bathroom floor, looking at the walls almost enclosing around her. It felt like a prison cell and the thought of that made her cry even harder. The world around her seemed to be spiralling and she wanted nothing more than to get off – to leave it all completely. This wasn't going to go away.

No matter how much she fought, the world had already made up their minds. They had taken the word of a child over that of a professional. Unless Ben rapidly changed his story, she was going to be known as the woman who seduced a teenager for the rest of her life. Worse than that, she could go to prison. She kicked herself. Why didn't she call the police herself? She could have got the upper hand then. Was it too late now? She looked up at the room surrounding her, the house she had built, all for nothing. All for her to never see it, or the people in it again. No one at work believed her, no one at home believed her. She was stuck in a nightmare with no one to turn to. Was this really the life she'd created? A life of objects but no people, no love, no support. She heard her laptop pinging in the kitchen. The noise was relentless, and it needed to stop. She wiped her mouth with the back of her hand and stood up. Without another thought, she walked back into the kitchen, picked up her laptop and threw it, with all her might, at the door. The smash rang through the empty house as Liz watched the laptop that she had carried for so long obliterate into pieces. She stood and stared at the fragments on the floor – her life had become the same. How was she going to fight this now?

Ben

(2 days earlier)

I went into school today knowing that I was going to get shit from the gang. I knew they'd be on my case about the evidence, about showing them everything as soon as I got through the gates, but I was ready, weren't I? Because I did it. I had it all. I had the messages from my mum's phone, the photo from the other night, and I'd managed to put one together that looked like she was in my room. Honest, it looks fucking mint. I mean, I couldn't work out how to make it look like we were next to each other, but I took the picture from the chippy and changed it so it was my bedroom in the background. Honestly, it's epic. It looks like she's just there, hanging out by my window, like I've caught her off guard. Perfect. I was ready.

'Today's the day, Bridges. You got everything?'

The whole 'Bridges' thing had stuck. I officially had a nickname. Jack has been using it for a while, yet hearing it again had me well buzzing as I brought my phone out me pocket.

'Yeah, I'm ready. Do you want to see it all?'

Jack and Lewis came swarming over to me. Almost running across the quad. Oh yeah... 'cause we'd be shouting across it. I'll be honest, I loved it. Everyone saw me having banter with Jack, everyone heard him call me Bridges. Everyone, in that moment, wanted to be me, and I hadn't even done anything yet. I could already tell that all my hard work was worth it.

When I reached them though, I saw it was still only them that had come up to me. Lynsey was sulking back, obviously. She hated anything that wasn't about her, and Lucy would never leave her side. But Ryan had stayed put too, because he'd stayed next to Mitchell.

Mitchell had his hood up again and his arms folded. He waited until me and the boys had met up and then pulled it down, looking right at me. Without moving forward, he shouted out,

'Woah, woah, woah. Not so fast. That weren't the deal. Put your phone away.'

Without even thinking I just did what I was told. Mitchell can do that sometimes. He seems to have this power that makes me do everything he says. That won't last though, will it? Not when the guys see everything I have. No one is going to tell the kid that nailed the hot teacher what to do. Still, I just stood there looking fucking dumb with my phone stuffed back in my pocket when Jack spun round to face Mitchell.

'What the fuck, Mitch? Why you saying that?'

'Because it ain't enough, is it? The deal weren't to show us. The deal was to show everyone. The deal was that he'd plaster her saucy pictures all over Facebook for the whole world to see.'

With that, the other kids in the quad started staring and mumbling to each other. I could feel my cheeks getting hot and the collar on my shirt started to rub. I almost rushed over to him, pushing Jack and Lewis out the way, so I could whisper without everyone else hearing.

'Come on, Mitch, I don't really need to do that, do I? I know I said I would, but surely showing you is alright? Look, I've got it all here. It's all on my phone. I don't want to piss her off by putting it on Facebook, do I?'

Mitchell started laughing. That stupid, loud laugh he does when he wants attention. Then he starts speaking even louder and everyone is looking on the quad.

'Oh, is that right? What happened to bros before hoes then, huh? I thought we were mates? Maybe we're not.'

'We are. You know we are.'

I sounded desperate. I knew I did, but I couldn't help myself. I couldn't lose Mitchell as a friend, could I? Where would that leave me? I could feel Lynsey's smirk burning into the side of my cheek and I wanted to be pissed off, super annoyed at the shit they were giving me and stand my ground, but all I could think of was keeping Mitchell on my side.

'Look, I can put it on there, of course I can. I just thought you might want to keep it to yourself?'

Then he just laughed again.

'Nice try, *mate.* Get it online tonight or I'm not interested anymore. Sick of playing bloody games. Come on, you lot, I'm sure Ben has tutoring to get to – wouldn't want to keep her waiting, would you, Benny Boy?'

Ben. Benny Boy. Not Bridges. Not best mate nickname territory. Just Ben. And what's worse? They all left. They all fucking followed him over to the basketball courts and left me standing in the quad on my own. I was back to square one. I was meant to be the one calling all the shots. The one with all the

street cred, yet there I was. Stood on my larry with my phone

still firmly in my pocket.

I looked around and tried to laugh it off, like shit like that

happened all the time. And then I made sure I went to the loos.

You know, make it look like I needed to go anyway. Couldn't

follow them to the courts if I needed a piss, could I? Then the

bell went. Thank Christ.

I spoke to Jack in Science. It's just us in our class and we

get on much better when no one else is around. I thought he was

going to ask to see the pictures, but he said Mitchell had told

them all not to ask me. I got it, I wouldn't go against Mitchell

either. But he told me not to worry too much, just reckons

Mitchell's pissed off because now he knows it's true. He said

Mitchell didn't believe me at first, but once I came in saying I

had evidence, he changed his mind and now he's angry about it,

so he's trying to make me wuss out of posting it and keep it to

myself. Jack thinks that if all the school know I shagged the fit teacher, then they'll all like me more than Mitchell and then he's

fucked. I can't even imagine it. Me being more popular than

Mitchell? That's mental. But what if it did happen? What if me

putting this on Facebook would make me the most popular kid in

school? If that's what Jack thinks, and that's what Mitchell

thinks, then that's what's bound to happen, right?

Then, on the walk home I thought of something.

Something from that conversation with Jack made me think that

Mitchell might not be the bezzie mate I thought he was. If he

would be pissed off that I got popular, does that mean he just

wants me around to be his dogsbody? Just wants me to do all of

his shit rather than have anything of my own? Because, he might

say I'm his mate, but is that just because it suits him? What if he

only chose me to hang around with so he had someone to boss

about? Think about it, since Jack has got with Lynsey, he's been

well full of himself. Telling me shit about Mitchell, like today,

even telling him he's being a knobhead to his face sometimes.

And the others… well… they're starting to notice that he's

getting away with it. That Mitchell ain't doing anything to stop

Jack. So, they're starting to turn to Jack a bit more than him.

Lucy always followed Lynsey anyway, so it makes sense,

doesn't it? It's like Beyonce and Jay-Z, or Kim and Kanye...

before they split... they're like the power couple of the school...

or that's what Lucy said the other day anyway. So, what if

Mitchell gets this? I mean, he was definitely pissed off when

Lynsey started going out with Jack because it's obvious that he

fancies the pants off her – to be fair we all do – but she didn't

want him, did she? She wanted Jack. Choosing Jack over

Mitchell was like a sign, weren't it? Like a hint saying that he

was losing his touch as leader of the gang. Well... then Mitchell

had to do something about it, didn't he? And the thing he did

was take on someone new – some loser that was so desperate to

have friends that they'd do anything he wanted without question.

So desperate that they'd be loyal even when they weren't invited

out, or even when their own family gets taken the piss out of for

the whole school to hear. Someone like me. Because then...

well, then Mitchell is back in charge, ain't he? He's the one ruling the show again.

But if I do this, if I post everything up online for the whole school to see, I won't just be a legend to my little gang. I'll be a legend to the whole fucking place. And then where does that leave Mitch? Obviously, I won't ditch him. I ain't like that, no matter what he clearly thinks, but I won't follow him around no more either, because I won't need him, will I? I'll have any mate I want. Imagine… me walking into school and everyone wanting to talk to me. Not the other way round, not on the outskirts anymore, but in the centre of everything, people on the outskirts of *my* conversations. Fuck, that's the dream. And I can make that happen if I just do this one thing. Doing this will show them who I am. It will show them that I won't sit back when they don't invite me out, that I won't ignore it when they say stuff about me or my family, and most of all, that I ain't a pussy. It's just something that I have to do. If I don't put this up on Facebook, not only will I not get that legendary status, but

Mitchell will turn all the mates I do have against me. It will be just like before. Or worse. I mean, if I get ditched by Mitchell's gang, I might end up even lower than Pissy Chris and I can't have that happen, can I?

I have to do this. I have to post it on Facebook. I've got no other choice. Besides… I spent so long on that Photoshop and risked loads with those texts from me mum's phone I might as well make it worth it. If she'd walked in and caught me, I would've got the bollocking of my life. As if I could waste all of that on just a few people? I might as well show everyone. It makes sense, so I'm going to do it. Right now. I've got all the stuff ready. The picture of her in her underwear, zoomed in so it looks like I'm in the room, the picture of her in my room, and all the screenshots of the text messages between us. Ain't nobody going to be able to say I'm lying now. Not Mitchell, not no one. I was going to try and catch her after school. Tell her it was OK, that I was going to out us so we could go public, but when I saw her in the corridor, she looked right through me. Like I weren't even there. Fuck, she's good at this, I'll give her that. But she's obviously too scared to even look at me in public, so I know this will help with that. She'll probably fancy me even more now anyway, seeing as I've been so brave just for us. I'll look like a proper man, you know, someone that takes control of the situation. I bet she likes that. In fact, I wouldn't be surprised if she runs straight over here and shags me tonight. I better shave my balls just in case. Fuck it… this is it… I'm about to become king of the fucking world. Let's do it.

Thomas

(Now)

I can't go to school tomorrow. I can't do it. I've had so many messages; my phone hasn't stopped. I've never had a message from anyone before, other than Pete, and I liked it that way. But now, it keeps buzzing. And it's never-ending.

When we first started Year 7, everyone added everyone on Facebook and WhatsApp; it was just the done thing. I remember feeling really sorry for Pete because his mum didn't let him have a phone yet. He had to wait until he was twelve and that wasn't until March. She did give in eventually, around Christmas, because she got an upgrade, but she wasn't happy about it. We were though. Mainly so we could text after every new episode of *The Mandalorian*. That was a great series. But now... well, now I'd do anything not to have a phone. In fact,

I'd do anything to have a mum like Pete's who limits his time on it… and, you know… doesn't have an affair with a Year 11.

We had everyone on WhatsApp, because one kid started a group for our form in September. No one has ever really used it before, other than a few random memes and GIFs, but tonight, the messages haven't stopped. Kids that have never spoken to me in my life are texting, asking whether my mum had sex with that Year 11 kid, whether it's the first time she's done it, whether I knew all about it, whether I'd seen him hanging out at our house. They want to know every disgusting detail. It's horrible. I haven't replied, of course I haven't. I mean, I don't know anything anyway, but if I did, I wouldn't be telling them anything. I thought if I just muted the group chat, I would have peace from it all. But when I didn't reply on there, the individual messages started coming. I don't have the numbers saved, so I can't tell who it is and none of them have profile pictures. Everyone has a profile picture on their WhatsApp, or at least they did, but now they all seem to have disappeared. Now it's just faceless people saying the nastiest things. They're calling Mum all sorts. Saying she's a whore and a slut and I guess they're right… in a way… I mean, isn't someone that has an affair a slut?

One of the girls in our class, Jenny, told everyone once how her sister's boyfriend had gone off with a girl in Year 10 and how we all had to call her a slut every time she walked down the corridor, and they all did, you know? Other than me and Pete, of course. But everyone else did and soon the whole school was doing it, so the boy ditched her and went back to Jenny's sister. I remember seeing the girl coming out the bathroom with mascara down her face once. She looked awful. Her cheeks were red, and she didn't look at anyone in the eye, just walked down the corridor on her own. I swear I haven't seen her since. Not once. I don't know what happened to her. It all died down and Jenny's sister dumped the boy the following week anyway, so I couldn't help but think it didn't really matter that much, but it did to that girl, it will to Mum, and it definitely will to me. I know I'm an easy target. I'm not stupid. I'm not exactly

someone that's going to stand up for themselves, but I can't

ignore it either. Especially when the messages don't stop.

Some of them seem almost nice, like a bit supportive.

People telling me not to bother coming to school tomorrow. Not

in a nasty way, I don't think, just telling me that if it was them,

then they wouldn't bother. They say it'll probably be worse than

today because Mum is definitely not going to be in, so there'll be

no one to protect me. Not that she would ever protect me

anyway. I see her at school during the day and she never even

looks in my direction, let alone smile at me or even wave back. I

feel like such an idiot when I wave, and she looks right through

me. I worked up the nerve to ask her why she did that once, and

she said that it was for my own good. She said that if everyone

saw me waving to my mum at school, I would get bullied, so I

thought she was protecting me. After tonight, I realise it was

because she was protecting herself. Didn't want the son she

didn't love embarrassing her at her precious work, did she? I bet she hated the day I started.

So yeah, I don't blame the kids that are telling me to stay away from school. I reckon Pete will say the same when I get to speak to him. He gave me a quick call earlier to say that his mum has banned him from talking to me. She doesn't want him associated with me because of '*all of this drama going on*'. And then he hung up. That's the last I heard from him; she must have taken his phone away again. Which sucks if I'm honest. It's harder not having him to talk to, but what can I do? She's really strict, Pete's mum, but she was always really nice to me, obviously not now though. I can't believe Mum has managed to ruin that as well.

The problem is, it's not just those messages I'm getting. Not just the ones that want gossip, or the ones that want to give me advice. There are others too. I don't know if they're banter or what, but... well... some of them are getting beyond a joke. Like this one – again, no idea who it is from – but they've said...

well... they've said if it were them, they'd jump off a bridge. They said that my life is going to be wrecked forever because of what Mum did and now everyone has seen her in her underwear and that I shouldn't ever show my face in school again. In fact, they've said I wouldn't be *safe* to show my face outside the *house* again. That people will take the mick out of me forever and I'm always going to be known as the son of 'Hall the Whore'.

That's what they're calling her now. It used to be 'Hot Hall' and that used to make me cringe, but this? It's even worse. And I guess they're right, aren't they? As if I'm ever going to live a normal life again. I've been googling what it all means. Ben is a minor. I don't know when his birthday is, but apparently even if he's already sixteen, it doesn't matter because she's his teacher, so Pete was definitely right on that one. It said on Google something about abusing her position of power? There was lots about that word... abuse. That's what people like Mum are apparently... abusers... and that doesn't just stop with a slap on the wrist or losing her job. That could mean prison. She could go to jail, and I'd never see her again. But then I guess she gets out of it that way, doesn't she? She gets to hide in prison and face no one, whereas me? I have to walk into school as the son of an abuser every day for the rest of my life. Even when I get a job, it will follow me, won't it? I mean, it's on the internet. It'll be on the news. I'd go for an interview, and they'd google me, and the first thing that will show up would be that my mum has a criminal record. I told Dad last week that I wanted to be a lawyer, but I can't now, can I? You can't fight for the law when your mum is the one who breaks it.

I mean, when you think of it like that, it's no wonder everyone thinks I should jump off a bridge. Wouldn't that be easier? What else have I got? I've got no friends if Pete isn't allowed to see me anymore. I've got no mum because apparently she's never loved me anyway, regardless of all of this, *and* she might be going to prison, and then there's Ellie, who hasn't spoken a word to me since she was about thirteen anyway.

Dad… Dad would be upset, I think. He would miss me, for sure, but he's got so much on. He doesn't have time to worry about me. I heard him speaking to Granny earlier about money. Something about whether he would be able to support me and Ellie on his own. It was clearly bothering him, like he didn't have enough, but also he's obviously leaving Mum for good, and of course I don't blame him, but that just makes me an extra burden, doesn't it? If I wasn't here, everything would be easier. I wouldn't have to face the kids at school, my mum wouldn't have to feel forced into loving me and my dad wouldn't have to be forced into paying for me. Ellie wouldn't be embarrassed by me either to be fair… Maybe it is the right thing to do.

Oh God. I don't know. I don't know what to do. The only thing I know for certain is that the messages keep coming. They've made memes up about Mum now. I knew that would happen. That's banter, I guess, but it's getting worse because they're turning on me. They're telling me they'll beat me up, they're telling me they'll find me, they're telling me to jump…

and I'm starting to think that's the right idea.

Ben

(1 day earlier)

I am the king of the world. Honestly. I'm pretty much a god I'm so loved. I walked into school this morning and I might as well have just walked out of fucking *Love Island*. People bloody flocked to me to hear all about how I'd shagged the fit teacher and how I'd become such a legend. I knew it was going to be big. To be honest I was a bit shit-scared this morning when I saw how far it'd gone. I sent the post last night, checked that Mitchell had seen it and then passed out with my phone on silent, so when I woke up this morning, I couldn't believe my eyes. People from all around the country had shared my post. I didn't realise that could happen to be honest. That's when I got a bit nervy because some people, the older folks, started getting on their high horse about our age gap and that, but I ignored them – figured it was just busybodies – but then I thought, what if it's got so big that people… you know… realise it isn't the whole truth? What if they notice the Photoshop and the pretend messages? But they never did, did they? They believed every bloody word of it. It was incredible.

I walked into the quad and couldn't move for people swarming around me. I've never known anything like it. Mitchell stood right by my side the whole time. Kept telling everyone that he knew, that he'd made me put it online. I didn't mind, because obviously that was true, but people didn't really seem to be listening to him anyway. Honestly. They ignored Mitchell and spoke to *me*. Fucking me. Ben Bridges, the kid that begs people to talk to him, couldn't even get to class on time because everyone wanted to chat. I even got fist bumped down the corridor. Honestly, it was mayhem – epic, awesome, perfect mayhem.

Some kids, like Ellie's mates, they seemed a bit shitty with me, but they were going to be, weren't they? They've just worked out their mate's mum's been shagging me… well… sort of. But I ignored them. I didn't need their shit when I was living my best life. There was so much banter and laughs in each lesson I was in, and the best part was, it weren't even me at the butt of them. Nah, I was the hero, the good one, the legend. Yeah... if I'm honest, she was the one they were taking the mick out of, but it's only jealousy, ain't it? That can't be helped. They wouldn't be ripping her if it was them that had ripped her clothes off... well... Anyway, the boys obviously wanted all the gory details. I had to make some more stuff up on the spot, but nothing I can't remember, and the girls... fuck me... they looked at me in a different way today, that's for sure. They wanted me. I could tell. Something about a lad with experience always seems to turn them on. I was thinking, as I was bowling home, that I'm lucky I'm a lad. Can you imagine if a girl had done this? As soon as she slept with someone... well... they'd know they were her first time, wouldn't they? They'd know that she'd lied about the time before, but with a lad like me... no one will ever know and that's the fucking beauty of it.

The only time I thought it was all going to go tits up was when Mrs Swann, the head teacher, called me into her office. I was sat in Science, being the legend that I now am, and a message came through that she wanted to see me right away. Everyone went 'oooo'. It was well embarrassing, but I just laughed it off, didn't I? Like a lad. Just strolled out of the classroom like I owned the place. I felt a bit panicked in the corridor if I'm honest, but everyone had lapped it up, and if they all believed me, there was no way some old teacher wouldn't – what would she know about Photoshop anyway? Probably didn't even exist in her day.

So, I walk into the office, which always smells really musty. It's weird. Mrs Swann always looks normal, but she smells like old lady, and it makes her office bloody stink. Anyways, she sits at her desk with her arms folded and I can't really read her expression. She's not angry, definitely not, but she's not happy either. It's like she's trying to be caring and old Swann is not a caring person in the slightest, so it all just feels awkward. Then she goes, '*Sit down, Ben, I just want a chat with you.*' I thought... fuck, it's spreading. No wonder she didn't look angry, no wonder she's trying to look like she cares and that, because she's heard what a top shagger I am and now she wants a bit of me too. I bet I'm the talk of the fucking staff room. Now, nothing against Mrs Swann, but old lady smell doesn't really do it for me, but how the hell do you tell your headmistress you don't want to shag her?

So, there I am worrying about whether I need to have an awkward convo with Swann when she starts talking about Hall. She'd obviously seen the post, but she weren't coming on to me or nothing; she just kept telling me I was in a safe space, and I would get my opportunity to talk when all the proper people were involved. I didn't really know what she was chatting about, but I just nodded along like I did – didn't want to look like a twat or anything, did I? So, there she is going on and on and on saying about how I will get a chance to speak about everything but about how they have to do it properly, etcetera, etcetera,

etcetera, when, all of a sudden, she goes, *'We've asked Miss Hall to stay at home today, so you can continue to feel safe at school.'* And I thought... fuck. I've done it. I've actually convinced them that me and Hall have been banging behind their backs. Because they weren't asking me to stay at home, were they? No – I was in a *safe place.* But her? They'd told her to stay away and why? Because they believed me. They believed that I had shagged the fittest teacher in the whole school. Mental. I stopped listening after that because I knew I didn't have to. Because I knew then that not only am I a legend with the rest of the kids in this place, but I'm now a bloody legend with the teachers too because they are all looking at me, at Ben Bridges, thinking... fuck... he shagged a teacher. And not just any teacher... the hottest one on the planet. I reckon there are *teachers* that are jealous of me now. Mr Smith for definite. He's always fancied her – everyone knows it. He follows her around constantly. Bet he's sat there wondering what I've got that he hasn't... Well, that's simple, Mr cock-blocking Smith, I'm a real man and you are just a knobhead. In fact, no, you're a dickhead. A loser dickhead. Just like the one I thought I was, but I'm not, am I? Because I'm a fucking legendary shagger that's owning this school.

So basically, the point of the meeting was to check I feel 'safe'. She did ask at one point if what I'd put up had been true and I told her it definitely was. She didn't need much convincing though and then she started saying that there'll be a proper meeting tomorrow with a load of other people. Not sure what that all means to be honest, but I reckon they'll just be asking me questions about how I turned out to be such a lad. She said my mum has to be there, so I told her I'd let her know. I mean… obviously I won't. I'll just say she's busy like I do at parents' evenings and that and they'll drop it. She never has a clue what's going on anyway. I wonder if Hot Hall will be there tomorrow. I reckon she'll be well chuffed that it's out in the open now. She'll probably tell the school they can stuff their job just so she can walk out with me. Shit… that would be insane. Walking out of the head teacher's office, holding hands with Hot Hall, in front of *everyone*, and then heading back to my place. Epic... beyond epic.

~

The rest of the day was great. Some of Ellie's mates said she hadn't come into school, but I didn't have time for that. And I did see her brother, Tim or something his name is, getting pushed around down the corridor for a bit, but that's just banter, ain't it? Can't have your mum shag someone else and not get grief for it. It was nothing bad though. Everyone was pissing themselves laughing. I've been in one of them before – everyone has. It's just something you have to go through. Mitchell calls it 'Shove Alley' and he starts them all the time. Everyone lines up on each side of the corridor and then you just start pushing someone from one side to the other. It's a right laugh. Honest. Tim – or whatever his name is – probably laughed too. You kind of have to in those situations... shit me, I would know. Not anymore though. Can't imagine I'll be shoved down the corridor again anytime soon. No one would dare. Not now.

So, now I'm walking back into the estate, finally on my own after having everyone crowd round me all day, when I see the usual blue flashing lights illuminating the houses where I live. It's always something. Probably Pissy Chris's dad flying off the handle again. Only when I've turned the corner do I realise that they're parked outside my house. Fuck. And Mum is on the doorstep. Shit. Something must have happened. I bet that new feller of hers has knocked her about, or nicked stuff from the house… not that there'd be much to nick to be fair. Anyway, as I'm walking towards her, she starts doing the weirdest thing I've ever seen my mum do… and I've seen her do some weird shit. She starts coming towards me with her arms outstretched like she's going to give me a hug… in public. What the hell? I mean, yeah, sure, I hug her on the sofa after her latest break-up, but that only lasts thirty seconds and then she draws her knees up, tucks them in her hoody and cocoons herself, making it bloody obvious she doesn't want any more affection. Now though, she's here… in the middle of the street… with coppers on the doorstep and her arms about to wrap themselves around me. Shit… maybe she's going to jail. I'm going to end up in care. Fuck.

'Whatever you do, just play along.'

Mum is hugging me now and whispering into my ear. She stinks of fags, but she's definitely tried to cover it up with perfume. I've never known her to wear perfume unless she's meeting up with someone from Tinder.

'What?'

'Just play along, you fucking idiot.'

Then she lets go of me and starts talking really loud. Loud enough for the whole estate to hear, let alone the coppers behind her.

'Oh darling. Why didn't you tell me? How could you keep such a thing from me? Did she make you? Did she tell you not to say anything? Is that why you hid it all?'

'What are you talking about?'

'The post on Facebook, honey. You don't have to hide it anymore. We've all seen it. I completely understand why you felt you had to do it all so publicly, and so do these nice men. They are not angry at you at all, darling. They just want to protect you. Just as much as I do.'

Before I can say another word, I'm being pushed into the house with my mum's arm firmly around my neck. I'm taller than her now, so it must be really uncomfortable for her, but she's determined to keep it there. I can't work out what the hell is going on. She's obviously seen it all, all the stuff about me and Hot Hall, but why are the coppers here? And why is she acting so weird? I've gone from feeling on top of the world to the fucking pits in 0.2 seconds and of course it's got something to do with me mum. When we're inside she tells the coppers to take a seat. Honestly. Actually invited them in and asked them to sit down... in *my* house... on *my* estate. This sort of shit don't happen around here, that's for sure. She's up to something, but I can't work out what. Then she goes, 'Sorry, but do you mind if I talk to my son in the kitchen first? I've not seen him all day and I need to make sure he's comfortable with me calling you. It will be a lot for him to take in. He is the victim in this after all.'

Victim? What the fuck? I ain't a victim. I'm a fucking legend. What the hell is she playing at? The coppers don't seem to mind, or they ain't got a choice – one or the other – because before I know it, I'm being led into the kitchen without them having a chance to answer.

'Listen, Ben. I saw your little post on the internet, and I don't know what the fuck you've been getting up to, but I got a phone call from *The Sun* today. Yeah, the actual newspaper. They want you to do an article about you shagging that teacher. I laughed when they said it. To be honest, mate, I've always thought you were a gay virgin, but they seem to think you ain't

chatting shit. So much so that they're planning on paying big

fucking bucks for your interview. Did you hear me? Loads of

cash, Ben. The problem was, they started asking about my

concern, and when I'd called the police, so I figured I better ring

them. Make it look convincing, you know? So, you tell the

police how that bitch molested you and then we can make a mint

from the papers. I've called Lee and told him to come over

too…'

'Who the fuck is Lee?'

'Don't be smart. You know me and Lee are seeing each

other. Just make sure you refer to him as your stepdad. I figured

it would look much more convincing if we were a proper family

unit. Always looks better when there's a father figure around,

doesn't it?'

'How would I know?'

'What have I told you about getting smart? Look, you owe me. You've robbed me of money all my life. I live in this shitty place because I got knocked up with you so young, so it's about time you started paying me back. Whatever you and that teacher of yours got up to, you need to tell them, and tell them it wasn't what you wanted. If we can get this all the way to court, think of how long it will go on for. There'll be more than just one interview, Ben. There could be hundreds, TV ones as well... I reckon they pay even better. Now stick out your bottom lip and start looking like a victim.'

Her hand is on my back. She's about to push me back into the living room. The back door is open. Fuck it. I need to run. Now.

Liz

(Now)

The sun shone through the window and onto Liz's face. The curtains hadn't been closed. She hadn't got undressed, or washed, or cleaned her teeth. She'd just stopped for the first time in what felt like forever. Stopped completely and allowed herself to fall into the grey sofa and into a world of dreams... well, nightmares. As Liz peeled open her eyes, the first thing to greet her was the bottles of red, empty on the coffee table, the glass next to them on its side. She had convinced herself she would be unable to sleep without it, thought it would be a good idea to help her feel rested for today, for the meeting she needed to attend, that she needed to be ready for. But it wasn't, was it? It was never a good idea to drink yourself into sleep. It was something she hadn't done in such a long time and the feeling was worse than she remembered.

As she lifted her head off the pillow, the weight of it seemed to want to bring her back down. Her eyes were heavy and stuck together with last night's mascara – half smudged through sleep and half smudged through the amount she had allowed herself to cry. She had finally let go, let go of the perfect persona she had created. She wanted to feel liberated, to feel alive and free. She felt the opposite of all of that. She felt completely surrounded by hurt, by pain and by grief. She had realised, during the second bottle of wine, that she was grieving – grieving for every part of her life that had been ruined in one fell swoop. The part a child had taken from her. Because that's what had happened. A boy... not more than fifteen... had been able to create a world with such conviction and credibility that she had been left with what? With nothing. Even Rob had believed it all without question, without any second guessing. She had been left alone in her house, her family gone, her career gone, while Ben got to strut around with no ramifications at all.

In fact, he was probably loving every second of it, and that made her even more sick.

The problem was no one saw it as unbelievable. No one saw her as innocent. In her head she knew she had to fight this. Call the police and put her side across. In her heart she already felt like she had lost. But her heart couldn't win today. She'd allowed her phone to die overnight, she couldn't bear to listen to the buzzing any longer, so she looked at the clock on the living room wall – 6am… Even with a hangover her body clock seemed to work very well. At least she had one thing going for her.

Focusing on her head, Liz cleared the bottles of wine from the living room and placed them in the recycling bin in the kitchen. It was there that she saw the remains of the smashed laptop. The mess she had created and left. She didn't have the time to deal with it now, or the strength if she was honest, so she stepped over the shards of glass and plastic, got herself some water and paracetamol and pushed herself upstairs and into the shower. One step at a time was all she needed to get through.

There was something odd about getting ready in an empty house. After stepping out of the shower, where she had let the water wash away the mess of the night before, she couldn't help but notice how easily she could put on the light. She could also put on the TV and watch the news if she wanted… not that she did. But the sentiment was there. The idea that she didn't have to sneak around, keep herself quiet to get the peace she craved for so long, because the peace was there. It was completely surrounding her; in fact, it was engulfing her. It was everywhere. And Liz couldn't help but notice that it didn't feel quite as calming as it should. She had wanted this to feel relaxing, to put her at ease, but it did the complete opposite and she felt herself feeling almost suffocated by the silence that filled the house. She looked for her phone. Whatever else would come through when she turned it on had to be ignored because she had promised Jo that she would be able to get hold of her about today's meeting. In fact, when she'd remembered that in the shower, she had kicked herself for letting it die and putting her own feelings before that of the school. That was the slippery slope, she had decided. If she allowed herself to look unprofessional, she would give more certainty to the boy's claims. She had to keep her head up and she had to maintain her professionalism at all times.

After plugging her phone into charge, Liz took herself to her dressing table. She stared at her face in the mirror. The red wine lips had been removed, the smudged mascara had been wiped away and now she had a blank canvas. This could be the beginning. If she fought to clear her name, everyone would have to make it up to her. And she would remember. She would never, ever forget the people that had turned, the people that were absent in her time of need.

Applying a full face of make-up, getting dressed and doing her hair had once again pulled Liz back to who and where she wanted to be. It was the beauty of being a woman. The idea that you could paint your face and instantly become someone else. Someone stronger. It was the power that had always fascinated Liz. She liked to have this mask, this look of togetherness that only a woman with expensive make-up could achieve. Thank goodness the outside world couldn't see how much her heart was pounding underneath it all. It gave her strength… or it certainly allowed her to look like she had strength in a time of pure uncertainty. Pulling on her favourite suit, and brushing it down with a lint roller, Liz finally felt ready to look at her phone and face the day ahead.

She had deleted Facebook in her rampage last night and therefore had no notifications to face as soon as her phone turned on. She did, however, have emails… and a lot of them. Now, Liz was used to a barrage of emails – that came with the territory of being deputy head – but this seemed to be more than usual. Tentatively, she clicked on the unread messages and instantly found a list of names that were not in her address book. Liz was meticulous with her emails; they were filed in folder after folder in a system she was sure only she understood. Every address was also saved with the full name of the colleague and listed under the department they worked for. These names were none of those. They were addresses she had never seen before and the people behind them were ones she had never interacted with; she was sure of it. So how had they reached her? Line after line of emails from people displaying their disgust, their outrage, throwing vulgar names in her direction like it was a common and casual thing to do. She dared herself to open one fully, despite the subject headings being hard enough to digest, and clicked on the first one on the list. The email address was 'littlemissbrat@hotmail.co.uk'. No indication of a real name, only hopefully a signal that it was from a child rather than an adult… although at Liz's school that was never that clear cut.

The email itself consisted of nothing more than one word. One word in large bold letters in the middle of the page… slut. Nothing else and nothing more. She clicked off it and onto another, 'dirrtygurl@gmail.com' – surely no one with that email address could be judgemental, but it turned out they could be. That one was longer. An entire paragraph of a badly spelt rant explaining how disgusting Liz was as a human being. How she might as well kill herself and do everyone a favour. That one hurt. As much as Liz didn't want it to, it did, and clicking off it did not make the words leave her head. She scrolled down, looking at the addresses. None of them consisted of a name; all of them consisted of hate. Until one, it had been sent last night, not in the early hours like the rest of them. In fact, it must have been sent just after Liz had smashed her laptop. It was from Annette Rawley, a parent. She knew the child, Lyla. She was a kind girl who worked hard and kept herself to herself. Surely this was a message of support? Someone who knew she would never do such a thing. She opened the email and read the following:

Dear Miss Hall,

I apologise in sending such an email to you, but I felt I would not be a caring parent if I did not. I was hoping to speak to you in person today at the school, but I was told you had taken the day to be at home. I must remark that I found this very

upsetting as by not showing your face, I assume you are hiding

your guilt in the matter of Ben Bridges. I therefore took your

email address from the school website in order to speak to you

more directly.

Of course. The school website. Liz remembered asking
Jo to set up a separate email for her to be public to parents,
different from the one she used with the staff so messages were
never missed. She had said she would but then had never got
around to it. Of course, Liz had never missed a message either, a
time where her efficiency had gone against her. She continued to
read.

Obviously in light of recent news, I am worried about

sending my daughter into school. You are supposed to be a

person of trust and you have abused that position with this boy

and who knows how many more. I am therefore requesting that a

full investigation takes place on every member of teaching staff

in the school to ensure nothing else untoward is happening while our precious children are placed in your care. I also politely

request that you hand in your notice and leave the school

immediately. If such an investigation or resignation does not

take place, I will have no other choice but to remove Lyla from

the school and I expect other parents will follow suit. As I'm

sure you are aware, Miss Hall, the safety of our children is of

utmost importance and by keeping you (or any others that follow

suit) in the school, you are putting our children at risk, and this

is something we simply won't tolerate.

Yours with concern,

Annette Rawley.

Liz read and re-read the email, yet it still didn't make any

sense. She knew the children would turn on her, and the staff

would do anything to keep their jobs, but the parents? Did they

not remember how much she'd helped their children? The

changes she'd made to the school? The number of hours she'd

put in to ensure they passed their OFSTED inspection? Clearly, none of that mattered... Nothing Liz had achieved in her whole career mattered. If they were happy to turn against her and believe this child over her so openly, then what hope did she have? She was starting to realise that not calling the police herself could have been the biggest mistake she'd ever made.

For the first time, she longed for Rob. She longed for someone to talk this email over with, to get another opinion on how to respond... or if to respond. She'd always been so certain of everything, never questioning her gut, but now she felt like she didn't even have one. She had no understanding of her life or what to do and she really needed someone to talk to, someone to help her prepare for this meeting, someone to hold her hand and tell her it was OK, and not just someone, she realised. *The* someone. The person who had been there, next to her, supporting her since she was a child herself. For the first time in what felt like forever, she needed Rob and no one else. She needed him here with her. He would know what to say. It would irritate her that he would, but then she would admit that he was right. In fact, she would admit that to his face right now if it meant him being here. But he wasn't. And he might never be again. Liz needed to step forward into today as she would have to step forward for the rest of her life, alone – ironically the one thing she'd always wanted… until now.

Staring at the mirror for one final time, she realised that she had been crying. The tears had ruined her perfect make-up and it was clear that she could no longer hide that she wasn't flawless. She got to her feet, took a deep breath, and prepared herself for the day ahead.

Ben

(Now)

So last night I ran. Ran like a dickhead. I don't know why. I'm meant to be a king now… a fucking god… and I saw the pigs and me mum and I just ran. Mum kept ringing my phone over and over again, but I just couldn't pick it up. I panicked. I'll admit it… I really panicked. When I saw the coppers, it all became a bit real. I mean… yeah, I want to look like a hot shot, I want everyone at school to think I'm awesome, but I don't want to ruin Hot Hall's life and… fuck… well, that's what I might've done. I thought – well, it seems stupid now – but I thought there was only two outcomes to this. I thought, either only my mates and some other kids at school would see, I'd be a legend and it would go no further or… well… *she* would see it and she would know that I liked her back and we would be together. I didn't think this would happen. I didn't think it would be all coppers and papers and formal meetings at school. Because that's what today's bringing. Some big fucking meeting apparently. And Mum knows all about it because the school rang her themselves.

When I finally got back home last night, I thought Mum would be asleep on the sofa, but she weren't. She was up, sitting at the kitchen table… well, plastic garden table that she puts in the kitchen for when she has her parties… or guests like coppers apparently. Anyway, she was sat on this white plastic chair and I'll be honest, the first thing I thought was that it was going to collapse under her weight. Not in a nasty way or anything, but Mum ain't small and the legs seemed to be pushing outwards as she sat on it. Then I realised I was probably staring at the legs because I didn't want to look at her face. I knew she'd be angry. And she was. The way her skin had gone pink showed me that before she even opened her mouth. She hates being embarrassed. I tried to play it cool, walked in the kitchen and got a glass of squash. I went, 'Alright, Mum.'

'Not really, Ben. Funnily enough. Where the fuck have you been?'

Yeah… I didn't expect a warm welcome. I ain't stupid. But I carried on looking at the cupboard, taking ages to choose a cup – even though there's only four without a chip in them and three of those were in the sink.

'I just had to get out for a bit. Why didn't you text me and say they were here? Give me a heads up?'

'What, like you did? With your fucking post last night? Where was the heads up with that one?'

I turned around and looked at Mum's face properly. Her hair was more shit than normal. It was always brushed all nice at the front and then looked like a bloody crow's nest at the back, but she must have been running her hands through the front like she did when she was stressed because the front was a trainwreck too this time. And her face was a lot redder than I'd realised. Not like, 'had too many ciders down the Queenie' red, but more like, 'I'm going to kill you' red. I figured it was better to look at the shit lino floor and avoid all eye contact.

'Yeah, fair enough. Look, I didn't think you'd see it.'

'Are you stupid? Of course I've seen it. The whole fucking town has seen it, Ben, and all before me. Honestly, if Lee hadn't rung me and told me, I would have walked out the door not knowing. What the fuck would I have looked like then?'

I mean, obviously, this is a bit of a lie. Think about it; Mum don't even leave the house until the afternoon, after *Loose Women*, and she spends most of the time she's 'watching' it scrolling through her phone anyway, so she would have spotted the post anytime between ten and one. The only reason this Lee would have seen it before her is because he works on the tools, so he's probably up and on Facebook before she's even opened her eyes. I didn't correct her though… figured it was safer that way.

'Look, I'm sorry I didn't tell you first…'

'Is it true?'

'What?'

'Is it true, Ben? Have you been shagging your teacher or not?'

Shit. It's one thing lying on social media, and to me mates, but to me mum's face? That's a whole other thing.

'She does fancy me, Mum,' I mumbled, feeling as bloody pathetic as I knew I just sounded. And that was when she laughed. Really laughed. Fucking hate it when she does that. It makes my shoulders go up and I get all defensive.

'What? She does. She comes on to me all the time at school, even Mitchell's seen it.'

I wanted to sound all cool and laid back about it, but it was like my voice had its own ideas. I was coming across like a whiny little kid and I knew it, but that's what she does to me.

She has this power that makes me act like a right stroppy girl and not a grown-up bloke. Which is rich when you think about it. Seeing as she's told me I'm the man of the house for my whole fucking life. That's not exactly been easy. But either way, the whiny voice did make her shut up laughing for a bit. I thought she felt sorry for me, so I looked up at her again and saw her staring me dead in the eyes. Her bird nest hair had got even higher, and she looked like she was going to have a heart attack, but she'd allowed a little smirk to spread across her face.

'Who's this Mitchell? One of your so called mates? What's he seen?'

'He's my *best* mate and the coolest kid in the whole school. And yeah, he's seen her come on to me. He even saw her take me into her office to get undressed.'

'Fuck. What a little bitch.'

'She ain't.'

'She fucking is. She's preying on my little boy, and we'll make her pay for it.'

Little boy? What the hell? So much for man of the house. So much for 'grow up, Ben'. That I've had since I was about five... but this? Her little boy? What a load of shit.

'What do you mean, make her pay?'

'Right, listen. I spoke to those coppers last night – after you bottled it like a prick. I told them that it was really unlike you to run like that. I said you must be completely traumatised by the whole thing and obviously you saw putting it on social media as the only way out. They said you were lucky, mind, said if she hadn't had her underwear on in that picture, it could have been revenge porn – you know that thing I watched on telly about. Anyway, it ain't on account of her being clothed and you being her student, so we don't have to worry about that. What we do have to worry about though is how long you can drag this on for. They said, if the school deem it to be true tomorrow, it will go to court, and she'll lose her job and potentially get prison time. Obviously, I could press charges now, but they said to follow the school's guidance on that and I'm thinking we need to stay on their good side. Because, if they find her guilty, you could be in for interviews. Like a shitload of interviews, with papers and telly, the whole fucking lot. We could even make it onto *This Morning*. And the best bit is that they all pay; the papers, the TV companies, they'll all pay you to speak and apparently, according to Janet next door, they pay really fucking well. Think about it… we earn enough from these interviews, and we can finally get out of this shit estate. More than that, me and Lee can go to Benidorm. I've always wanted to go there. And if you want to come too, you better make sure they believe every word that comes out of your mouth. You need them to feel so sorry for you. You're not some horny teenager; you are a sweet, innocent kid that she took advantage of. You get me? You play it like that, and they'll be eating out of the palm of your hand. No one wants to watch some smug prick talking about how he banged a married woman, but they do want to hear about the poor boy that was abused by his teacher and had his childhood ruined. They're the interviews that make the big bucks. So, you better get upstairs and practise your fake crying ready for tomorrow. I don't care what sordid fun you've had up till now; from tomorrow onwards it was hell and you've been through the worst few weeks of your life. Oh, and text that Mitchell and tell him he better be prepared to open his mouth too. I'm going to look at holidays. Off you fuck.'

And I did. I didn't say another word. I just walked up to my room and shut the door, leaning against it to make me feel safe from her, from Lee and his bloody holiday and from the whole pissing world if I'm honest.

I haven't slept all night thinking about what Mum said. I get it… of course I do… we ain't ever had money. Honestly, it's been shit for my whole life. Yet if I did this, if I made a mint, then I could quit the chippy and actually spend weekends with my mates… in new trainers… and new trackies… I'd fit in, proper this time. Only, to do that, I've got to fuck everything. Not only will I fuck it up with Hot Hall, but I won't get to be a hero. If I do what Mum says… crying and that… I'll look like a right twat, won't I? If I play the victim, I can't tell anyone what a top shagger I am because I've got to make it sound like she forced me into it – not that I won her over with my top moves. I don't know what's worse. Everyone thinking I was a little wimp that was made to have sex with the hottest teacher alive or having to work at the chippy for the next twenty years. I mean, let's face it, I ain't going to get any GCSEs to get a proper job, am I? And if I can't earn much, I'm stuck. Stuck in the same estate as me mum for the rest of my life. It's fucking bullshit. Why can't I get paid to do interviews where I just get to brag about what a legend I am by bagging Hot Hall? Surely they'd still pay me for that? Now that would be awesome. Can you imagine? I'd be hitting up the red carpet at film premieres as the sixteen-year-old stud. I bet even Megan Fox would want a bit of me then.

Oh fuck. Even I know that ain't going to happen. Kidding myself again, ain't I? Rich and a wimp or skint but a legend – they are my only two choices. Oh, I don't know what to do. And I've got to decide quickly because this bloody meeting is this morning. Mum's already got up and gone in the shower. I couldn't believe it. She's fucking washed. And in the morning, *before* school. She said she needed to look respectable or something. I don't think she's ever looked respectable in my whole bloody life, but apparently today is that day. Can't believe the school rang her about it. They must have known I wouldn't tell her. Stupid school.

'Ben, hurry the fuck up. We can't be late, can we? And don't do your hair. It will look better if you look dishevelled and hard done by.'

Well, that ain't hard, is it? I've looked hard done by every day of my pissing life.

'Oh, and Lee will be here in a minute. He's coming too so we look like a proper family. Don't fuck it up, mind. He's still pissed you did a bunk last night and he's losing a day's wage for this. I've told him you'll pay him back out of your first interview packet.'

Jesus. I've got no choice, have I? At least if I can earn a packet, I'll be able to get away from here. All this *we* bullshit Mum keeps spouting on about ain't happening. This will be *my* money and *I'll* be the one spending it. I'll leave Mum on the shitty estate, and I'll rent a place in town, near all the pubs and that. Mitchell could be my roommate and it wouldn't matter that the world thinks I'm a wimp because Mitchell will know the truth and we'll have our own lads' pad. In a couple of months, it will all be over, and we'll be living our best lives. Bringing girls back to our place and living like rockstars. I've got all the time in the world to prove what a top shagger I am, and it will be much easier to prove with money. Fuck it... bring on the meeting and bring on 'stepdaddy Lee'. My life is going to be epic once again and it will start by getting away from the two people I'm about to walk into school with. Deep breath, Ben. You got this.

Thomas

(Now)

I packed a bag last night. Well… the bag was already packed from when we got here, but I moved it into my school bag and put my books under my bed at Granny's house. They won't notice until it's too late. The messages didn't stop last night. They kept coming and coming. So many people with so many opinions. I didn't hear anything else from Pete at all. That's why I kept my phone on – just in case he called – but he didn't. His mum must have taken his phone for good. But I needed him. Everyone else in the house had ignored me all evening. Granny and Dad were in deep conversation and Ellie had stormed out to her mate's house when Dad brought up the messages Mum was chatting about on the phone. So, without Pete, there was no one.

Granny's is one of those old-fashioned houses that still has a landline, and I know Pete's mobile number off by heart. So, last night I went downstairs to ring him from it so his mum wouldn't recognise the number and know it was me. Problem

was, it went straight to voicemail. Literally, the only thing I can

talk to at the moment is the O2 messaging service – sounds

about right, doesn't it? I was so angry when I got the message

that I slammed the phone down a bit too hard, and Granny came

running out into the hallway.

'Thomas, are you OK?'

I didn't even say a word to her. Didn't even look at her

really. All I wanted to do was fall into her arms and cry, but

what good would that do? That's the exact reason why Mum

hates me. She said so herself. I'm too wimpy. So if I do it to

Granny as well, she'll end up hating me too. Then what have I

got? Ellie already hates me, so does Mum. Dad must hate me if

I'm the one that made them fall out of love and now Granny will

hate me if I start being a wuss to her too. So I ignored her and

ran straight back up to my room. She didn't follow me – why

would she?

The more I think about it, the more I can't help but shake the feeling that it isn't Pete's mum that's stopping us from talking. Maybe it's Pete. I mean, I wouldn't blame him. He's now friends with the worst kid in school. Why would anyone want to put them through that? I heard that this Ben... the one Mum... you know... well, apparently, he used to be friends with someone called Chris but then he wet himself in the middle of school and so he ditched him. Maybe that's what Pete's doing to me? I mean, let's face it, if pissing yourself is social suicide, then why wouldn't this be? Having your mum hook up with a Year 11 and not being able to stand up for yourself is pretty low. Pete's obviously realised he would be better off without me and who could blame him? I wouldn't.

That's why I took my books out of my bag and put my overnight stuff in instead, because why would I go to school? Why would I walk into somewhere on my own? Somewhere that I will hate every second of for the rest of my life. I might as well just leave. So that's what I'm doing.

This morning I put my uniform on as normal and went downstairs as if nothing was happening. Dad looked straight at me and obviously wanted to talk about what I'd heard Mum say, but I didn't give him the chance. I just avoided all eye contact and got some cereal out of the cupboard. When he went back to looking at his phone, I stuffed some breakfast bars into my pockets just in case. I wanted to grab some crisps too, but me and Pete always eat in the cafeteria at school, so Dad would know something was different. Bars you can hide... crisps... no chance. Then I sat down and ate the cereal in complete silence. We were the only ones in the dining room, yet neither of us spoke. I looked at my cereal bowl and he looked at his phone. Part of me kept wishing he would talk to me, make it all better, but I guess that isn't possible, is it? After a few spoonfuls, I dared myself to look up at Dad. He was too engrossed in his phone to notice, so I stared a little deeper. He looked awful. I don't think he slept last night. I heard him and Granny talking until really late and then I only heard her feet on the stairs coming up to bed. He put the TV on as soon as she left and that's all I heard. Every time I woke up… which was a lot… the TV was still going. I'd assumed he was asleep on the sofa, but looking at him this morning, I don't think he was. His hair was all over the place, not gelled like usual, and his eyes seemed darker. I can't really explain it, but they just looked dull. Dad is a morning person. He wakes you up with a smile every day and *hates* phones at the table, yet here he was, sat in his own world and a smile couldn't be further from his face.

Every part of me wanted to look after him, to ask if he was OK, but how could I? I can't be the person he speaks to, be his shoulder to cry on and then leave him. And, besides, what if he asked me back? What if he said… *how are you, Thomas?* I can't exactly say… 'Oh, I'm terrible to be honest, Dad. I've only got one friend and he isn't talking to me. My mum doesn't love me or you for that matter… oh yeah, and all my class think I should kill myself.' No. No conversations could happen this morning, so I ate half my cereal and scraped the rest in the bin.

That's when I saw the beer bottles. More than I'd ever seen Dad drink in my life, and they must have been him – Granny only ever has a glass of sherry at Christmas, never anything more, and Ellie didn't come home last night. Not that even she would be brazen enough to put them in the kitchen bin – she hides hers in her wardrobe and then puts them in the public bin outside our house, on her way to school. Seeing the bottles made me realise that Dad couldn't take anymore. He had enough on his plate, and me staying around would only make his life harder. So I left the table, grabbed my bag and walked out the front door. I'll be honest, I don't think Dad even noticed, which is probably for the best.

I walked the normal way to school. I wasn't really sure where else I would head, but as soon as I got nearer and saw other kids, the shouting started.

'Ain't you the son of Hall the Whore? Fucking hell, mate, I wouldn't be walking the streets if I were you.'

'Shit… it's Hall's son. Left her shagging someone else, have you, mate? Who is it this time? Someone in your year? Or does she like teenage kids rather than little wimpy kids?'

'I heard your mum's getting the sack today. No one to protect you then, is there?'

That's the last one I heard. Mum was getting the sack. She didn't want to be my mum and now she wasn't going to be my teacher either. I was never going to see her again. Dad would have to take on everything and by the look of him this morning, that's the last thing he could cope with. I ducked into a side alley, trying not to listen to the jeers as I did so, and walked through the streets, keeping out of everyone's way. I'd never walked this bit of town before. Mum and Dad always called it the 'rough end' and told us not to go near it. It was where the old market once stood, but now it was just where drunks and homeless people hung out. I walked past the Wetherspoons, the one Ellie always wanted to go to. She said all her mates were getting served down there, but Mum and Dad never let her go. I mean, they didn't realise that she would just drink down the park when they said no anyway, but that's what Ellie's like. Every time she said she was staying at her mate's house, she'd really be at the park, drinking and smoking. I tried to tell Mum once, but she wasn't interested. I thought it was better to tell her that she would probably be safer at the pub than the park, but when I saw it, it made me think otherwise. There were men in there. Horrid old, grey-haired men, drinking pints first thing in the morning. They had the same dead look in their eyes as Dad at the table. Maybe that's how he'll end up after all of this.

I kept walking and that's when I saw the train station. My first thought was to pick a train to board and get out of here, but then I thought, where would I go? I didn't have enough money for a hotel, or food, so where would that leave me? It seemed I had two choices – I could either stay here and be lonely and bullied for the rest of my life, or leave and become the homeless man I'd just walked past in the old market. Neither felt like much of a choice, or much of a life, and that's when I thought of the third option. The one they had given me last night. The one where I got to end it all. That's when I climbed the bridge over the tracks. That's when I dropped my bag and walked further down, away from my phone and my belongings. And that's where I'm sitting right now. I need to watch and work it out. Work out how fast the trains come, how often and when I'd have to jump. But I have to do it at the right time. If I'm going to do this, it needs to work. It's my only choice.

Liz

(Now)

The green gates that surrounded the playground had once seemed so reassuring to Liz. The idea that they held in everything she needed to control her life gave her a sense of comfort she'd never really been able to explain. However, looking towards them today, they seemed overwhelming, uncomfortable, and more like a prison than a place of security. She wondered if this was how the children felt when they started their school day. Not with a sense of belonging and safety, but in a place where they felt trapped and forced to be somewhere they didn't want to be. Coupled with the looming jail bars, as she now saw them, were the leering faces looking back at her from the other side. She couldn't help but picture all those police dramas that Rob watched in the evenings while she worked. The ones where the newbie inmate would walk through the hall and the prisoners would be banging cups on the bars of their cells from the other side. It was a haunting image and yet one that seemed so real. Only these weren't prisoners. They were students. Kids. But what seemed like hundreds of them. All at once, they had turned towards her as she had driven into the car park. The black Mercedes was obviously too noticeable to a bunch of teenagers with big dreams, probably way above their station. She'd hoped, more than anything, that this meeting would have been scheduled early in the morning, or last thing at night. Or anytime really that meant the playground would be empty and the children would all be wreaking havoc on the streets, and not in the school premises. Nevertheless, as Liz knew well, wishing and hoping got you nowhere, and she also knew that asking Jo to move it to a time when no one would be around would make her look even more guilt ridden. So here she was at 10:30am… break time.

Stepping out of her car, she had intended to hold her head up high, but the night before was taking its toll. Despite the layer of make-up under her eyes, nothing could rid them of the swelling and bloodshot appearance she had seen in the visor mirror only moments ago. So, instead, she looked at the ground and she walked quietly through the playground and towards the staff room. This had to be another blow from Jo. She said Liz didn't have to go to the main office because, '*of course*', she was still a member of staff. However, walking up to the main office at breaktime would mean avoiding the majority of children. Walking to the staff room meant the staff car park and the playground. It was 1-0 to Ben. Or Jo? At this moment, she trusted no one.

Ben. The drive to school this morning had been the first time she had thought of Ben properly throughout all of this. She couldn't fathom the reason. Why had he fabricated this? Had it only been from the mistake at the window? If that was anyone else, would they have done the same? Or had he purposely sought out her house and hidden in the bushes to watch her? She'd realised only this morning that this was the angle she should have gone down. She was so worried about playing it down, keeping her mouth shut to save herself and the school, her reputation, that she missed the right tact. *She* should have played the victim from the start. The woman that had been stalked by an overzealous, sex-driven teenager. She couldn't have been the first. But what did she do? She stood her ground. She defended herself with pig-headedness. In short... she'd lied. She'd said the underwear wasn't hers. Not that he was outside in the bushes. She kicked herself thinking of it.

As she walked past a group of Year 10s, the whispering flooded over her like a wave. Yet no one spoke louder than that. Had they been told not to approach her? Not to talk to her? Yes, she was deputy head, but there were always characters that didn't seem to give a stuff about that on a normal day, let alone one where she was about to get sacked. But there was nothing. No shouts, no jeers, no outward laughing. Sure, there was sneers, some side looks and nudges to their mates, but that was it. There was only one thing for it. They had been warned. Threatened –

probably – with a Saturday detention. That was always hated the most. But then, if they had, was Jo protecting her still? Was it that she simply couldn't have the meeting any other time and so had done her utmost to shield her most loyal member of staff? Liz didn't know. And to be fair, she didn't care. Right now, she just needed to get into the staff room. No doubt there would be more stares coming her way from in there.

The musty smell hit her first. Schools always had a smell. It was hard to put your finger on it. Primary schools smelt more of art supplies and fabric softener, whereas secondary schools were more unwashed blazers and Lynx Africa. It was amazing how being away for one day could heighten her senses so much. Yet it did, and she had to stop herself from clinging onto her nose as soon as she stepped into the building. She didn't need to look up – she could walk these corridors in her sleep – but she knew she had to. If things were to go her way, and that felt like a very big *if* at the moment, she would still be these people's boss, their line manager, and she needed to remind them of that, regardless of the turmoil that was bubbling up inside her stomach. So, she lifted her head from the ground and, despite the state of her eyes, stared forward. Not just forward, but at them. She stared straight into their eyes. Who knew? Perhaps her bloodshot eyes would pull on their heartstrings and she could still play the victim after all. As long as they showed her tears… and not her hangover. She didn't smile though. She couldn't. The fake forced smile she'd given these people every morning for over a decade was not about to greet them today. Staring at her staff as she walked the familiar room made her reminiscence about the old Liz. The confident Liz. The Liz who, on the surface, had it all. And it made her shoulders straighter and her head higher. She needed to show them she had done nothing wrong. But *they* had. *They* had let her down and they would feel guilty for that in time. But for now, she just needed to prove her innocence and their guilt.

With that, the door in front of her opened.

'Liz, hi, thanks for coming. Do come in.'

The idea of stepping into Jo's office had haunted her mind and her dreams ever since her phone call. She'd imagined the HR representative as nothing short of a monster. A tall figure with a sinister smile and evil eyes. Instead, sat in front of her was a youngish woman, probably in her early forties, with sleek black hair, warming brown skin and deep brown eyes that seemed to give a sparkle of hope. She smiled as Liz entered the room, and her nose stud glinted in the sunshine that was coming through the vertical blinds at the window. Whatever Jo or the rest of the staff thought, this woman had not made up her mind. It was clear that she was prepared to give Liz the benefit of the doubt, and Liz intended to grab that with both hands.

The room seemed less daunting than she'd pictured now. Especially as all that was in there were the three women. HR lady in the corner, Jo behind her desk and Liz. She had decided not to quickly sign onto a union. She knew how it would look. That it would make Jo believe that she needed guidance, help and more than anything, a case for defence. And she didn't need any of those things. She'd always backed herself in life and Jo knew that, so Liz didn't intend to change anything now. Although, as she stared around the room, one person did enter her head that she wished was here. The one, she'd realised only recently, that had always been there to back her up no matter what.

Liz had prided herself on independence all her life. But was she really? Had she really gone through it all alone? Of course she hadn't. If it wasn't for Rob, Ellie wouldn't be here. And if it wasn't for Ellie, perhaps she wouldn't have fought so hard for the career she had gained. She wouldn't have pushed herself to be more because there would be no stigma to fight against. She had always seen her family as a trap, something to escape, but perhaps they were what she needed. Perhaps they were the ones pushing her forward all this time. Either way, they weren't here now, and neither was anyone else. This was the time Liz would need to prove to herself that she was as strong as she always claimed. She took a deep breath and nodded at Jo to start.

'We all know why we are here. There has been an allegation of indecency towards you and the school board, as well as the council, need us to get to the bottom of it. Now, when we spoke before I know you proclaimed your total innocence and before we proceed, I need to know if this is still the case. Do you deny any relationship with the pupil Ben Bridges?'

'Other than a professional one, yes. I am his teacher and nothing more.'

'OK, thank you. I will now pass this over to Primera, the HR representative from the county council. She is going to ask you some questions. I am simply here as a witness.'

'Thank you, Jo. Hello, Liz.'

The voice was as calming as the face. Liz felt herself turning towards this woman and away from Jo. Her words, her demeanour, was like ice. This woman was the direct opposite of that. Liz wondered what hers would be like if she was sat in Jo's chair right now. Although she didn't need to think for too long on that one.

'Hello, Primera.'

'The first thing I want to do is to understand your thoughts and views on the matter at hand. I'm not here to make judgements; that will be for the council and the police to do... if it goes that far... I'm simply here to obtain as many facts as I can and paint a picture from both sides. I must tell you that I will be speaking to Ben directly after this, so I have a fair comparison of events. Can I ask what you felt about your relationship with Mr Bridges?'

Liz took a deep breath to steady her voice. She pulled down her trousers to straighten the crease that was appearing on her thigh and then looked up to make eye contact with Primera. She wanted to ensure she was ready to speak clearly and slowly. There was nothing more guilty-looking than a shaky voice.

'There is no relationship, other than a professional one. He is just a pupil. A struggling pupil whose grades needed improving. He had little support from home and so I started to tutor him. He was bringing down my data in the English department and with OFSTED around the corner, I needed to improve it as much as possible.'

Liz decided not to mention the fact that she was also hoping for Jo's job by next year at the latest. She wanted to look like a team player, despite the lack of members on her side presently.

'I see. Now, looking at your data here, Liz… May I call you Liz by the way? Or would you prefer Miss Hall?'

'No, Liz is fine, thank you.'

'Lovely.'

Primera carried on in her calm and passive tone. 'So looking at your data, Liz, I can see that there are a few children that are hindering it, if you don't mind me putting it that way. Why was it only Ben who was offered your tutoring?'

Liz knew this question was coming. She'd practised her response to it in her head so much that it almost felt false as she spouted it out in front of the women opposite her.

'A few reasons really. I had hoped to tutor all the children as the year went on, but I would be unable to commit to everyone. I wanted to demonstrate to the rest of the department what a difference it could make in the hope that they would be willing to have a go too. As you know, I cannot force the team to give up their lunch breaks to help struggling students, so I thought this would be a good way to... let's say... encourage them to want to do right by the children... and by the school. When I looked at the children that needed help the most, Ben seemed the perfect candidate. He isn't a difficult child. Well, not usually. He is well behaved in lessons and doesn't have a record for disruption, but he has no... natural gift of academics and his home life gives him more disruption than help and therefore his grades have suffered. I thought he would be a good one to start with, someone that I could show improvement with straight away as a good example. There are also, if I am permitted to say, a number of safeguarding issues with Ben, and as DSP I thought it was another way of keeping a close eye on him and making sure he was OK.'

'That all sounds very magnanimous, I must say. So how do you think you went from helping a struggling student to being accused of sexual misconduct?'

Direct. She was definitely direct. Liz knew she needed to meet this woman with the same manner she was dishing out.

'Your guess is as good as mine, I'm afraid. I cannot give you a concrete reason as to why such allegations have been fabricated. Children have wild imaginations as I am sure anyone who has worked in a school will tell you. Perhaps he got carried away with the idea of our one-to-one sessions.'

'And can you tell me a bit more about your one-to-one sessions? What happened in them?'

She was leaning forward now, twisting her pen in her hand as she did so. She looked like someone trying to play 'good cop' in some old American movie. Did this mean that Jo was going to be 'bad cop', or did it just mean that she was the villain? She didn't want them getting the wrong idea.

'Work. Schoolwork.'

When a silence filled the room, Liz knew she needed more and so continued. 'We met either at lunchtime or after school, depending on when he could stay. He works in a chip shop down the road on a Friday evening, so we would do lunchtimes on a Friday and usually two other sessions during the week, depending on my timetable. If you'd allow me to go to my office, I could get the file for his sessions. I have detailed plans of each one we completed and a record of the work he achieved.

You will see from there exactly what we did in each session...

which, as I say... was schoolwork and nothing more.'

'Yes, we have seen that file. Jo brought it with her this

morning. We saw that you did one session on *Romeo and Juliet*,

despite Ben learning about *King Lear* for his exams. Why was

that exactly?'

Liz felt her throat go dry. She wasn't sure if it was

because they'd brought up *Romeo and Juliet* and the thought of

the note flashed through her mind, or because they had been

through her things. She was a very private person and having her

files looked at without her permission left her feeling vulnerable

and on the back foot, which is not where she wanted to be.

'To get him more in touch with the language. As you can

see from the file you obviously have possession of, I was going

to look at a few Shakespearean texts with him to help him

become accustomed with the way he wrote. The next session

was going to be *Hamlet* if I remember correctly.'

'You do. I saw from your paperwork that was your intention,' she said before pausing slightly. 'I am just curious, why *Romeo and Juliet* first?'

'Why not? It is a more famous one that the children tend to know. Most of them would have studied it in some capacity in Year 6, so I thought he might be aware of the storyline.'

'I see. Can you understand why we would worry about that sort of story, in light of recent events?'

'Well, of course I can now, but that didn't even cross my mind before.'

'Not at all?'

'No.'

'So, what about when you'd found this note?'

And there it was. The picture Ben had left her. The one she had stuffed back in her desk drawer as if it was nothing, before all of this had happened. Thinking nothing of it, being so naïve and reckless. Of course they had been through her desk.

She knew she could argue it, that there was some impeachment

of privacy, but the desk was the school's property and admitting

that she had hidden it would've made things look a hundred

times worse. There was only one way to play this, and Liz had to

make sure she seemed calm. So, before she answered, she

pushed her hair behind her ears. She wanted to show them how

steady her hands were, how steady her voice was, how innocent

she was. She hoped more than anything it didn't look like she

was fumbling around for something to say.

'What note is that?'

'The note written to you, from Ben. It was found in your

desk.'

'I've never seen that note before in my life.'

There it was. Another lie. But this one had to be told.

There was no other choice.

'Are you sure about that, Liz?'

'I'm certain. I have no idea what that note is, or what it says.'

'OK, but I have to tell you that we will be asking Ben when he placed it in your desk, or put it in your hand. Of course, we don't know such things, and if it was before you were asked to leave the school premises, we will be inclined to believe you had indeed seen the note before today.'

Liz felt this last statement was an attack. This seemingly sweet woman was now, it seemed, trying to get a rise out of her, and she wasn't going to allow it. She was, however, going to gain back some control. Once again, she straightened her trousers and sat further upright in her chair. She crossed her legs and tucked them neatly to the side and this time she made sure it was her that leant forward in the direction of Primera.

'And there I was thinking you were not here to make such decisions, Primera? As I have already stated, I have not seen that note before today and I do not profess to know what words it contains.'

'I see.'

'So, am I allowed to be privy to that information?'

'I think it's best we move on. I have heard your take on the matter, and I don't wish for us to hit a stumbling block. Can we move on to your phone?'

'My phone?'

'Yes, do you have it with you today?'

'Yes. It's in my bag.'

'OK. Obviously, I can't force you to allow us to look through it, only the police can do that, but I wondered if you would be happy to show us your messages and photographs? Just to see if anything matches up with what Ben posted online.'

Liz allowed herself a small smug smirk to appear on her face. Perhaps not wide enough for the others to notice, but enough for her. She made sure she looked in Jo's direction as she answered. It was the first time she had given her any eye contact since Primera had started talking.

'Of course I will. I have been happy to show my phone all along. I think you'll find I offered to show it to Jo yesterday, did I not?'

Jo shifted in her seat as she gave a slight nod of the head in Primera's direction. Over the last conversation, Liz had almost forgotten she was in the room. She had looked directly at Primera and her pinstriped pencil skirt and pink blouse. The woman had crossed her legs over to the side as if she was an interviewer on a television programme and she had given her such intense eye contact that Liz had not noticed anything else around her. Now, shifting her focus and reaching for her bag, however, she had seen how messy Jo's desk was. Very unlike her to not have order when she had a visitor coming. Her hair, which was always pulled tight into a crocodile clip, had also loosened and wisps of hair could be seen poking out of her hairline. That was when Liz realised that Jo was stressed. Perhaps not as badly as Liz – or perhaps she was – but the last twenty-four hours had obviously taken its toll on her too. And of course it had. The emails Liz had received must have been minimal compared to the ones Jo must have found in her inbox. But worse than that: phone calls, parents at the gates, pupils within the school. She must have been dealing with it all and her body language showed everything. Her shoulders were hunched, and her eyes seemed sunken. She sat low in her seat, almost showing defeat. In fact, Liz was unsure whether Jo had decided she was guilty, or whether she even had the fight in her to care enough. If this is how she looked after day one, what sort of support would she gain further on down the line? Because Liz knew this wasn't the end.

Taking out her phone, she was instantly distracted by her screen. Missed calls. All from Rob. Fifteen of them in total. Why would he be ringing her so frantically? Surely not to just have another go at her?

'Is something wrong, Liz?'

Primera was waiting with her hand out expectantly for the phone. Liz decided to hold on to it.

'I seem to have a lot of missed calls from my partner. I had it on silent, you see, so I didn't know it was ringing.'

'Oh, I see. Did he... want to be here? To support you? You are allowed someone with you. It doesn't have to be a union rep.'

'No. He isn't ringing for that.'

'I see.'

The words hung in the air. The admittance that the father of her children had also turned his back on her seemed to leave a sick feeling in her throat and an entirely different one in Primera's – for her it was obviously the confirmation she needed. He disbelieved her, so why would anyone else think differently? Or did he? Perhaps he was ringing because he did want to support her, to be there in the meeting? Maybe Liz was clutching at straws, but maybe he trusted her after all. The most surprising thing of all, however, was how much Liz wanted that to be true.

'It doesn't matter. He knows I'm in this meeting. I will call him back afterwards. Besides, you wanted to see the phone, yes? Well, If I open my messages, feel free to read as many as you wish. You will see there is nothing on there that shouldn't be. Messages from Rob about the children, messages from the children about the children, perhaps a couple of updates from the gym or my yoga instructor but… nothing else.'

The last words seemed to get stuck in her throat. Nothing else. No one else. No friends arranging catch-ups, no family checking in. That had all stopped years ago. None even from Rob's mum. She knew she despised her, always had, and Liz had to admit the feeling was very mutual, but still… nothing but work and the gym and Rob… which up until now had always felt fine.

As Primera was about to take Liz's phone from her, however, there was a knock at the door, which made Liz pull it back and cling on to it a little harder. She looked at Jo, who seemed more exhausted with the idea that someone would interrupt this meeting than cross. 'We're busy,' she shouted through the door. 'There is a sign.'

'I know, Mrs Swann. I'm very sorry to interrupt, only it's quite urgent.'

With that, the door opened without another word being said and in walked Annette Marshall, the busybody secretary that Liz had a very love-hate relationship with. Although today, she looked more worried than smug, which was definitely a change for her.

'I'm so sorry to interrupt, Jo, really I am, but there's been a bit of an incident and I could really do with talking to Liz.'

'We're in the middle of something...'

'No, I know, it's just... well, Thomas...'

Liz spun round in her chair and faced Annette. Her heart was pounding, and she instantly knew something was bad. Maybe this was it. Maybe this was the mother's instinct she had heard so much about but never felt herself.

'*My* Thomas? What's happened?'

'Well, we don't know, Liz. It's just, he didn't turn up for school this morning, very unlike him obviously, and when we rang your husband… sorry… partner… he said he had left first thing, but he's not here. Now, Rob's just rung the school and said Thomas had packed his bag this morning and taken all his belongings with him. He was worried he'd run away…'

'Run away? Run where? Where would he run?'

'That's all I know. He took his bag from his granny's house… because they stayed there last night, didn't they? Rob did say he'd been trying to call you, but there was no answer…'

And there it was. The smugness. The smirk she would expect from the school gossip. When do these women grow up?

The smirk annoyed Liz, her knowing all of this annoyed Liz, but

not knowing where Thomas was annoyed her more than

anything else. In fact... it broke her. She felt tears rising up in

her eyes and for once in her life, she didn't care who saw it. She

had done this to her son. She had told him she didn't love him

and now he was gone. Gone to God knows where and all she

knew was that she did. She did love him... more than anything,

and nothing was as important as telling him that. Right now.

Liz picked up her bag, stuffed her phone in it and walked

towards the door. She knew Jo had asked her to stop, she could

hear Primera talking about protocols, but none of that mattered.

All that mattered was Thomas and getting him home. That's

when she opened the door and walked right into Ben. The boy

that had created all of this was stood in the corridor waiting to

walk into that room to spout off more of his lies, to ruin more of

her life. His mum stood next to him, and some man she had

never seen before was playing on his phone as if they were just

waiting in the queue at the supermarket. Like none of this

mattered. And it did matter. It mattered *so* much, and she needed to stop all of it.

'Ben. Ben, please stop this. I'm begging you. My Thomas is missing. He left because of everything. Because of your lies. It's too much. I don't hate you. I'm not angry. I just need you to tell them the truth so I can find my son and bring him home. *Home*, Ben… where he should be… with me. Please tell them the truth. Please make this all stop.'

She ignored Primera calling her to stop talking to Ben, she ignored his horrific mother's act of being concerned about her son and more than anything she ignored the fact that begging a teenage boy for help was something she had promised herself she would never do again. Nothing mattered anymore. None of this drama, none of Ben's lies and certainly not the school's reputation. All that mattered was Thomas. And that was why, despite every bit of chaos surrounding her, she walked down the corridor towards the car park, fumbling with her phone as she did so. She needed to get hold of Rob and she needed to piece

everything in her life back together, not for her, but for her son.

Ben

(Now)

Fuck. That's literally all I have to say. Fuck. Fuck. Fuck. Today was the worst. The worst day ever in my whole life and that's saying something because I've had some pretty shit times – beyond shit times – but nothing compared to today. It was horrible. I'm horrible. I'm the shittiest person on the planet. I deserve to have no friends. No life. No nothing.

It all started while I was waiting to see Mrs Swann and the woman from HR. I'd woken up feeling a bit shit about everything I was going to do. I knew I needed to, but it was the way Mum was acting round me. It was like she was two completely different people… One minute she was in character, being all loving and concerned, and the next minute she was usual Mum with her threats and crap. And when I was stood there with them, outside the office, I thought, this is bullshit. Me, stood there with me mum who doesn't take an interest in me from one week to the next, and this bloke Lee, who I've never

even spoken to in my whole bloody life. And we were stood

there, together, trying to look like the perfect family. Like the

victim teenager and his concerned parents. I mean, seriously?

What utter crap is that? I've never had a perfect family and I

never will. I accepted that years ago. But as I was stood shuffling

my feet, I couldn't help but think of something.

I don't have that perfect family, but I know who does...

well, did... and that's Hall. They always looked perfect to me.

Her kids had a mum and dad... a proper one. Not a supposed

'stepdad' like mine whose surname I don't even know and will

probably be gone next week. And their mum works hard to bring

in money, not like mine that sits on her arse claiming benefits

and nicking the extra off me. I mean, their mum, she works in

their school; she must be so involved in her kids' futures and

lives and that but mine? She has nothing to do with her day and I

still reckoned today was the first time she had stepped into this

school since I was in Year 7. She came on the open day; I know that because she made a right scene chatting to Chris's mum really loudly while Mrs Swann was giving her speech. It was so embarrassing. One teacher actually told her to shut up as if she was still a pupil, and she reacted like she was by pulling a face at him and folding her arms in a hump. Honestly, I could have died there and then.

Since then, she's never stepped through the door again. I thought I was so clever not telling her about any meetings she was meant to come to, or sports days she could watch because I thought she'd embarrass me again. I honestly thought I was really conning her by keeping her away from the gates, but then, as I'm stood outside that office today, I thought… I haven't really been keeping her away, have I? She's been keeping herself away, from the school, from her duties as a mum and most of all, from me. Think about it, what other mum doesn't notice she's missed parents' evening twice a year, for four years? What other mum has never once met a teacher or been to a meeting about GCSE options? I would bet my life on the fact that she doesn't have a clue what choices I picked or what lessons I'm studying. I mean, shit me, it weren't that long ago since she was here herself – she must know how it goes. She must have known that I'd chosen my options, that they'd run meetings about sixth form and shit, but she chose not to notice, didn't she? I didn't keep it from her like a clever little shit... She ignored it because she chose to... because then she didn't have to take any notice of me at all. And that's fine, ain't it? I guess it kind of suited both of us. She didn't show up to school in a tracksuit with her tits hanging out and embarrassing me and she didn't have to spend any time with the son that ruined her life. It was win-win.

Yet here she was. Today she was all dressed up in a shirt, standing in the school like the world's best mum. Like she gave a shit. Stood there trying to put her arm round me whenever a teacher walked past. And all because of what? Because her kid had been abused by a teacher like the rest of them thought? Nah, because she wanted to cash in on some money from the papers while she could. So she could take Lee the dickhead to Benidorm and make him hang around for a week longer than he was going to. The more I thought about it, the more it made me feel sick and every time she tried to put her bingo wing on my shoulder, I wanted to knock it off and run.

Then… well… then it got worse. We're stood there waiting to go in and Mum's trying to whisper in my ear about what to say and how to behave. She even asked me if I could fake cry… Honestly… that's what she said to me. It made me sick, so I was just about at the end of my tether, about to tell her not to bother coming in with me, when Hall burst out the office. Fuck. She looked awful. I've never seen her like it before. She still had make-up on, and a nice suit and that, but her eyes looked puffy and swollen and her hair looked like she had been running her hands through it constantly and not in a sexy way – in a shit way, like she'd been panicking. And then when she spoke to me. Not spoke, fucking begged me. (Funny how all the times I'd dreamt about her begging me for something, it was never quite like this.) When she did that, she looked... well... broken. She was speaking really fast and desperate like, and it took me a while to work out what she was saying, but it was something about Thomas – her kid. Something about how he was gone or missing, and it was my fault. She told me to tell the truth. Fucking pleaded with me to make it all stop and then just left. Ran down the corridor, clacking in her high heels, and didn't look back. I could hear Mrs Swann calling after her, the other lady too, and Mum was being a gobshite as per, but she ignored them all. She ignored everyone around her and just carried on running until she'd gone out the door and out of sight.

As soon as she was gone, we were pushed into the office with Mrs Swann and the other woman. I could hear Mum kicking off, saying how she shouldn't have spoken to me and that she was angry that I had been in contact with the woman that abused me. It was bullshit. Everything Mum was saying, everything I'd said, I knew it was all bullshit, but I just sat there frozen. They were talking all around me. A woman I'd never met before, a teacher who had nothing to do with me and a mum that was pretty much the same. Three women who all pretended to give a shit about me, while one... one who had actually taken an interest and tried to help... had just run away like a bloody scared kitten. And all I could think about was what she'd said. How Thomas had done a bunk. How he was missing because of... because of me.

I'd seen him yesterday. I'd seen him get pushed down the corridor... but that's just banter, ain't it? Every kid goes through that. Surely, he wouldn't run away just because of a Shove Alley. That's pathetic. But still... what if it wasn't because of that? What if that had only been the start of it? What if he'd been bullied... or beaten up... because of the shit I'd done? I kept picturing him lying on the floor being kicked in the stomach and then I couldn't focus on what the fuck was going on. I just sat there. And then I felt Mum reach for my hand and squeeze it so hard I jumped out my skin. When I looked up, she was looking at me, in a way that the others couldn't see, and she was glaring.

Proper glaring. Like I needed to buck up or get the beating of my life. So that's when I woke up and started listening to the questions.

They asked me about our relationship, about how we had started seeing each other and without even thinking I started spurting out all the shit I'd been practising last night. I'd laid awake for hours thinking about what I was going to say, and it was like I'd rehearsed it so much it just came out. Honest, it was like word vomit, and I couldn't stop myself. The shit I was talking, about how she had come on to me in my one to ones and how she had suggested we do it at my house. My mum piped up then and said she wasn't around when I got back from school because she was at work, and I nodded along like it was all real. Honestly… my mum at work… That's even more laughable than me shagging Hot Hall. And that was the moment. That's when I realised that this was all laughable. As if I ever thought Hot Hall would want to shag me. The dickhead from Year 11. She could have anyone… why the fuck would she choose me? And I knew then that she hadn't. She'd never chosen me. She didn't teach me *Romeo and Juliet* as a hint… She taught me it so I'd pass my GCSEs. She didn't give me a strip tease from the window… She got undressed and had no fucking idea I was in the bushes. Because that's where I was, wasn't I? In the bushes like a childish perv. That's all I was. And there I was… sitting around a load of people that didn't give a shit… ruining the life of the one person that actually did. The one person that had actually tried to help me. The first person in my whole fucking life that cared about what happened to me and I was there spouting a load of rubbish. It all got too much. I couldn't handle it.

Look, I ain't saying it's cool. Fuck me – no way – but I cried. I sat in that room, stared at everyone around me and burst into tears. Mum looked so chuffed she totally lost character. She obviously thought I was laying it on thick. And so did the others. Mrs Swann looked so worried and the other woman… Pri something… she leant right forward in her chair and offered me a tissue. They all looked at me like I was the victim. But I weren't, was I? She was… and Thomas. Thomas didn't deserve none of this. He didn't deserve having his whole family ripped apart. I didn't get it until I saw Hall. Until I saw the look in her eyes, the desperation, the love. 'Cause I ain't never had that, have I? I ain't had anyone look at me with love the way she did. Only it weren't directed at me. It was directed at her own kid that had done a bunk because of me. And that's when Mum tried to put her arm around my shoulder, just like I'd done for her every time some new bloke had run off with someone else. The difference was… this was the only time she'd done it back to me. Fifteen, not sixteen, but fifteen years and I swear it was the first time she'd put her arm round me like this. I mean, I'm sure she carried me around when I was a baby and that, but I don't really remember, and any photos we have, I'm in the bloody bouncer chair and she's on the sofa anyway – or one of her mates is holding me. The only thing I've seen her cradle is a bottle of fucking beer. And here she was, arm round me, pretending to care, all for show, and I was sick of it. I was crying, yeah, but I think it was more anger. I was angry that the person that should be asking me if I was OK was counting pounds and pennies in her head. And I was even angrier that she was all I had. Yet someone with so much more than me had felt the need to run. It was all bullshit, and it was all my fault. And so, I flipped. I told her to get off me. Well, I was in school, weren't I? She couldn't hit me there; she had to keep up the pretence no matter what. So, I told her. I told her to fuck off. Told her to stop pretending she cared because she didn't. Told her that I didn't even know who Lee was, let alone make the teachers believe he was my stepdad, because that was a lie. In fact, it was all a lie. And then it came out… proper word vomit… I told them everything. How I thought Hall was coming on to me, how I'd bragged about it in the playground to look cool and how my mates had jumped on it. That they'd told me I needed evidence and how I'd fucking panicked. How I'd made up all the posts. I told them I thought she wanted me because she was in her window in her underwear… and that's when I had to admit it was in the window because I was in the bushes outside. That's when I looked like a perv. That's when I shut up.

The whole room went silent. Proper silent. Mrs Swann had given up trying to keep her hair neat and was pulling it out at the sides. The other woman, she'd stopped writing. She was holding the pen in mid-air, and I swear her mouth was open for fucking ages. Mum... well... she looked well angry. Like the angriest I've ever seen her. There was a vein in her forehead I'd never noticed before, but I reckon there and then you could have seen it from space. Lee looked fed up too... but I also don't know how much he'd heard... he had kind of zoned out at the very beginning. And there I was... tears down my face, snot coming out my nose, my face must have been red because so were my arms and my hands. I must have looked a right fucking mess. But still, no one spoke. No one... until Mum.

'You mean... You made all this shit up?'

So much for not swearing, hey? I knew the best behaviour lark wasn't going to last, but I didn't think she'd crack so early. And for some reason, it made me even more pissed off. And for those few minutes I didn't give a shit that it was Mum I was speaking to, or that I was in front of my head teacher, and so I told her, in front of everyone.

I said, 'Don't pretend like you didn't know. You know you did. You said so yourself that you didn't think she'd shag me. But you told me to come here anyway, didn't you, Mum? And why was that?'

Then there was silence again.

'I don't know what you mean,' she said. Definitely trying to sound calmer than she was. She kept glancing from me to Mrs Swann and back again. Her face had gone all red and sweaty, like she'd been running, and she was holding her hands so tight her fingers had gone white. 'I had no idea what you were up to... There I was, worrying about how some old trout had been playing away with my innocent teenager and there you were sitting on your phone making the whole thing up. I should never have let you have one in the first place.'

'Let me have one? *Let* me have one? I had to bribe you to give me your old one, just so I could fit in, and why was that? Hey? Because one of your old fellers whacked me so hard when he was pissed that you were worried the school would start asking questions when I had PE. That's why you let me have your old phone – so you could get me out of PE for two weeks with me pretending to have 'growing pains'. You gave me that phone so I would lie to the school... and not for the first time.'

Yeah, I went too far. I went way too far. I don't know why it happened, but it did, and once I'd said it, I couldn't take it back. Mrs Swann and the other woman kept looking between themselves, obviously not knowing what shit to deal with first. The shit that I'd made up about Hot Hall, or the shit I'd revealed about my mum. Either way, I didn't give them much time to think about it because I legged it. Literally, jumped off my chair and ran from the room. I felt like a prat, but I didn't know what to do. If I stayed, I'd be dealt with double shit. I'd have it from the teachers about making stuff up and I have it from Mum for opening my mouth. The only good thing was that Lee seemed completely oblivious to everything and so at least he won't belt me one.

To be fair, he probably would have been the best stepdad ever because he didn't take a blind bit of notice of anything. Life would have been alright then. In fact, life was a lot easier when no one noticed shit about me. I realise that now. Yeah, I was a loser, but I weren't in this state. I weren't sitting in my bedroom, shitting myself in case the door opens. I don't know what would be worse – the school or Mum? Or the police? I'll probably get done for wasting their time or something. You see shit like that on *EastEnders* all the time. I'm not doing anything though. I'm not running like earlier; I'm not packing my bags like Thomas; I'm just sitting here. Waiting for the next thing to happen to me. That and staring at my phone.

Turns out me legging it out of the school in floods of fucking tears didn't go unnoticed. Loads of people saw me and loads of people are messaging already. I guess I can kiss goodbye to Mitchell and all me mates now. As if they'll want to hang out with me after all this. I reckon even Pissy Chris will be too good for me now. Shit... that's depressing. It's a good job I was going to fail all my exams anyway because there is no way I'm going back to that school. As soon as Hot Hall walks back into the building, they'll all know it was just bullshit. Then what? I've got no choice, have I? I can't go back there... ever again.

Liz

(Now)

Rob was in the car park when she made it outside. Annette could have told her that one, but Liz was so relieved to see his face that she didn't give it a second thought. She put her phone away and almost ran towards him. Her mind was racing – this was the first time she'd seen him since he'd walked away from her, and the first time she'd spoken to him since the phone call in the car. So much had changed in her head since then, but she hadn't communicated any of it to him, and she had no idea how he would take it if she did. When she'd called yesterday, she had been so worried about Ellie and so dismissive about Thomas and yet here they were having to join forces to find *him*. She couldn't make head nor tail of it.

The one thing she couldn't allow to cloud her judgement was the school and for the first time in a long time, her career had to come second... perhaps even lower down the list than that. She had ignored any stares she got from pupils or staff as she ran out of the building; their opinions were irrelevant right now. She knew speaking to Ben was a bad idea, she knew that they would try and tell her that she influenced him in some way, but what choice did she have? How else would she be able to get through to him? That could have been her only opportunity to speak to him and maybe that was all she needed. Despite everything, she knew he wasn't a bad kid. Naïve? Definitely. Under-supported? Without a doubt. What role model did that boy have? But he needed to know. He needed to know exactly what he was creating. It was beyond childish banter now, or whatever he thought it was, and Thomas going missing was the final straw. No one around him would be able to show him an ounce of sense, so Liz had to be that person. What did they care about her life? What did anyone care? Jo was clearly annoyed she'd walked out of the meeting, and even the prim and proper HR representative looked disgruntled at the thought of rescheduling. But that's because they didn't understand or didn't want to understand the pressure her family had faced, the torment they had endured during all of this. And why would they? If Liz was honest, she hadn't properly considered her family's feelings once through any of this, so why would an outsider care? The only person that did care was standing in front of her.

Stood by his car in the staff car park, Rob heard her heels on the pavement and looked up from his phone. He looked as dishevelled as she felt, and Liz shocked herself at how much she wanted to throw her arms around him. How much she wanted to tell *him* that everything was OK. Rob had always been the sensitive one, Liz forever logical. That was why… in some ways… they worked so well. She took hold of situations and made them manageable, no matter what the circumstances, while he got all emotional and soppy. What was once irritating all of a sudden felt endearing.

'Any news?'

'Obviously not. Otherwise, I wouldn't have rung you.'

He was trying to stay mad at her and she got it, but his body language gave him away. His shoulders were hunched, his hair was on end and his eyes had tears in them. In fact, he looked just like she did this morning when she'd tried to plaster on the same conviction – only he didn't have make-up to help. She couldn't rise to any of his bait, no matter what he wanted to throw at her. They needed to focus on one important thing: Thomas.

'OK. So, have you tracked his phone? That GPS app you put on it?'

'Yeah, but he must be somewhere with no signal… or he's dumped it… The last tracking signal was just past these gates and then it goes dead.'

'Well, at least we know he walked past them, and not overly long ago. He could still be close. Have you spoken to Ellie?'

'She's not answering my calls.'

'Why? Where's she?'

'At Diane's. I called her mum to double check she was there, and she is, but she's mad at me, so she's going to stay there for a bit. Mel was really good about it all actually.'

'I bet she was… She's always had a thing for you.'

Liz had meant for this to sound light-hearted, to break the ice, but she saw as soon as she finished the sentence that was not the way it was going to be taken.

'Brilliant, so you're matchmaking now, are you? Running off with a kid and setting me up with another single parent at the school. You're unbelievable.'

He turned to open his car door, either that or he just turned his back on her again, but Liz knew she had to fight for him this time. To make things right instead of making things worse.

'You know that's not what I meant… I was… I was just trying…'

Rob turned back round, but his tone of voice had changed. He was whispering, clearly conscious of being in public, but trying to sound cross all the same. Despite that though, Liz knew it was hurt that was pouring out of him. He really did believe she had done everything she was accused of.

'Trying to what? Make light of this shit situation we're in? Look at us, Liz. I'm at Mum's, you're about to lose your career, Ellie hates us and won't come home – not that she really has a home – and Thomas is God knows where. He's not street smart. He can't survive running away. It's all a fucking shambles and it's all your fault. I hope he was worth it.'

Liz stepped towards Rob and lowered her voice to match his. She agreed that the last thing her children needed was another public spectacle to embarrass them further, but she needed to stay strong and get Rob to believe her. If they were past reconciliation, she would have to live with that, but their kids needed them to be on the same team, now more than ever.

'Look. I'm going to say this once and only once more. I did not sleep with a teenager. I haven't slept with anyone but you… ever. And you know that deep down, I know you do. Now I take it Ellie's mad because of the Facebook snooping, am I right?'

He didn't answer; he just nodded and looked at the floor. For a grown man, Rob often reminded Liz of one of her teenage pupils and it occurred to her that perhaps men never really grew up.

'Well, at the end of the day, that can wait. I'm assuming Mel isn't going to allow her to run off and meet some man she doesn't know, so Thomas needs to remain our top priority. He's either walking the streets towards the town, unsure what to do, or he's cut through the woods and is walking that way. I'll go through the woods if it's all the same to you – don't really fancy walking through a crowd of people – and you go into town?'

The last sentence gave off a bit more vulnerability than she was hoping to portray, but it seemed to soften Rob slightly and that was going to be nothing less than a positive through all of this. He looked up at her, his bloodshot eyes showing through the gaps in his fringe, despite his face still pointing toward the floor. It surprised Liz how much their images must mirror right now. She'd always seen Rob as scruffy – appearance was important to her – but maybe this was just what it looked like when you cared more about other people than yourself.

'Yeah, that's fine. Keep your phone on loud and I'll call you if I find him. He can't have gone far… This is Thomas after all.'

For the first time in a while, Liz managed a small smile. As she climbed into her car, and Rob simultaneously climbed into his, Liz couldn't help but feel like she finally had someone back on her team, and she realised at once how much that meant to her. Before she drove off, Rob wound down his window and beckoned for her to do the same.

'Ellie hadn't met him by the way. She was adamant that she wouldn't do something like that, but she was annoyed that I told her not to talk to him again… and that you'd looked at her laptop obviously. But you know… secretly… I think she was pleased that you cared so much. That's not something you show that often, you know? Not to any of us. That's why it's so hard to believe you when you say nothing happened. But… anyway… let's go find Thomas and discuss it later, yeah?'

'Yeah…'

With that, Rob put his window back up and drove out of the staff car park. Liz felt tears in her eyes again but for a completely different reason. Of course they didn't trust her; they had no reason to, but if she could find Thomas and talk to Ellie… and to Rob… He'd said 'discuss it later', which was more than she could have hoped for this morning. Perhaps whatever was facing her on the road ahead would be much easier to deal with if they were on her side. They were a long way off 'happy families' because, in all honesty, they'd been a long way off that for years... but perhaps there was a glimmer of hope of having them back in her corner. And this time she would know how important that was. Now to find Thomas. She was sure he hadn't gone far... sure he hadn't done anything stupid... He was probably just sitting in a coffee shop somewhere keeping his head down. Rob would call her in just a second and tell her everything was OK. Still, she drove towards the woods anyway... It led to the train station and if he had been daft enough to get on a train, it would be a whole other kettle of fish. Surely, he wouldn't have gone that far though. Or would he? How bad had it been for him? Liz had no idea, and the shame of that seemed to swallow her whole.

Without another thought, she missed the turning to the woods and drove straight towards the station car park instead.

She didn't know why, but it felt right, like that was the way she needed to head. Maybe that was what they called mother's intuition? Liz had never felt it before. All of a sudden, she put her foot down and felt the urgency back in her stomach. The one that had made her leave the office so quickly. It had been muffled by her conversation with Rob, but now it was back with full force, making her feel sick. She couldn't get to the train station quick enough and despite her logical brain questioning her decision, the forcefulness of her belief drove her forward.

Turning the corner and pulling into the car park, her fears became panic when she saw a police car and an ambulance. Blue lights still flashing, and doors left open. They'd been abandoned... quickly. So, Liz abandoned hers. She knew she didn't have any practical reason to believe it was for Thomas, but something in her gut told her that it was. Or that it could be. And 'could' was all that she needed. Running towards the station door, she could see a security guard standing at the sliding door, his large frame blocking the entrance.

'Sorry, Miss, station is closed for a bit. And you can't leave your car there anyway.'

'I know. Can you tell me *why* the station is closed?'

'There is an incident that needs dealing with.'

She realised, at this moment, that the assertiveness of his voice and stance did not match the fearful look that was showing in his eyes. She knew something was happening behind him and she needed to know what it was.

'Well, obviously. I can see the rapid response vehicles… Can you tell me what kind of incident? Who or what does it involve?'

'I can't tell you things like that. I've been told so. Please can you move your car and come back another time.'

This man seemed to have all the intelligence of a brick and yet had been given the authority of the queen's personal bodyguard for some reason. Liz could feel the anger burning inside her. He could tell she was distressed; he could tell she needed to get inside, yet he clearly didn't care… either that or he was too stupid to notice.

'Look… my son is missing. If this has anything to do with a twelve-year-old boy, mousy brown hair, about 5 foot 3ish, then I need to get inside right now.'

The man didn't need to say anything else. His face said it all. He had immediately gone ashen and had apparently forgotten how to blink. It was all Liz needed to know. It was all any mother needed to know. She pushed past him and made her way towards the platform.

Thomas

(Now)

I climbed over the fence. I left my bag on the bridge and I hung over the side. I could barely hold on. Stupid small hands. Stupid black iron railings. They're too wide. They made it harder to steady myself. But I managed it. And I saw the train. I had watched enough to know exactly when to jump. People had seen me studying them, but nobody had asked why. I'll be honest, I wanted them to. I wanted to tell someone my plan so they could stop me, but no one did. No one asks in this place. Everyone walks down with their heads pointing to the floor, or to their phone. Most people probably didn't even notice. Too busy looking at Facebook, too busy staring at pictures of my mum looking like a slut. Because that's what everyone thinks, isn't it?

So that's what I think. But if I'm the sort of person that thinks their mum is a slut, then what chance do I have at life?

Dad won't be able to afford to keep us. Mum has all the money – they argue about that all the time. And Mum won't give him any money because she'll be locked up. So, me and Ellie will go into care. Only Ellie hates me, so she'll ditch me, and I'll be left with a family I don't know. More people that only pretend to care. Like Mum… like Pete. I thought Pete might have noticed I wasn't in school. I thought he would have told the teachers and they would have come looking for me. I gave them enough time to find me. I counted way more trains than I needed to, to know when they would come… and when I would need to jump. But still I kept counting… kept waiting. But no one came. And if that isn't a sign, then I don't know what is.

If I had disappeared all morning and no one noticed, then what's the point of hanging around for any longer? In fact, they might never notice I'm gone. Everyone says suicide is selfish. They say it makes the lives of the people you've left behind harder. But if the people you've left behind don't love you, then really you're just making it all easier, aren't you?

That's why I climbed over the fence and that's why I'm clinging on to the railings. That's why I stared at the train, knowing when to let go. All I had to do was let go. But I didn't. I didn't let go. I couldn't. My hands were sweaty enough. It would have been easy. But my fingers stayed enclosed around the railings. They didn't open and in a flash the train was gone. And that's when people started to notice. That's when they screamed and shouted. That's when they wanted someone to call the police. But by then it was too late, wasn't it?

No one had asked me before if I needed help. No one had offered to help a boy sitting on a train station bridge on his own in the middle of the day. They probably saw the uniform and thought I was just bunking off. I knew I should have ditched the blazer somewhere. Maybe then they would have seen a clue and knew where to come… if they were looking, of course. But no one is looking. I know that now. Well… the people at the station are. More and more of them are looking as I hang here. Some of them have got their phones out. They could be showing this to the world. To everyone. I'm going to be just like Mum. Just another face on the internet doing something wrong. I know it's wrong.

I'm scared. If I'm honest, I'm really scared. But they're all looking. And as soon as this goes on the internet, they'll know that I'm her son. She might not know it, not really – she doesn't act like a mum. But everyone else will know she is, and they'll know it's her fault. Maybe that will show her how much I loved her. That I would do this rather than live without her? Maybe then she'll love me back. I might not be around to see it, but I'll know it. Because if someone dies because of you, you have to love them, right? You have to love them forever.

I don't want to die. Not really. But I'm here. I did this. Everyone told me to, and nobody told me not to. And now I'm standing on a bridge with another train coming in about two minutes. If I don't go through with it, everyone will think it's all for attention. And that would be worse. Wouldn't it? It would. I know it would. I thought this would be the worse it got, but it will just be the beginning if people see me hanging here, crying, and doing nothing. All for show. Just like Mum. That's what they'll say. Getting attention, just like Mum. So now I have no choice, do I? What else can I do but let go?

Liz

(Now)

'Thomas!'

The scream rang out around the station as Liz pushed her way through everything and everyone and got the first look of her twelve-year-old son hanging from a railway bridge. The police were attempting to hide him from view with their yellow high vis jackets almost blinding the crowd below. But Liz could see. She could see everything. She could see, as clear as day, that he was one wrong move away from doing something terrible. One wrong move away from the end. He looked so small. Too young to be in that uniform, too young to be… there… in that place. What had she done?

'He's my son. Let me through. That's my boy.'

They didn't stop her. No one could, but still… they didn't try. She ran up the steps and towards his frail figure. She didn't stop for caution, she didn't try to talk to him; she just acted on impulse and that was to throw herself towards him and pull on his blazer, trying to lift him like he was a baby, once again, in her arms. But no matter how hard she tugged, he didn't move. When did he get so strong? Despite all her efforts, he clung to the railings, with no part of him moving.

'Please. Please don't do this. You can't…'

She hugged his back so tight that she felt like she couldn't breathe. Her face was buried in his blazer and her arms barely reached around him and the railings, but she didn't care. She needed to cling on tight. She was so surrounded by his clothes that her ears were muffled, and she nearly missed the words coming out of his mouth.

'Mum… Mum, I'm scared.'

She lifted her head and saw the tears on his cheeks, she heard the warble in his voice. He didn't want this as much as she didn't. The one thing she could easily recognise was someone that was in over their head.

'It's OK. I'll help you. I'll get you down. Trust me.'

'Why would you? Why would you get me down?'

'What do you mean?'

'You don't care about me. You said so yourself. Why would it matter to you if I jumped?'

His voice wasn't stroppy, or cross. It was hurt. The most hurt she had ever heard him sound and it was all her fault. He heard her say those terrible things on the phone and not once had she rung him to explain. Not once had she tried to fight for him, because... well... because she thought it was true. She thought there was no love inside of her for him. But she knew, she knew the moment she thought she'd lost him that there was.

'Of course I care,' she told him, clinging on harder to his body, his clothes, anything. 'I care so much. I was lost, I'll be honest with you. I had no idea what was going to happen, and it made me angry at everyone around me. I felt like no one was listening to me… and I know… I know that's how you feel now, but I'm here and I'm listening and… and I love you.'

She said it. She knew she needed to; she knew it was what he needed to hear to be safe… but also… she felt as if she meant it. For the first time in her life, she really meant those words with every fibre of her being. But still, he didn't move. Still his hands remained clasped to the iron railings, facing away from her and towards the gap in front of him. The bridge, the tracks, the idea of the end. That was the way he was looking, and she needed that to change.

'Please, Thomas, please let me help you get down. Please let's talk on our own, away from all of this, from all of them.'

'Is that it? Is that why you want me down? Because you're embarrassed of people seeing?'

'God no. It's because I need you to be safe… I really, really need you to be safe.'

Liz cried harder then, harder than she ever had in her life, harder than the day she found out she was pregnant. She moved her arm to around his neck and hugged her little boy just like she should have done every day of his whole life.

'I've let you down. I know that. I haven't had any form of affair, I promise you, but I've not been a good enough mum. Not ever. And I know that now. It's too late to change what's happened, but it's never too late to change what will happen… But I can't do that without you here. Please… please get down… and let me be the mum I should have been, the mum I want to be.'

There was a pause. It felt like an eternity, but she knew she needed to give him space. To give him time to process. To understand.

'I… I'm scared to let go… What if I fall?'

'You won't. I'm here. I won't let you.'

This was it. Liz allowed herself to look towards the officers that had been about six feet away the entire time. She gave them a nod in case they could help. Then she moved her hands from around his neck and put them under his armpits, trying with all her might to take all the weight of her boy.

'I've got you. It's OK. You can do this.'

With that Thomas let go with one hand. But the panic was clear, and he rushed to put it back again.

'I can't, Mum. I don't know how.'

'Hold on, son, hold on tight.'

Liz looked towards the officers at the side. They had inched closer when he took his hand off, but they were staying back now. They needed to know it was time to step in.

'Please,' she called to them, aware of the rising mobile phones from down below as she did so. 'Please come and help us. He wants to get down. Help me get him down.'

That was all the officers needed. Within what felt like a flash, they had grabbed either side of her son and lifted him back over the edge like he was nothing more than a sack of potatoes. He'd fallen away from her as they did so, and his feet had gone from underneath him. He slumped to the ground, his blazer almost covering his face and his shoulders, and his palms hit the concrete of the bridge. For a moment, there was calm. Everyone stood back and allowed Thomas the space he needed. He didn't lift his head or look at anyone. All that could be heard was the muffled but undistinguishable noise of him sobbing uncontrollably. Liz stepped forward, trembling, and put her arms around him. It was all he needed. He pulled her closer and buried his head into her chest, just like he did as a toddler, as he continued to cry. Liz allowed herself to fall to the ground with him and encase him in everything she had. She was crying too – no, sobbing. Sobbing harder than ever. Never in her life had she felt so grateful for human contact.

'I'm sorry. I'm so sorry.'

The only words she could muster but hopefully the one that mattered most. She knew there were people around her, she knew they wanted to speak to Thomas, to check he was alright, but she couldn't let him go. And in that moment, they allowed her just that. A time where she could hug her son and apologise for every moment in his life that she believed she hadn't wanted him. Because right now all she wanted was on the floor with her, on a cold railway bridge with a frost in the air and stares on people's faces.

'Thomas, I do love you. I do. One day you will understand. It's not always black and white, but I know now that you and your sister... and your dad. You are everything to me and I'd be lost without you. I would never have forgiven myself if... if... Why, Thomas? Why did you do this? Why did you think of... this?'

Thomas didn't lift his head, but he moved. His hands were wrung together, and he wiped his face with his cuff. He started to mumble, and Liz had to move in closer to hear.

'The messages wouldn't stop, Mum. They just kept coming. They said I should. Said I should just jump.'

'What messages? Who said?'

'Everyone. They kept coming. Kept saying if they were me, they wouldn't want to be here anymore. Said it would do everyone a favour. It would make everything better.'

'Why?'

And that's when he lifted his head and met her gaze.

'Because of you. Because of what you did with that boy.'

Liz felt a lump stick in her throat. She felt like she couldn't talk. That if she opened her mouth, she would vomit there and then. Who were these kids? They'd pushed her boy to do something... horrendous... and because of what? Because of her. That was what hit her the hardest. She felt as if she'd just jumped in front of a train herself. Gripping him tighter still, she managed to say the words she needed to get out.

'I didn't do it. I promise you. It has all been made up. I saw him earlier… at school… and I begged him. I pleaded with him to make it stop. I don't care how that makes me look anymore, Thomas. I really don't. As long as you were safe, that was all that mattered. I don't know how he did it. How he made it look so convincing. But he did. Turns out we all underestimate people. But I will fight this. I'll fight it for all of us. I will clear my name and we will be a family. A proper family. Not just on the surface.'

She meant for this to feel powerful. To give him strength, hope and most of all, belief. Belief in her and the words she was saying. But rather than any form of relief, she saw sadness.

'But Dad…'

Rob. Who knew how he felt? Liz certainly didn't. But she knew how she felt, finally, and that was what he needed to hear.

'The truth is, Thomas… I love your dad. I always have. Yes, I've worked hard, I've provided money, but that only goes so far. You need support, someone to back you and… it's taken me a while… but I've realised that's what he's done. He's always been there. Never put a blocker on anything, stopped me from achieving anything. He's only ever built me up, made me stronger, never knocked me down or told me I can't do anything. Not like I have to him. Really… he's never given up on me. And that's what I intend to do for him now. No matter what he throws at me, I will never give up on him. I will fight for him and for us more than I've ever fought for anything else. I will show all of you that I'm innocent and that I love you. Every single day if that's what it takes.'

Thomas reached forward and held on to her tighter. He didn't say anything more, but he gripped her arm with such emotion that Liz allowed her head to fall onto his. It was only then, as it was quiet, that she heard a rustling behind her. She knew it would be a police officer. She couldn't blame them;

they'd allowed her long enough. But no part of her wanted this moment to end. She needed to hug her boy for as long as he needed her to. She moved her head gently so her arm was still close, reassuring him that she would stay by his side, but allowed herself enough room to look up and see who was standing behind. Perhaps ask for some more time together despite the cold and wet seeping through her trousers. She had expected a yellow high viz. A man with authority looking down on her. Judging her for the state they were all in. But instead, she saw the kind eyes of the man she had spent so much of her life with. His floppy brown hair in front of his face, a drip of rain forming on the front of it, about to drop onto his nose. He had tears in his eyes – complete disbelief at what he was seeing – yet he had allowed her time. He hadn't pushed in; he'd left her to say what she needed to say. How much had he heard? Why Thomas had done it? That she was innocent? Or how much she loved him? Liz couldn't help but hope with all her heart that he had heard that bit. That he knew how she felt. And something told her he had. The anger had gone from him. He looked vulnerable. Not quite relieved, not happy in any way, but open. Open to working things out? Open to putting their family back together? Who knew? Right now, they needed to focus on Thomas… and Ellie…

'He's OK. He's shaken, but he's OK. How many people know? I don't want Ellie finding out from anyone but us.'

'Don't worry. Someone I work with was here at the station. He rang me and I rang her. She answered this time – thank God. She's going back to my mum's to wait for us there. But maybe it will be better if we all talk at home? Just us?'

Without looking up from the floor and still clinging on to her arms, Liz heard Thomas mutter the words, 'I'm so sorry, Dad.'

'I think we all have things to be sorry for, Thomas. But for now, let's take it one step at a time. I've spoken to the officers; they are happy for us to go home, and they will pop over later to see you and speak to us all. They'll still have to be involved for a while, but that's nothing we can't handle. Not if we're all together.'

Liz thought that was aimed at her… or hoped… or wished so hard she surprised herself. She looked deep into his eyes for some sort of reassurance. He stared back and put his hand out.

'Let's go home. We've got a lot to talk about still, but I'd rather not do it in the pouring rain with an audience if it's all the same to you.'

And there was the smirk. Rob's signature side smirk that had made her go weak at the knees and made her feel sick at different times of their relationship. This time though, it gave her the biggest sense of reassurance, a glimmer of hope that things may be OK. She knew she needed to get him to believe her, but she also had some things she wanted to say herself too. This would be an opportunity for them all to start again, for them all to say what they needed to say, and there were things that Rob would need to listen to as well. But maybe they would give each other the respect that had been lacking for too long. Maybe they would all get a chance to be listened to.

They all got up from the floor. Thomas still snuggled into his mum's arm, keeping his head under his blazer. And who could blame him? The police had managed to move most people away, but there were still some lingering. Vultures. Preying on vulnerable kids. Then the thought struck Liz. Is this what people had thought about her? The venom she just had in her mind about those people, the opinion she had just formed in a split second. She had been on the receiving end of that. Maybe they had their own reasons for being here. Maybe things just aren't always what they seem. Maybe that's something she should have worked out a long time ago.

Ben

(Now)

Mum's still not back. And I've still not gone out. I don't know what to do. If I stay here any longer, she'll come home, drunk as shit probably. She'll come in, banging on my bedroom door, no doubt raging about missing a holiday or worse. If Lee's split up with her because he weren't getting any money, my life will be over. But if I go out… I don't know who I'm going to bump into…

Turns out word travels fast. Enough people saw me running out the school to put two and two together. Either that or they've held an assembly saying it was all bullshit. Probably wanted all the parents to know sooner rather than later… save the school's arse rather than mine. I get it – who would want to save me anyway? But now the messages have started coming. And not good ones either. Not ones saying I'm a legend. Nah, they've all gone, haven't they? And now there's just shit. Tons and tons of it. Some just taking the piss… you know, banter and all that… some more serious. Like Ellie's friends. They've been going in. And I guess I deserve that.

Apparently, Ellie's little brother jumped off a bridge or something. One text said he was in hospital in a coma. It said that if he dies, it's my fault. And it would be, wouldn't it? How do I live with that? I didn't mean for none of this to happen. All I wanted to do was show Mitchell and the others. Just to keep my mates. No one else was meant to see. It weren't meant to go everywhere. Talking of Mitchell, I've heard shit all from him. Nothing. Not even abuse. I expected abuse. But he's just gone off the grid. I text him to see if he knew what was going on with that Thomas kid. If anyone had the gossip, it would be him. But I had no response. I think that's worse than getting shit. Just frozen out like you don't even exist.

I took the post down. Deleted all the shit that I put up, but nothing's really changed. It didn't take anything away.

That's when more messages came. Loads of stuff about how I'd

deleted the post, so I must have been lying. I mean, it's true, but

still. I've got WhatsApps and Facebook messages. They're

writing liar and shit all over my wall. I might just delete the

whole page. Wish I could delete my life. How the fuck am I

meant to walk into school after all of this? I won't even be able

to walk down the road let alone through the gates. I thought

Pissy Chris was brave going in after what he did, but that's

nothing now, isn't it? Pissing yourself just ruins *your* life… no

one else's.

That's why I text Mitchell. I thought if he was still in my

corner, still backing me regardless like mates should, then I'd

have nothing to worry about. But he's not, is he? He's turned his

back on me like everyone else. I've got no one… and I guess

that's what I deserve. Fuck it. I ain't going to school tomorrow. I

ain't going to school ever again. I ain't going to get any GCSEs

anyway, so what's the point? I can still have the life I want

without the money from the papers. I'll pack a bag and jump on a train to London. There must be something there I can do. Mum said my dad used to work on Billingsgate Fish Market. Maybe I could go there and see if he's still around? I don't know who to look for, but surely there'll be a feller that looks like me? I could tell him I'm his son and then just work on the market with him. Then he'll ask me to live with him… probably… and all of this will be nothing but a memory. No one in London will know anything about Hot Hall and the Facebook post. I'll be free *and* earning money. Bollocks to all this, that's a much better life anyway.

Shit… someone's just knocked on the door. It can't be Mum… obvs… she'd have a key, but who else could it be? The filth? They'll be here soon enough, I'm sure. But it seemed too soft to be them? Could be anyone coming to have a go. Or just to start something. Shit, what if it's Hot Hall's bloke? What if he's brought a load of mates with him to kick my head in? I mean… I wouldn't blame him, but fuck… I can't handle that on my own.

Actually, what if it's Mitchell? Come to check I'm alright. I bet it is. I knew he wouldn't ditch me.

I head downstairs and dive into the living room. You can see the front door from there and then there's no need to second guess. No need to risk getting my head kicked in from a pissed off bloke, is there? Jesus… I've not been this close to the net curtains in ages. They're yellow at the bottom, and they stink like fags. No wonder my mates never wanted to step foot in here. You see it on that advert all the time, *'you've gone nose blind…'* Well, clearly I fucking have because my house reeks. Bet even Billingsgate Fish Market smells better than in here.

Shit… it's Pissy Chris. What the fuck does he want? Surely he's not going to kick my head in. I'd like to see him try. But still… why would he come out and knock on my door? Maybe he's waited all this time to tell me how much of a prick I am. Maybe he's come to rub it in my face now I'm the laughingstock of the school and not him anymore. That's how bad it is. I'm hiding behind a stinky net curtain, refusing to answer the door to Pissy-fucking-Chris. My life is over.

'I know you're in there. I can see you through the window. Open the door.'

Shit.

'Seriously, open up. If my dad catches me standing outside yours…'

Well, I've got no choice now, do I? Can't have him pissing himself on my doorstep… or his dad knocking me out for that matter. So, I go to the door and open it. He comes in quick, looking behind him to check no one is watching, and then we're both just standing there, in the hallway. Not really sure what to say to each other.

Chris starts. He looks proper awkward. Maybe he ain't here to take the piss after all.

'I… look… I just wanted to check you were OK.'

'Yeah, I'm alright. Why wouldn't I be?'

'Ben. Drop the act. Everyone knows you made it all up. It's everywhere. People were chanting "Benny's full of Bullshit" all round the quad earlier.'

'Fuck…'

'Look, I know how it feels to be the one everyone laughs at. But it gets better. Well… it gets… alright. Point is, it's not as bad as you think it's going to be.'

'Oh really? Chris, all you did was fucking piss yourself. I made up that I'd shagged a teacher. There were police and papers, and fuck knows what else. Why did I have to put it on Facebook? It made it so much bigger. And worse than that… Mitchell ain't texting me back. None of them are. I've got no one. I can't go back to school tomorrow. I can't walk in on my own.'

'Yeah… that must suck…'

I hear the tone in his voice. I know what he's getting at. Of course, he walked into school on his own every day because... well, because of me. But I had nowhere near the power that Mitchell has. That's what he doesn't understand. It's going to be so much worse for me because Mitchell can make it that way.

'Look... that's kind of what I wanted to say. You don't have to walk in by yourself tomorrow. I'll meet you at the top of the road, at the lamppost, like we used to when our mums stopped talking, and I'll walk in with you.'

'What? Why would you do that?'

'Because you're my mate.'

Shit... I ain't been much of a mate lately, have I? And I still ain't. Because I know he's being nice and I know I should say thanks, but all I keep thinking is, what's worse? Walking in on your own or walking in with Pissy Chris? Nah... I'm not walking in at all.

'Look, cheers… mate… but I'm not going in tomorrow. I've decided I'm going to head up to London, to see my dad. Going to stay with him for a bit and work at the fish market. It's going to be epic. I don't need school anyway – not like I'm going to get anything out of it.'

'You don't know that.'

'Yeah, I do. It's fine – I'll like working at Billingsgate, I reckon.'

'So, when did your dad get in touch?'

Shit. How do I get round this one? I can't look at his face, so I stare at the floor. Bloody carpet is almost threadbare out here – I can see the concrete poking through underneath and everything. God this house is a dump.

'Well… he ain't… but Mum said he worked there, so I figured I'd just go and see if there was someone that looked a bit like me.'

Yeah, saying it out loud makes me feel like a dick. And I can tell from his face he thinks so too. But what else can I say?

'Come off it. That was nearly sixteen years ago. He won't still be there... if he ever was.'

'What does that mean?'

'Come on, Ben. You know your mum. She talks shit, like they all do around here. For all we know your dad could be pulling pints at the Queen's Head rather than in London. You could go all the way there for nothing. Just come to school tomorrow. I'll meet you by the lamppost.'

Now he's turning round and heading for the door. Like it's a done deal. Like I'm going to just go to bed, wake up in the morning and stroll into the fucking lion's den. Oh yeah, don't worry though, it will be OK, because I've got Pissy bloody Chris to defend me. What a load of bollocks. We'll be eaten alive... and that's if I survive Mum first.

'Pls… Chris. I can't stay here. I can't. When Mum comes back, I don't know what she'll do. I've never seen her angry like she was today. Only she had to hold it in then, didn't she? She won't have to do that here. You know you always said about your dad's eyes? About how they went red around the edges when he was going to kick off? That's what happened to Mum's today. I can't stick around to see what that means.'

I saw him flinch when I mentioned his dad. I knew I shouldn't have, but he needed to know how I felt. In fact, he's probably the only one who does know how I feel, come to think about it. Not just about school either, but about being an estate kid, with shit parents. Do you know, maybe school would have been easier if I hadn't ditched Chris. Maybe it would have blown over and we could have looked out for each other. Too late now though. I ain't ever going back no matter what he says. He turns from the door and looks at me. As he does, he moves his hair with his hand, and I can see a purple bruise from between his fingers. His head looks battered.

'Your mum's at Karl's down the road. She's pissed as a fart already. You can hear her screaming from down the street. I walked past when the window was open, and she was telling everyone how you'd lied to her and mucked up her holiday. None of them were really listening though because she's slurring her words that much you could barely understand her. The way she's going, she won't even make it home, let alone be in any fit state to do anything. Put a chair up against your door, under the handle. That's what I do… I don't think she'd do anything bad but just in case. Then turn your phone off and go to sleep. Meet me in the morning. I promise, it ain't going to be as bad as you think it is. And if it is, it won't last very long. There's always some other shit that takes over eventually.'

And then he walks out… checking before he does so, obviously, but he just leaves. And now I'm stood here, in the hallway, wondering what the fuck to do. I go upstairs and check my phone one more time. I don't open any messages; I just look for one name, for Mitchell's, but it ain't there. He must have told the others to stay away from me too because I've heard from no one. Not Jack, not Lynsey or Ryan. I don't know what that means. Does it mean they're done with me completely or they're biding their time to get me back? Problem is, I ain't never going to know unless I actually go back to school.

Chris was right… I don't know if me dad's in Billingsgate. It's shit, but I don't. So, what if I rock up to London and there's no one there? Where do I go then? It might be shit in this house, but at least I know I've got a bed and food… most of the time. Fuck… food… the chippy. Will Mr Chang have seen all of this? I'm meant to go to work tomorrow. What am I going to do about that? I never thought I'd say this, but hopefully he'll let me hide at the back by the fryers.

I pick up a chair and put it under my door handle, just in case, and think of Chris. That was decent of him to come over, to be fair. Can't believe he has to do this every night. I wonder if kids like us will ever get out of this estate. I guess there'd be more chance if we did it together, and with money in our pockets. Money I would get from showing up at the chippy tomorrow. Actually… I wonder if Chang has any jobs going. I could get Chris one and we could both put our money away to get out of here. Fuck new trainers, we could get our own flat somewhere really, really far away, where no one knows I pretended to shag a teacher, and no one knows Chris pissed himself. That's what we need, I reckon. Maybe I'll tell Chris tomorrow? Guess I could always walk into school and see how shit it is? Then make my decision on what I'm going to do. Fuck it. I'm turning off my phone and getting into bed. Let's just see what tomorrow brings. What else can I do?

Liz

(Now)

The car journey home had been silent. Liz had sat in the back with Thomas like she did when she first brought him home from the hospital. She'd forgotten all about that until she climbed in and sat beside him. How she had stared at this little boy from his car seat, the guilt she had felt even then. She remembered looking at his closed eyes and his squashed nose. At the red marks on his bald head and his small hands, tucked up together across his stomach. More than anything, she remembered willing herself to feel something, anything that made her heart know that this little boy was hers, her son, who would depend on her for the rest of his life. She knew she had felt something with Ellie... at the very beginning... but with Thomas? She couldn't help but wonder if things would have been different if she had perhaps spoken out then. Told somebody how she was feeling? Would they have helped her... or taken him away? She had already had a lifetime of judgement, even at that age, and she knew she could never have dealt with any more. Perhaps that was why she'd buried her feelings so deep for so long and focused entirely on her work.

Work... even as she thought of the place, she felt sick. The way she'd left, ran out the building like a scene in *EastEnders*. Of course, it hadn't mattered then, not when Thomas needed her. But now... when would she ring them? When would she explain? At that very moment Thomas tightened his grip on her arm. Like he could sense her thoughts and was reminding her to focus. Obviously, there was no way that was true – she hadn't changed so dramatically that she believed in a higher power – but he definitely had intercepted her thoughts at the precise moment she had needed him to. He hadn't let go of her arm since the beginning of the journey, and she'd never tried to move away either. Thomas needed his mum. Perhaps he had needed her for a lot longer than just today, but today she had noticed. Her eyes had been opened and she wasn't about to let him down again. Not anymore.

As they pulled up at the house, Rob had glanced in the rear-view mirror. Thomas still had his head down, so it was Liz he had looked at directly. For a moment it was as though they were the only two people in the world. She allowed herself to meet his look and hoped that she was showing a mixture of remorse and love. Because she did love this loyal old puppy staring back at her... she'd just forgotten. They seemed to keep the stare for a while before the silence was broken by her phone ringing.

'Perhaps it's Ellie,' Rob had said, without taking his eyes off her reflection. Liz took this as a sign to reach into her bag and look for her phone. Thomas clung tighter, but other than that he didn't react. Liz was unsure how long it was going to take to get any real words out of him, but she was determined to help him discuss anything he needed. Ironically, in just the way she had wished someone had done for her all those years ago.

Looking down at the phone, however, she was disappointed not to see her daughter's number flashing back at her, but that of the school. The questions she had thought of earlier were about to be answered and now she wasn't sure if she wanted to know. She felt a lump in her throat and her heart began to race. She looked from her phone, back to Rob's eyes in the mirror in front of her. The blue of his pupils giving the only light in the darkness of the grey car.

'It's the school…'

'Answer it. We can go inside, can't we, Thomas?'

'No. Stay in here with me… please?'

There it was again. The smirk, just as he nodded his head. She felt herself breathe, and her heart slow slightly. It was just what she needed, the reassurance she should have fought for all this time.

'Hello.'

'Liz, hi. Jo here… obviously. Look, Ben has explained everything. Said he made the whole thing up. He's gone home and we will have him in isolation tomorrow. It will probably be best for him anyway; you know what these kids are like. We'll get the school counsellor involved; she'll know what to do. Anyway, I need you back in pronto. We need to discuss a plan of action. Obviously there are some "untruths", shall we say, that will need ironing out, but we can work on those together. I was thinking maybe you could do an assembly. Social media and the lark and together we can compose an email to the parents. If we get started straight away, we could have it out by the end of the school day and we can start tomorrow as normal.'

Liz was dumbfounded. Had Jo completely forgotten *why* she had left the meeting? Or did she not care?

'Jo… Thomas…'

'Oh yes, I hear you found him. All OK, I presume?'

'Er… no. No, not really. I can't come in, not now. I'm needed here.'

Liz caught Rob's eye once again. She didn't know how much he had heard of the conversation, but the tear in his eye had shown her that he had heard that bit.

'No, you're needed here. The school's reputation is on the line, and we need to act fast. I expect you to be with me in the next half an hour. Thomas will still be there when you get home.'

The lump in Liz's throat was immediately swallowed. The thought of this woman dictating her life, telling her what to do after the disbelief she had shown, brought Liz back to exactly where she needed to be. The fight inside her began to burn once again, and she cleared her throat, ensuring she spoke clearly and articulately, with the most force she'd had for a long time.

'Jo. I will not be returning to work today. In fact, I will be taking the rest of the week off. I feel completely let down by your lack of belief and I will want to contact HR before I even think of stepping back into the building. More than that, my son is struggling because of bullying at *your* school, and I will be taking compassionate leave to deal with it. If that is not signed off by yourself, I will happily speak to the doctor about the stress I have been feeling and I am sure he will be more than happy to sign me off for a while. Now, as we both know, our insurance does not cover sick leave due to stress, and the budget will not be able to cope with a supply teacher. It does, however, cover compassionate leave, which is why I am certain that *will* be granted until I feel ready to discuss things further. I will also be requesting a full interview with yourself and HR before I take my position back. For now, I need to be with my family, and I would respectfully ask that you do not contact me until next week… Oh, and feel free to compose an email to the parents *yourself.* You are the head teacher after all.'

She put the phone down. Only then did she notice how much she was shaking, but she didn't care. She had to end it before the tears spilled out of her eyes and the crack in her voice gave her away. She looked back at the rear-view mirror and into the blue eyes looking back at her.

'He admitted it was all a lie. No truth in it at all.'

Now it was Rob's turn to allow the tears to fall.

'I'm so sorry. I should have believed you.'

'As you said to Thomas, we all have things to apologise for. But not in the car.'

Liz had, all of a sudden, become very aware of curtains twitching in the neighbours' houses. They had obviously been sat in the car far too long. As she reached for the door handle, she squeezed her son's arm and smiled at her partner's reflection. This wasn't going to be a quick fix, but she was determined for it to be fixed, no matter what. It was going to be OK, regardless of how long it took. As she stepped out, into the rain, she saw her daughter walking towards her. Another apology that needed to happen. She looked sullen, awkward, stroppy – her usual teenage self – but she was home. They all were. That was the step they had all taken together, and the others would follow. No matter how much they had to pick each other up. From now on, they would.

Ben

(Now)

This is bollocks. It's all bollocks. As if I can walk into school. As if I can show my face. I can't do that. I left my phone off all night, but I didn't sleep. Do you know how hard it is to do nothing without your phone? I couldn't even play *Candy Crush* or nothing. But being bored was better than facing all the shit that would have been on there. It must have been the middle of the night when I heard Mum come in. The front door swung open so hard it hit the wall – that will be another dent in the plasterboard, without a doubt. Normally it's her fellers that do shit like that though, not her. Thought there might be someone with her, maybe even Lee checking she'd got back OK. Thought maybe he would be decent. But there were no voices, just her, drunkenly mumbling to herself. Definitely no one with her.

She stayed downstairs for ages. I was hoping she'd pass out on the sofa, then I could just sneak past in the morning, but she didn't. Eventually, she started dragging herself up the stairs. You could tell she was swaying because I could hear her knock into the side of each wall on the way up. Then I heard a crash. There's one picture on the wall. It's not a picture, actually, it's a record, in a frame. 'London Calling' by The Clash. She's always told me it was my dad's. The only thing he'd left behind. Claims she hates the man, but it's the only thing on the wall. No school pictures of me, not even a photo of the two of us, just this well old album that no one has ever heard of before. Especially since HMV closed in town. They used to have T-Shirts with it on in the window. You know, like vintage ones? I thought of buying one once, thought Mum would like it, but I bottled it.

Don't matter now though because it's in pieces on the stairs. I heard her shout 'shit', but she kept coming up… I wonder if she trod on any of the glass.

Anyway, she came up the stairs and rattled my door handle. Thank fuck for Chris's idea about the chair because she soon gave up trying to get in. She didn't shout or nothing. Just called me a prick and went to bed. Now it's morning and I should be getting ready for school, but I don't know what I'm meant to do. I can't go in and face everyone. It's nice and everything of Chris to say he'll walk in with me but... really? What's that going to do? Just draw more attention to me. Problem is... if I stay here, I have to face Mum and that could be well worse, depending on how bad her hangover is, so I'm kind of stuck. Fuck. I guess at least Hot Hall will be happy. Thomas obviously didn't die because I reckon Chris would have told me last night, so he's probably back at home and she'll be heading back to work today just like normal. Like nothing's even happened. I wish that made me feel better, but it don't really. Her life is great and mine is... well... fucked.

Shit.

I was just about to hide under the covers when I swear I just heard a knock at the door. Can't be Chris already, can it? One thing going in... another going in this bloody early. And besides, he said he'd meet me at the lamppost, not knock the door. Maybe he thought I'd bottle it, so he's come knocking. But I can't go in this early. I can't just be sitting in the quad waiting for the shit, can I? Or is that his plan? Get in early and try and hide in one of the classrooms? In the Science block or something? That's a good idea actually. Could work. I mean, I ain't ready, but it won't take me long.

Shit. He just knocked again. Calm down, Chris. One more knock and he'll wake Mum up. Fuck's sake, he knows better than that surely? I've got no choice. I need to quietly move the chair from under the door handle. Then I can go and let him in. He'll have to wait in my room until I'm ready. I wonder when the last time was that Chris was in my room. Bet it's been bloody ages. Not that it would have changed at all; same shit different day and all that.

Bollocks.

I knew I'd forget about that glass. I was trying so hard to be quiet that I didn't look where I was going. Now there's glass in my foot. I hobble over to the door, muttering under my breath, swing it open to usher Chris inside and... what?

'Miss Hall? What are you doing here?'

'I don't really know. Well, I do. I need to talk to you. Can I come in?'

I look upstairs, hoping that's enough for her to work it out. How can I invite her in when Mum could come down at any minute? I don't know how she'll react with all of this and I ain't about to bloody risk it. But then, she does the same, doesn't she? Only she looks out into the road before she looks back at me and I know what she's thinking and she's probably right. What if someone looked out of their window now and saw her standing on my doorstep? What if they were snapping pictures on their phone as we speak? So, I give in and let her in the door but open the living room door so we can go straight in there. The curtains are closed, and it smells proper dingy. Mum must have had a fag when she got in because the ashtray's out on the coffee table and her lighter's on the floor. Thank God she remembered to stub it out this time. I saw Hall stare at the smashed glass on the stairs and now at the ashtray on the table and it feels shit. I look at my foot quickly to make sure it ain't bleeding. It doesn't look like it is, but still... it's pretty embarrassing. I look up at her for the first time, properly, and it's obvious she's been crying. I can tell by her eyes. That makes me feel shit. Doesn't stop me cringing about the house though.

I move Mum's bag off the sofa, but she stays standing. I don't know whether that's because she isn't staying or because she's scared she'll catch something from sitting down, and I don't blame her.

'Look, Ben,' she starts, 'I just needed to ask you something. First, I want to check you're OK. Of course, that's important. But I also wanted to ask you why? I didn't want to ask in front of everyone in some meeting, or at school at all for that matter. But I need to know for my own peace of mind. Why did you do this?'

Well, what the hell do I say to that? My mouth's bloody dry and nothing's coming out. All I can do is keep looking at my foot. It's still not bleeding, but I can feel something in it and that's enough to distract me and make me keep my mouth shut. But she's not getting the hint.

'Ben, please. This is important. I need to know why. Did I do something that gave you the impression I was interested? If I'm going to carry on teaching, I need to know the answer.'

If? Why would it be an if? And what do I tell her? Yeah… you stood near me in a corridor, and I ran away with it? Honestly. The more I've thought about it overnight, the more ridiculous I sound. When you say it out loud, I just sound like a prick. I still can't bring myself to open my mouth. I glance up quickly and see she is getting pissed off now. She wants me to tell her things that I can't. What am I meant to do?

'Nothing? That's what you're giving me? You ruin my life, and I don't even get an explanation?'

What the hell? Ruin her life? Suddenly my mouth is back, and it's in overdrive.

'Your life? Yours isn't the one that's ruined. I told the truth... in the end. Everything will go back to normal for you. It's my life that's fucked.'

Shit. I've never spoken to a teacher like that in my life, but it's true, isn't it? Besides, it doesn't exactly feel like you're talking to a teacher when you're stood in a room that stinks of fags in your pyjamas, does it? This is a right mess.

'Oh, is that true? You think everything in my life will snap back to the way it was because you admitted you made it all up? Come on, Ben. Don't be ridiculous. You have no idea what you've created, or how big this all is, do you? That post has been seen by thousands of people.'

'I deleted it.'

'It doesn't matter. It's been seen. It's been shared. You just have to google my name to know this isn't going anywhere. What if I want to change jobs? Go to a different school? You think the pupils there won't google their new teacher? Or they won't want to know my HR records? This will follow me, wherever I go, for a long time. That's what the internet does. And more than that… what about my kids? What about when Ellie goes to uni and some idiot finds the online report that was done in the local paper yesterday? What about Thomas? He's in Year 7, Ben. He's going to go through years at that school with everyone knowing what happened. Everyone knowing the accusations you made. Everyone seeing the pictures you posted. He's in a bad way over this. Kids can be cruel. I thought you'd understand that. That's why I thought you'd help. I thought you'd explain to me how you came up with all of this. I need to protect my children, Ben; I need to know what they are walking into when they go back. That's why I'm here. I need to know whether I can send them back or whether they need to be at home.'

Now I'm the one crying. I can't look her in the eyes, but I can feel the tears dripping down my cheeks and my nose and hanging off the end like a kid that isn't getting an ice cream. I know I need to help, but I don't know how.

'You did nothing, OK? It was all in my head. I thought you fancied me and then the more I spoke about it, the more it became real. Then I told people, and they wanted evidence, and I didn't have any, did I? Because you hadn't done anything. But they wouldn't let it go.'

'Who wouldn't? What people?'

'You know. My mates... Jack, Lynsey... Mitchell.'

Why does saying his name hurt so much? Why is that making me cry more? God, this is so embarrassing.

'So, they are such good mates that they were peer pressuring you? Is that it? All of this, just to impress some kids that are going nowhere in life? That was worth putting me through all of this? I'm trying to understand, Ben, I really am, but this doesn't make sense. If I didn't do anything, like you say, how could you let it get this far?'

'You wouldn't understand, would you? That's the point. I bet you have no idea what it's like to be the kid that no one wants to be around. The one that walks in on their own and stands at the edge of every conversation. Never knowing the inside joke. Then all of a sudden, I *was* the chat. I was the one they were all talking about, and I ran with it. I didn't know it would get this big.'

'And would you have done it if you did?'

'No.'

I mean… I don't know really. Would I? Was this worth the moments when I felt like a legend? Let's face it, I'm never going to have that again. I'm never going to rock into school like a hero ever again for the rest of my life. So maybe it was worth it? Looking at her though, I don't reckon I should say that bit out loud. So instead, I say, 'I'm sorry.'

'Thank you. I appreciate the apology, but nothing is going to change this and it's definitely not over, so I need to know the truth. Are you sure there was nothing I did?'

'Nothing other than be the only one that's ever cared. Ever tried to help.'

Yeah... now I feel bad.

'You can still do well, Ben. You just need to keep working hard. Trust me, I do know what it's like to be the outsider and I do know what it's like to be the one they're all talking about. I would say, sometimes the outsider has the better chances. You've got those chances still. Get your head down and work hard and make sure people are talking about you for the right reasons. Trust me.'

'I can't go back to school, Miss.'

'Yes, you can.'

'I can't face them.'

'If I can, and Ellie can, and Thomas can, then the least you can do is try. Besides, you'll be in isolation for a couple of weeks anyway, so you won't need to face anyone just yet.'

Jesus. I've never been so happy to get a detention in all my life.

When she turned to leave, she looked again at the glass on the stairs and the ashtray on the table. I could see her taking it all in and looking at me with sympathy. It never gets easier being on the end of one of those looks. But then she turns, lowers her voice and whispers, 'The school counsellor will be chatting to you today as well. Maybe try being completely honest... for once. I think it might help you this time.'

And then she turns the door handle and goes. She must be bloody strong because I normally have to kick it to open first time. I go back to the living room and watch her drive away in a car that definitely does not belong on this estate, and I know it's weird, but all I keep thinking is how strange it was to see her in jeans. I mean… I know she's older and that – she's my teacher – but when you see them in normal clothes rather than work shit, they look different. Older. Mum-like if anything. As if she could have ever been my missus. I can't believe people believed all that shit. I can't believe *I* believed it.

Fuck, that's a point. I need my phone.

I bomb back up the stairs, not stepping on glass this time, and head into my room and under my pillow. I can hear Mum snoring through the door, so I don't need to worry about waking her up. She really must've had a skinful last night. I think about what Hall said. About the counsellor and telling the truth and that… and about googling her name. So, I turn my phone on and ignore the WhatsApps that are pinging through one after another and open Google instead and type in Liz Hall. Fuck. There's so many hits.

No smoke without fire. Teacher still under questioning for having an affair with teenage boy.

Former pupil speaks of her shock after discovering her old teacher has been accused of luring a teenage boy into bed.

School urged to keep suspension up until investigation is over.

Parents' fury over reinstatement of paedophile.

Shit. She was right. This isn't going anywhere anytime soon. I need to go into school today. I need to do something to put this right. More than anything, I need to be brave. Probably the bravest I've ever had to be. And I reckon Hall was right. I reckon I do need that counsellor after all.

Ben

(Twenty years later)

I never thought I'd step back into these corridors, and I must admit, it feels stranger than I thought it would. The green gates haven't changed, the quad is the same, and the buildings look just as run down, but there's new signs around, with a new head teacher's name. Not one that I recognise. In fact, none of the staff list looks familiar, but I guess that's to be expected. When I walk into reception though, I am met with one very familiar face. Is it strange that I still want to call her Miss?

'Ben? I thought it was you.'

'Hi… Liz. Nice to see you again.'

She looks different. Blonde for a start and obviously older, but the features are still the same. She's still in good shape and she's still well presented, but she seems more approachable than she did when I was a kid. More warmth coming from her. I see the yellow visitor's sticker stuck to her blazer and wonder how strange that must be for her. Then I see the bags she's brought with her and the label of her business and realise she must be doing OK.

She contacted me about three months ago. I hadn't recognised the email address at first. Elizabeth Kirby... She must have finally married Ellie's dad. It didn't click though until I opened it and read it. She'd left teaching, not long after I'd left school, and had used the experience to start her own CPD business, looking into the dangers of social media in education. Reading that had hit me hard. It was so long ago now, yet it had clearly shaped both our futures. She said she often thought of me and always wondered what I'd got up to, but it wasn't until she was doing an assembly in a school that she thought to get in touch. Apparently a child had approached her afterwards and said that she'd heard that story before.

Sophie was a girl from one of my group therapy sessions that was particularly struggling with fitting in. I'd spent a lot of time with her and had eventually opened up to her about my experience at school. Of course, Liz didn't use my name in any of her talks – she assured me of that – but Sophie was adamant that she must have been discussing her own social worker. And she wasn't wrong. Liz then got in touch and asked me if I would be willing to do a talk with her. It took me three months to come to the decision, but when she said it was here, back in the school where it had all started, I couldn't turn it down, could I? How can I tell the children I work with that I have moved on with my life and still be too scared to come back here? Especially when it was Liz's words that had shaped my future this way.

So that's why I find myself back in reception with Liz Hall… sorry, Kirby. A yellow sticker on my chest, a briefcase in my hand and a trainer on my foot that's about to walk into the school hall and be greeted by a swarm of children. There could be a Chris in there, hiding at the back, a Mitchell, that will probably shout out at some point during the talk, but there could also be a Ben. A kid that's so desperate to fit in he's about to do something stupid, without understanding the consequences.

That's the kid we're here to reach today. And anyone else that needs it. Just like I did.

Out of the door struts the new head teacher. High heels and a pencil skirt suit, thinking she's helping by having us in today. Beside her is the new school counsellor, the one that actually makes a difference.

'Hi, you must be Ben, the social worker?'

'That's me.'

'Welcome. Have you been to our school before?'

Acknowledgements.

To my sister, Becky, who told me not to stop. I'm so grateful that I didn't. Thank you for keeping me going.

To my mum, my best friend. The strongest and most loving person I know. Thank you for always telling me to follow my dreams. I love you.

To my Grandma, 'my biggest fan', thank you for your belief and for keeping all my writing. You always knew I would do this.

To my Dad. I'm sorry you didn't get to see this, but you always knew it would happen. Thank you for being my rock. I miss you.

To my children, I hope I've shown you to follow your dreams, thank you for being my biggest reason.

And to my husband, Jonny. There will never be enough words to thank you for being my biggest cheerleader and never questioning my ability to succeed. You're support means more to me than you'll ever know. This wouldn't have happened if it wasn't for you – my hero.

And to all my friends and family: my brother in law, my in-laws - who have always treated me like one of their own and supported me every step of the way, Becky for reading the very first draft and making me continue and everyone else I am beyond lucky to have in my life. Nothing is unachievable when you have support behind you.

Printed in Great Britain
by Amazon